Books by Isaac Bashevis Singer

Enemies, A Love Story

Isaac Bashevis Singer

ENEMIES,

A LOVE STORY

FARRAR, STRAUS AND GIROUX · *New York*

· *AUTHOR'S NOTE* ·

A LTHOUGH I did not have the privilege of going through the Hitler holocaust, I have lived for years in New York with refugees from this ordeal. I therefore hasten to say that this novel is by no means the story of the typical refugee, his life, and struggle. Like most of my fictional works, this book presents an exceptional case with unique heroes and a unique combination of events. The characters are not only Nazi victims but victims of their own personalities and fates. If they fit into the general picture, it is because the exception is rooted in the rule. As a matter of fact, in literature the exception *is* the rule.

The novel was first published in *The Jewish Daily Forward* in 1966 under the title "Sonim, di Geshichte fun a Liebe." It was translated by Aliza Shevrin and Elizabeth Shub and edited by the latter, Rachel MacKenzie, and Robert Giroux. My gratitude to all of them.

I.B.S.

· PART ONE ·

· CHAPTER ONE ·

1

HERMAN BRODER turned over and opened one eye. In his dreamy state, he wondered whether he was in America, in Tzivkev, or in a German camp. He even imagined himself hiding in the hayloft in Lipsk. Occasionally all these places fused in his mind. He knew he was in Brooklyn, but he heard Nazis shouting. They were jabbing with their bayonets, trying to flush him out, while he pressed deeper and deeper into the hay. The blade of a bayonet touched his head.

Full awakening required an act of volition. "Enough!" he told himself, and sat up. It was mid-morning. Yadwiga had been dressed for some time. In the mirror on the wall opposite the bed he caught sight of himself—face drawn, his few remaining hairs, once red, now yellowish and streaked with gray. Blue eyes, piercing yet mild, beneath disheveled eyebrows, nose narrow, cheeks sunken, the lips thin.

Herman always woke up shabby and rumpled, looking as if he had spent the night wrestling. This morning there was even a black-and-blue mark on his high forehead. He touched the bruise. "What is this?" he asked himself.

Could it have been caused by the bayonet in his dream?
The thought made him smile. He had probably bumped
against the edge of the closet door on the way to the bathroom during the night.

"Yadwiga!" he called in a sleepy voice.

Yadwiga appeared in the doorway. She was a Polish
woman with rosy cheeks, pug nose, light-colored eyes; her
hair was light as flax, combed back in a bun and held in
place by a single pin. She had high cheekbones and a full
lower lip. In one hand she held a dust mop and in the
other a small watering can. She wore a dress with red and
green squares in a design uncommon in this country, and
on her feet were run-over house slippers.

Yadwiga had spent a year with Herman in the German
camp after the war and had been living in America for
three years, but she had retained the freshness and shyness
of a Polish village girl. She used no cosmetics. She had
learned only a few English words. It even seemed to Herman that she carried with her the odors of Lipsk; in bed
she smelled of camomile. From the kitchen now came the
aroma of beets cooking, of new potatoes, of dill, and something else summery and earthy that he couldn't name
but that evoked a memory of Lipsk.

She looked at him with good-natured reproach, shaking
her head. "It's late," she said. "I've done the laundry and
the shopping. I've had my breakfast, but I'm ready to eat
again."

Yadwiga spoke a peasant Polish. Herman talked to her
in Polish or sometimes in Yiddish, which she did not
understand; he would throw in a few Biblical quotations
in the holy tongue or even phrases from the Talmud, as
the mood struck him. She always listened.

"Shikseh, what time is it?" he said.

"Almost ten o'clock."

"Well, I'll get dressed."

"Would you like some tea?"

"No, it's not necessary."

"Don't walk around barefoot. I'll get your slippers. I polished them."

"You've polished them again? Who polishes slippers?"

"They were all dried up."

Herman shrugged. "What did you polish them with? Tar? You're still a peasant from Lipsk."

Yadwiga went to the clothes closet and brought his bathrobe and slippers.

Though she was his wife and the neighbors called her Mrs. Broder, she behaved toward Herman as if they were still in Tzivkev and she still a servant in the house of his father, Reb Shmuel Leib Broder. Herman's entire family had been wiped out in the holocaust. Herman was alive because Yadwiga had hidden him in a hayloft in her native village of Lipsk. Her own mother had been unaware of his hiding place. After the liberation in 1945, Herman learned from an eyewitness that his wife, Tamara, had been shot after their children had been taken from her to be killed. Herman left with Yadwiga for Germany and the camp for displaced persons and later, when he obtained an American visa, had married her in a civil ceremony. Yadwiga had been ready to adopt the Jewish faith, but it seemed senseless to burden her with a religion that he himself no longer observed.

The slow, hazardous trip to Germany, the voyage on the military ship to Halifax, the bus trip to New York had so bewildered Yadwiga that to this day she was afraid of traveling alone on the subway. She never went farther than a few blocks from the house in which she lived. She really did not need to go anywhere. Mermaid Avenue provided her with everything she needed—bread, fruit, greens, kosher meat (Herman did not eat pork), an occasional pair of shoes or a dress.

On the days Herman stayed home, he and Yadwiga would stroll together on the Boardwalk. Though he told her repeatedly that she needn't cling to him—he was not about to run away from her—Yadwiga always held him firmly by the arm. Her ears were deafened by the noise and clamor; everything vibrated and shook before her eyes. Her neighbors urged her to go with them to the beach, but since the crossing to America Yadwiga had a dread of the ocean. A mere glance at the leaping waves and her stomach began to churn.

Occasionally Herman took Yadwiga to a cafeteria in Brighton Beach, but she could not accustom herself to the trains hurtling by on the El with their deafening roar, or the screeching automobiles racing this way and that, or to the hordes of people in the streets. Herman had bought her a locket to wear, containing a slip of paper with her name and address written on it in case she got lost, but it was no comfort to Yadwiga; she didn't trust anything in writing.

The change in Yadwiga's life seemed like an act of Providence. For three years Herman had depended on her utterly. She had brought food and water to him in the loft and carried out his waste. Whenever Marianna, her sister, needed to go to the hayloft, Yadwiga would climb up the ladder and warn Herman to burrow himself deeper into the space he had hollowed out in the depths of the hay. During the summer, when the fresh-cut hay was being stored away, Yadwiga hid him in the potato cellar. She put her mother and sister in constant jeopardy; if the Nazis discovered that a Jew was hiding out in the barn, they would have shot all three women and perhaps burned down the village as well.

Now Yadwiga lived on an upper floor of an apartment house in Brooklyn. She had two princely rooms, a foyer, a bathroom, a kitchen with a refrigerator, a gas oven, electricity, and even a telephone on which Herman called her when he was away on his book-selling trips. Herman's business might be in distant places, but his voice brought him close to her. When he was in the mood, he would sing her favorite song to her over the telephone:

"Oh, if we were to have a boy.
Praise the Lord on high!
In what would we cradle our joy?
Praise the Lord on high!
In the street below
There's a tub in the snow.
In that would our little son lie
As we sang him a sweet lullaby.

Oh, if we were to have a boy.
Praise the Lord of the poor!
In what would we swaddle our joy?
Praise the Lord of the poor!
In your apron full
And my muffler of wool.
In these would we wrap him secure
Against the cold, he'd be safe and sure."

The song remained a song: Herman took care not to make Yadwiga pregnant. In a world in which one's children could be dragged away from their mother and shot, one had no right to have more children. For Yadwiga, the apartment he gave her made up for not having children. It was like an enchanted palace in the stories that old village wives used to tell while spinning flax or stripping feathers for down. You pushed a button on the wall and lights went on. Hot and cold water flowed from faucets. You turned a knob and a flame appeared on which you could cook. There was a tub for daily baths that kept you clean and free of lice and fleas. And the radio! Herman would set the dial on a station that broadcast in Polish in the morning and evening, and Polish songs, mazurkas, polkas, on Sunday a sermon by a priest, and news from Poland, which had fallen to the Bolsheviks, filled the room.

Yadwiga could neither read nor write, but Herman would write letters for her to her mother and sister. When a reply came, written by the village teacher, Herman would read it to her. Sometimes Marianna enclosed a kernel of grain in the envelope, a little stalk with a leaf from an apple tree, or a small flower—reminders of Lipsk in faraway America.

Yes, in this distant country Herman was Yadwiga's husband, brother, father, God. She had loved him even when she was a servant in his father's house. Living with him in foreign lands, she realized how right she had been about his worth and intelligence. He knew his way in the world —he rode on trains and buses; he read books and newspapers; he earned money. If she needed anything for the house, all she had to do was tell him and he would bring it himself or an Express man would deliver it. Yadwiga would sign her name with three little circles as he had taught her to do.

Once on May 17, her name day, Herman had brought her two parakeets, as they were called here. The yellow one was a male and the blue one a female. Yadwiga named them Woytus and Marianna, after her beloved father and sister. Yadwiga had never got along with her mother. After Yadwiga's father died, her mother had taken a second husband, who beat his stepchildren. Because of him, Yadwiga had to leave home and work as a servant for Jews.

If only Herman stayed home more often, or at least slept at home every night, Yadwiga would have considered her good fortune complete. But he traveled about selling books for a living. When he was away, Yadwiga kept the door chained for fear of thieves, and also to keep the neighbors out. The old women who lived in the apartment house talked to her in a mixture of Russian, English, and Yiddish. They pried into her life, asking where she came from and what her husband did. Herman warned her to tell them as little as possible. He taught her to say in English, "Excuse me, I have no time."

2

HERMAN shaved while the bathtub filled with water. His beard grew fast. Overnight his face became as prickly as a grater. He stood before the mirror of the medicine cabinet—a man of slight build, somewhat taller than aver age, his narrow chest covered with tufts of hair resembling the clumps of stuffing that stick out of old sofas and armchairs. He ate as much as he wanted, but he remained lean. The outline of his ribs could be seen, and there were deep hollows between his neck and shoulders. His Adam's apple moved up and down as if of its own accord. His whole appearance expressed weariness. Standing there, he began spinning a fantasy. The Nazis had come back into power and occupied New York. Herman was hiding out in this bathroom. Yadwiga had had the door walled up and painted so that it looked like the rest of the wall.

"Where would I sit? Here on the toilet seat. I could
sleep in the bathtub. No, too short." Herman examined
the tile floor to see if there was enough room for him to
stretch out. But even if he were to lie down diagonally, he
would have to draw his knees up. Well, at least he would
have light and air here. The bathroom had a window
opening on a small courtyard.

Herman began to calculate how much food Yadwiga
would need to bring him each day for him to survive: two
or three potatoes, a slice of bread, a piece of cheese, a
spoonful of vegetable oil, from time to time a vitamin pill.
It would cost her no more than one dollar a week—at the
most, one dollar and a half. Herman would have some
books here, and writing paper. Compared to the hayloft
in Lipsk, this would be luxurious. He would keep a
loaded revolver at hand, or perhaps a machine gun. When
the Nazis discovered his hiding place and came to arrest
him, he would welcome them with a volley of bullets and
leave one bullet for himself.

The tub almost overflowed; the bathroom was filled
with steam. Quickly Herman turned off the faucets. These
daydreams had taken on the character of obsessions.

As soon as he was in the tub, Yadwiga opened the door.
"Here's some soap."

"I still have a piece left."

"Perfumed soap. Smell. Three for a dime."

Yadwiga smelled the cake of soap herself and handed it
to him. Her hands were still as rough as a peasant's. In
Lipsk, she had done the work of a man. She had sown,
mowed, threshed, planted potatoes, even sawed and
chopped wood. Her neighbors in Brooklyn gave her all
kinds of lotions to soften her hands, but they remained as
calloused as a laborer's. Her calves were muscular, hard as

stone. All the other parts of her body were feminine and smooth. Her breasts were full and white; her hips were round. She looked younger than her thirty-three years.

From sunup until she went to sleep, Yadwiga never rested for a moment. She always found work to do. The apartment was not far from the ocean, but a good deal of dust blew in through the open windows, and all day Yadwiga washed, scoured, polished, and scraped. Herman remembered how his mother had praised her for her industriousness.

"Come, I'll soap you," Yadwiga said.

Actually, he felt like being alone. He hadn't finished figuring out the details of how to hide himself from the Nazis here in Brooklyn. For instance, the window would have to be camouflaged so the Germans wouldn't see it. But how?

Yadwiga started to soap his back, his arms, his loins. He had frustrated her longing to bear children and so had taken the place of child for her. She fondled him, played with him. Every time he went away from home, she feared that he would not return—he would lose his way in the turmoil and vastness of America. His every homecoming seemed a miracle. She knew that today he was to go to Philadelphia, where he would stay overnight, but at least he would eat breakfast with her.

The aroma of coffee and of bread baking drifted in from the kitchen. Yadwiga had taught herself how to make poppyseed rolls like the ones in Tzivkev. She prepared all kinds of delicacies for him and cooked his favorite dishes: dumplings, matzo balls with borscht, millet with milk, groats with gravy.

She had a freshly ironed shirt, underwear, and socks ready for him every day. She wanted to do so much for

him, but he needed so little. He was more often on the
road than at home. She had a burning desire to talk to
him. "What time does the train leave?" she asked.

"What? Two o'clock."

"Yesterday you said three o'clock."

"A few minutes past two."

"Where is this city?"

"You mean Philadelphia? In America. Where should it
be?"

"Is it far away?"

"In Lipsk it would be far, but here it's just a few hours
away by train."

"How do you know who wants to buy books?"

Herman was thoughtful. "I don't know. I try to find
buyers."

"Why don't you sell books here? There are so many
people here."

"You mean Coney Island? Here they come to eat popcorn, not to read books."

"What kinds of books are they?"

"Oh, different kinds: how to build bridges, how to lose
weight, how to run the government. And books of songs,
stories, plays, the life of Hitler—"

Yadwiga's face became serious. "They write books about
such swine?"

"They write about all kinds of swine."

"Well." And Yadwiga went into the kitchen. After a
while Herman followed her.

Yadwiga had opened the little door of the birdcage and
the parakeets were flying about the room. The yellow par-
akeet, Woytus, perched himself on Herman's shoulders.
He liked to pick at Herman's earlobe and nibble crumbs
from his lips or the tip of his tongue. Yadwiga was amazed

at how much younger, fresher, and happier Herman appeared after he had bathed and shaved.

She served him warm rolls, black bread, an omelet, and
coffee with cream. She tried to feed him well, but he
didn't eat properly. He bit off a piece of the roll and put
it aside. He only tasted the omelet. His stomach had
surely shrunk during the war, but Yadwiga recalled that
he had always eaten sparingly. His mother would quarrel
with him about it every time he came home from Warsaw,
where he was studying at the university.

Yadwiga shook her head in concern. He swallowed
without chewing. Even though there was plenty of time
before two o'clock, he kept looking at his watch. He sat on
the edge of his chair as if he were about to jump up at any
moment. His eyes seemed to be staring off beyond the
wall.

Abruptly he shook off his mood and said, "Tonight I'll
be eating supper in Philadelphia."

"Who will you eat with? Alone?"

He started talking to Yadwiga in Yiddish. "Alone.
That's what you think! I'll be eating with the Queen of
Sheba. I'm as much a book salesman as you're the Pope's
wife! That faker of a rabbi I work for—still, if it weren't
for him, we'd be starving. And that female in the Bronx is
a sphinx altogether. What with the three of you, it's an
absolute miracle I haven't gone out of my mind. Pif-pof!"

"Talk so I can understand you!"

"Why do you want to understand? 'For in much wis-
dom is much grief,' Ecclesiastes said. The truth will be
known—not here, but in the hereafter, providing anything is left of our miserable souls. If not, we'll have to
make do without the truth—"

"More coffee?"

"Yes, more coffee."

"What's in the newspaper?"

"Oh, they've made a truce, but it won't last. They'll start fighting again soon—those buffaloes. They never have their fill of it."

"Where is this?"

"In Korea, China—you name it."

"The radio said that Hitler is still alive."

"If one Hitler is dead, there are a million ready to take his place."

Yadwiga was silent a moment. She leaned on her broom. Then she said, "The neighbor with the white hair who lives on the ground floor told me I could earn twenty-five dollars a week in a factory."

"You want to go to work?"

"It gets lonesome sitting in the house by myself. But the factories are so far away. If they were nearer, then I'd work."

"Nothing is near in New York. You have to ride on the subways or you're stuck where you are."

"I don't know English."

"You could take a course. I can enroll you in one if you like."

"The old woman said they don't accept anyone who doesn't know the alphabet."

"I'll teach it to you."

"When? You're never at home."

Herman knew she was right. And at her age it was diffi-cult to learn. When she had to sign anything with her three little circles, she reddened and perspired. It was hard for her to pronounce even the simplest English word.

Generally, Herman understood her peasant Polish, but sometimes at night, when she was overcome with passion, she would chatter a village gibberish that he couldn't follow—words and expressions he had never heard before. Could it be the speech of ancient peasant tribes, perhaps from pagan times? Herman had long been aware that the mind contains more than is gathered in one lifetime. The genes seem to remember other epochs. Even Woytus and Marianna seemed to have a language inherited from generations of parakeets. They obviously carried on conversations, and the way they would take flight together in the same direction, within a fraction of a second, indicated that they knew one another's thoughts.

As for Herman, he was a riddle to himself. The entanglements he involved himself in were mad. He was a fraud, a transgressor—a hypocrite, too. The sermons he wrote for Rabbi Lampert were a disgrace and a mockery.

He got up and went to the window. A few blocks away, the ocean heaved. From the Boardwalk and Surf Avenue came the noises of a Coney Island summer morning. Yet, on the little street between Mermaid and Neptune Avenues, everything was quiet. A light breeze was blowing; a few trees grew there. Birds twittered in the branches. The incoming tide brought with it a smell of fish, and something undefinable, a stench of putrefaction. When Herman put his head out of the window, he could see old shipwrecks that had been abandoned in the bay. Armored creatures had attached themselves to the slimy hulls—half alive, half sunk in primeval sleep.

Herman heard Yadwiga saying reproachfully, "The coffee is getting cold. Come back to the table!"

3

Herman left the apartment and ran down the stairs. If he didn't disappear quickly, Yadwiga might call him back. Every time he went away, she said goodbye as if the Nazis were ruling America and his life was in danger. She laid her hot cheek against his, begged him to be careful of cars, not to forget his meals, to remember to phone her. She clung to him with the devotion of a dog. Herman often teased her, called her silly, but he could never forget the sacrifice she had made for him. She was as direct and truthful as he was devious and enmeshed in lies. Still, he couldn't stay with her day and night.

The house in which Herman lived with Yadwiga was an old building. Many elderly refugee couples who needed fresh air for their health had settled there. They prayed in the little synagogue nearby and read the Yiddish papers. On hot days they brought benches and folding chairs out on the street and sat around chatting about the old country, their American children and grandchildren, about the Wall Street crash in 1929, about the cures worked by steam baths, vitamins, and mineral waters at Saratoga Springs.

Herman occasionally had the desire to strike up an acquaintance with these Jews and their wives, but the complications of his life made it necessary to avoid them. Now he hurried down the shaky steps and turned quickly to the right into the street before any of them could stop him. He was late with his work for Rabbi Lampert.

Herman's office was in a building on Twenty-third

Street near Fourth Avenue. He could get to the subway at
Stillwell Avenue by walking down Mermaid, Neptune, or
Surf Avenues, or by the Boardwalk. Each of these routes
had its attractions, but today he chose Mermaid Avenue.
This street had an Eastern European flavor. Last year's
posters announcing cantors and rabbis and the prices of
synagogue pews for the High Holy Days still hung on the
walls. From the restaurants and cafeterias came the smells
of chicken soup, kasha, chopped liver. The bakeries sold
bagels and egg cookies, strudel and onion rolls. In front of
a shop, women were groping in barrels for dill pickles.

Even if he never had had a large appetite, the hunger of
the Nazi years had left Herman with a sense of excitement
at the sight of food. Sunlight fell on crates and bushel
baskets of oranges, bananas, cherries, strawberries, and
tomatoes. Jews were allowed to live freely here! On the
main avenue and on the side streets, Hebrew schools dis-
played their signs. There was even a Yiddish school. As
Herman walked along, his eye sought hiding places in
case the Nazis were to come to New York. Could a bunker
be dug somewhere nearby? Could he hide himself in the
steeple of the Catholic church? He had never been a parti-
san, but now he often thought of positions from which it
would be possible to shoot.

On Stillwell Avenue, Herman turned right, and the hot
wind struck him with the sweet smell of popcorn. Barkers
urged people into amusement parks and side shows.
There were carousels, shooting galleries, mediums who
would conjure the spirits of the dead for fifty cents. At the
subway entrance, a puffy-eyed Italian was banging a long
knife against an iron bar, calling out a single word again
and again, in a voice that carried over all the tumult. He
was selling cotton candy and soft ice cream that melted as
soon as it was put into a cone. On the other side of the

Boardwalk, the ocean sparkled beyond a swarm of bodies. The richness of color, the abundance, the freedom—cheap and shoddy as everything was—surprised Herman each time he saw it.

He went into the subway. Passengers, mostly young people, streamed out of every train. In Europe Herman had never seen such wild faces as these. But here the young seemed dominated by lust for enjoyment rather than for mischief. The boys ran, screeching, shoving one another like rams. Many of them had dark eyes, low foreheads, and curly hair. There were Italians, Greeks, Puerto Ricans. The small girls with their broad hips and high breasts carried lunch bags, blankets to spread out on the sand, suntan lotion, and umbrellas to protect them from the sun. They laughed and chewed gum.

Herman went up the stairs to the El, and a train soon arrived. When the doors opened, he felt a blast of heat. The ventilators hummed. Bare lightbulbs dazzled the eye; newspapers and peanut shells were strewn over the red cement floor. Some passengers were having their shoes shined by half-naked black boys, who knelt at their feet like ancient idol-worshippers.

A Yiddish newspaper that someone had left behind was lying on a seat and Herman picked it up and read the headlines. Stalin had declared in an interview that Communism and capitalism could co-exist. In China there were battles between the Red and Chiang Kai-shek's armies. On the inside pages of the paper, refugees described the terrors of Majdanek, Treblinka, Auschwitz. An escaped witness gave an account of a slave-labor camp in north Russia, where rabbis, socialists, liberals, priests, Zionists, and Trotskyites were digging for gold, dying of hunger and beriberi. Herman thought he had become inured to such horrors. Yet each new outrage shocked him.

This article ended with the promise that some day there would be established a system based on equality and justice that would cure the sickness of the world.

"So? They are still intent on curing?" Herman dropped the paper to the floor. Phrases like a "better world" and a "brighter tomorrow" seemed to him a blasphemy on the ashes of the tormented. Whenever he heard the cliché that those sacrificed had not died in vain, his anger rose. "But what can I do? I contribute my share of evil."

Herman opened his briefcase, took out a manuscript, and read it, making notes. His livelihood was as bizarre as everything else that had happened to him. He had become a ghost writer for a rabbi. He, too, promised a "better world" in the Garden of Eden.

As Herman read, he grimaced. The rabbi was selling God as Terah sold idols. Herman could find only one justification for himself: most of the people who listened to the rabbi's sermons or read his essays were not completely honest either. Modern Judaism had one aim: to ape the Gentile.

The doors of the train opened and shut; Herman looked up each time. No doubt there were Nazis roaming about New York. The Allies had proclaimed amnesty for three-quarters of a million "small Nazis." The promises to bring the murderers to trial were lies from the very beginning. Who would sentence whom? Their justice was deceit. Lacking the courage to commit suicide, Herman had to shut his eyes, stop up his ears, close his mind, live like a worm.

Herman was to have changed from the express to the local train at Union Square and then get off at Twenty-third Street, but when he looked out, he saw that the train had already reached the Thirty-fourth Street station. He took the stairs to the opposite platform, where he boarded a train going downtown. But again he missed his station and rode too far—to Canal Street.

These mistakes in the subway, his habit of putting things away and not remembering where, straying into wrong streets, losing manuscripts, books, and notebooks hung over Herman like a curse. He was always searching through his pockets for something he had lost. His fountain pen or his sunglasses would be missing; his wallet would vanish; his own phone number would slip from his mind. He would buy an umbrella and leave it somewhere within the day. He would put on a pair of rubbers and lose them in a matter of hours. Sometimes he imagined that imps and goblins were playing tricks on him. Finally he got to his office, located in one of the buildings owned by the rabbi.

4

RABBI MILTON Lampert had no congregation. He published articles in Hebrew journals in Israel and contributed to Anglo-Jewish periodicals in America and England. He had book contracts with several publishing houses. He was in demand for lectures at community centers, and even at universities. The rabbi had neither the time nor the patience to study or write. He had amassed a fortune from real estate. He owned half a dozen convalescent homes, had built apartment houses in Borough Park and Williamsburg, was a partner in a company that contracted for building projects worth millions of dollars. He had an elderly secretary, a Mrs. Regal, whom he continued to employ although she neglected her work. He had been

separated from his wife, but they were again living together.

The rabbi referred to what Herman did for him as "research." Actually, Herman ghosted the rabbi's books, his
articles, his speeches. He wrote them in Hebrew or in Yiddish, someone translated them into English, and a third
person edited them.

Herman had been working for Rabbi Lampert for several years. The rabbi was many things at once: thick-
skinned, goodhearted, sentimental, sly, brutal, naïve. He
could recall obscure commentaries from the Prepared
Table, but make errors in quoting a verse from the Pentateuch. He played the stock market, gambled, and raised
money for all sorts of charitable causes. He was over six
feet tall, had a potbelly, and weighed two hundred and
sixty pounds. He played the role of a Don Juan, but it
soon became apparent to Herman that the rabbi had no
luck with women. He was still searching for his true love
and often made himself ridiculous in this seemingly hopeless quest. It had gone so far that once he was punched in
the nose by a husband in an Atlantic City hotel. His expenses were often greater than his income—at least that's
what he reported on his tax return. He went to bed at two
and woke up at seven in the morning. He ate two-pound
steaks, smoked Havana cigars, drank champagne. His
blood pressure was dangerously high and his doctor kept
warning him about a heart attack. At sixty-four, his energy had not flagged and he was known as "the dynamic
rabbi." He had served as an army chaplain during the war
and boasted to Herman that he had reached the rank of
colonel.

No sooner had Herman crossed the threshold of his office than the telephone rang. He answered it and from the
other end of the line the rabbi immediately began shout-

ing at him in his strong bass voice. "Where the heck have you been? You were supposed to check in the first thing this morning! Where is my speech for Atlantic City? You forget that I still have to go over it, in addition to everything else I have to do. And what do you mean by moving into a house that doesn't have a telephone? When a person works for me, I have to be able to reach him, not have him stuck in a hole like a mouse! Ach, you're still a greenhorn! This is New York, not Tzivkev! America is a free country; you don't have to hide here. Unless you're making money illegally or the devil knows what! I'm telling you today for the last time—get a telephone where you live or our business is goodbye. Wait, I'm coming over. I have to talk to you about something. Stay where you are!" Rabbi Lampert hung up.

Herman started writing quickly in small letters. When he first met the rabbi, he had been afraid to admit that he was married to a Polish peasant. He had said he was a widower and had rented the spare room of a poor friend from the old country—a tailor who didn't have a phone. Herman's telephone in Brooklyn was listed under the name of Yadwiga Pracz.

Rabbi Lampert had often asked if he might visit Herman at the tailor's. It gave the rabbi special pleasure to drive his Cadillac down the streets of a poor neighborhood. He also enjoyed the impression made by his great bulk and smart clothes. And he loved doing favors—finding jobs for the needy, writing letters recommending admission to philanthropic institutions. Herman thus far had been able to talk the rabbi out of visiting him. He had explained that the tailor was too shy for company, and that as a result of his life in the camps he was somewhat unbalanced and might not even let the rabbi into the house. Herman had also dampened the rabbi's interest by casually mentioning that the tailor's wife was lame and that the couple had no children. The rabbi preferred families with daughters.

The rabbi told Herman over and over again that he should move. He went so far as to suggest a match for him. He offered him an apartment in one of his own houses. Herman explained that the old tailor had saved his life in Tzivkev and needed the few dollars of rent money that Herman paid him. One lie led to another. The rabbi made speeches and wrote articles opposing mixed marriages. More than once, Herman himself had to expound on this theme in his writings for the rabbi, warning against mingling with the "enemies of Israel."

How could his actions ever be explained to make sense? He had sinned against Judaism, American law, morality. He was deceiving not only the rabbi but Masha. But he was unable to behave differently. Yadwiga's sheer goodness bored him; when he talked to her, it was as if he were alone. Masha was so complicated, stubborn, and neurotic that he couldn't tell her the truth either. He had convinced her that Yadwiga was frigid and he had made a solemn vow that as soon as Masha divorced her husband, Leon Tortshiner, he would free himself from Yadwiga.

Herman heard heavy footsteps and the rabbi opened the door. He could barely get through the doorway: tall, broad—an enormous man with a red face, thick lips, a hooked nose, and bulging black eyes. He wore a light-colored suit, yellow shoes, and a gold-stitched tie with a pearl stickpin. In his mouth was a long cigar. His gray-streaked black hair stuck out from beneath his Panama hat. Ruby cuff-links glittered at his wrists and a diamond signet ring shone on his left hand.

He took the cigar from his mouth, flicked the ashes on the floor, and shouted, "*Now* you're starting to write. It should have been ready days ago! I can't wait like this till the last minute. What have you got scribbled there? It looks too long already. A conference of rabbis isn't a meeting of the elders of Tzivkev! This is America, not Poland. Well, and how about the essay on Bal Shem? It should have gone off. There's a deadline! If you can't manage it, please tell me and I'll find someone else—or I'll talk into a dictaphone and let Mrs. Regal type it."

"Everything will be ready today."

"Hand me the pages you've done and, once and for all, give me your address. Where do you live—in hell? In Asmodeus' castle? I'm beginning to think that you have a wife somewhere and are hiding her from me."

Herman's mouth felt dry. "I wish I had a wife."

"If you wanted one, you'd have one. I picked out a fine woman for you, but you won't even meet her. What are you afraid of? No one is going to drag you to the wedding canopy by force. Now what's your address?"

"Really, it isn't necessary."

"I insist that you give it to me. I have my address book right here. Well?"

Herman gave him an address in the Bronx.

"What is your landsman's name?"

"Joe Pracz."

"Protsch. An unusual name. How do you spell it? I'll have them put in a phone and tell them to send the bill to this office."

"You can't install one without his consent."

"Why should he care?"

"The ringing frightens him. It reminds him of the camp."

"There are other refugees and they have telephones. Have it put in your room. It will be better for him, too. If he's a sick person, he should be able to call a doctor or get help. Lunatics! Crazy people! This is why we have a war every few years; this is why Hitlers rise up. I insist that you spend six hours a day in the office—that's what we agreed. I'm paying rent and taking it off for tax purposes. If an office is always locked, then it's not an office. I have enough trouble without you."

Rabbi Lampert paused, then he said, "I wanted us to be friends, but there's something about you that makes it difficult. I could help you a great deal, but you shut yourself up like an oyster. What secrets are you hiding behind those proverbial seven locks?"

Herman didn't reply at once. "Anyone who's gone through all that I have is no longer a part of this world," he said finally.

"Clichés, empty words. You're as much a part of this world as the rest of us. You may have been a step away from death a thousand times, but so long as you're alive and eat and walk and, pardon me, go to the toilet, then you're flesh and blood like everyone else. I know hundreds of concentration-camp survivors, some of them were practically on the way to the ovens—they're right here in America, they drive cars, they do business. Either you're in the other world or you're in this world. You can't stand with one foot on the ground and the other in the sky. You're playing a role, that's all. But why? You should be open with me of all people."

"I am."

"What's troubling you? Are you sick?"

"No. Not really."

"Maybe you're impotent? That's all nerves. It's not organic."

"I'm not impotent."

"What is it then? Well, I won't force my friendship on you. But I'm calling today and having them put in a telephone."

"Please wait a while."

"Why? A telephone isn't a Nazi; it doesn't eat people. If you have a neurosis, go see a doctor. Maybe you need an analyst. Don't let it scare you. It doesn't mean you're crazy. The best people go to them. Even I went to an analyst for a time. I have a friend, a Dr. Berchovsky from Warsaw. If I send you to him, he won't overcharge you."

"Honestly, Rabbi, there's nothing wrong with me."

"All right, nothing. My wife also insists there's nothing wrong with her, but she's a sick woman just the same. She turns on the stove and goes shopping. She lets the water run in the tub and leaves a washcloth in it that stops up the drain. I sit at my desk, and suddenly I see a puddle on the carpet. I ask her why she does these things, and she becomes hysterical and begins to curse me. That's why there are psychiatrists—to help us before we get so sick that we have to be put away."

"Yes, yes."

"Well, wasted words. Let's see what you've written."

· CHAPTER TWO ·

1

WHENEVER Herman pretended to be on the road selling books, he spent the nights with Masha in the Bronx. He had a room in her apartment. Masha had survived years in the ghetto and concentration camps. She worked as a cashier in a cafeteria on Tremont Avenue.

Masha's father, Meyer Bloch, had been the son of a rich man, Reb Mendl Bloch, who owned property in Warsaw and had had the honor of sitting at the table of the Alexandrover rabbi. Meyer spoke German, became a Hebrew writer of some reputation, and was a patron of the arts. He escaped from Warsaw before the Nazis occupied the country, only to die later of malnutrition and dysentery in Kazakhstan. Masha had attended the Beth Yaakov schools at the insistence of her Orthodox mother, and later had studied at a Hebrew-Polish high school in Warsaw. During the war, her mother, Shifrah Puah, was sent to one ghetto, Masha to another. They didn't see each other again until they met in Lublin after the liberation in 1945.

Even though Herman had himself managed to survive the Hitler catastrophe, he could never figure out how

[27]

these two women had been able to rescue themselves. He
had spent almost three years hiding in a hayloft. It was a
gap in his life which could never be filled. The summer
the Nazis invaded Poland, he was visiting his parents in
Tzivkev, while his wife, Tamara, had gone with both children to her family in Nalenczew, a spa where her father
owned a villa. Herman had hidden himself first in Tzivkev, then at Yadwiga's in Lipsk, and so avoided the forced
labor of both ghetto and concentration camp. He had
heard the shouts of the Nazis and the sound of their guns,
but had been spared looking into their faces. Weeks had
passed without his seeing the light of day. His eyes had
grown accustomed to darkness; his hands and feet had become numb with disuse. He had been bitten by insects,
field mice, rats. He had developed a high fever and Yadwiga had cured him with herbs she picked in the fields
and with vodka she stole from her mother. In his
thoughts, Herman had often likened himself to the Talmudic sage, Choni Hamagol, who according to legend
slept for seventy years and when he awoke found the
world so strange that he prayed for death.

Herman had met Masha and Shifrah Puah in Germany.
Masha was married to a Dr. Leon Tortshiner, a scientist
who was said to have discovered, or to have helped discover, some new vitamin. But in Germany he spent entire
days and half the nights playing cards with a band of
smugglers. He spoke a flowery Polish and dropped the
names of professors and universities with which he
claimed to have been associated. He managed financially
on what the "Joint" gave him and on the meager income
Masha earned mending and altering clothes.

Masha, Shifrah Puah, and Leon Tortshiner had pre-
ceded Herman to America. When Herman arrived in
New York, he ran into Masha again. He worked first as a

teacher in a Talmud torah and then as proofreader in a small printing shop, where he met the rabbi. By that time Masha had been separated from her husband, who as it turned out neither had made any discoveries nor had any right to the title of Doctor. He was now the lover of a wealthy elderly woman, the widow of a real-estate man. Herman and Masha had fallen in love when they were still in Germany. Masha swore that a gypsy fortuneteller had foretold her meeting with Herman. The gypsy had described him down to the smallest detail and had warned her of the pain and troubles their love would bring. While predicting Masha's future, the gypsy had fallen into a trance and fainted.

Herman and Tamara, his first wife, had both grown up in well-to-do homes. Tamara's father, Reb Shachnah Luria, had been a lumber dealer, and partner with a brother-in-law in a glass business. He had two daughters —Tamara and Sheva. Sheva had died in a concentration camp.

Herman was an only child. His father Reb Shmuel Leib Broder, a follower of the Rabbi of Hushatin, was a wealthy man who owned several houses in Tzivkev. He hired a rabbi to instruct his son in Jewishness and a Polish tutor to teach him secular subjects. Reb Shmuel Leib hoped his only son would become a modern rabbi. Herman's mother, who had attended a German gymnasium in Lemberg, wanted her son to become a doctor. At nineteen, Herman went to Warsaw, passed his matriculation exams, and enrolled in the school of philosophy at the university. He had shown a leaning toward philosophy even as a youngster. He had read all the philosophic books he could find in the Tzivkev library. In Warsaw, against the wishes of his parents, he had married Tamara, a student of biology at the Wszchnica, who was active in

leftist movements. Almost from the very beginning they
did not get along. A disciple of Schopenhauer, Herman
had determined never to marry and bring new generations into the world. He had told Tamara of his resolve,
but she became pregnant, refused to have an abortion,
and enlisted her family to force him into marriage. A boy
was born. For a time she was an ardent Communist and
even planned to go to live in Soviet Russia with her child.
Later she dropped Communism and became a member of
the Poalay Zion Party. Neither Tamara's parents nor Herman's were in a position to continue supporting the
young couple and they earned their living by tutoring.
Three years after their marriage, Tamara gave birth to a
girl—according to Otto Weininger (at the time considered by Herman to be the most consistent philosopher), a
creature with "no sense of logic, no memory, amoral,
nothing but a vessel of sex."

During the war and in the years after, Herman had
time enough to regret his behavior to his family. But basically he remained the same: without belief in himself or
in the human race; a fatalistic hedonist who lived in pre-
suicidal gloom. Religions lied. Philosophy was bankrupt
from the beginning. The idle promises of progress were
no more than a spit in the face of the martyrs of all generations. If time is just a form of perception, or a category of
reason, the past is as present as today: Cain continues to
murder Abel. Nebuchadnezzar is still slaughtering the
sons of Zedekiah and putting out Zedekiah's eyes. The pogrom in Kesheniev never ceases. Jews are forever being
burned in Auschwitz. Those without courage to make an
end to their existence have only one other way out: to
deaden their consciousness, choke their memory, extin-
guish the last vestige of hope.

2

When Herman left the rabbi's office, he took the subway to the Bronx. People were hurrying and shoving in the heat of the summer day. On the Bronx express train, all the seats were taken. Herman gripped a strap. Above his head a fan whirred, but the air it stirred was not cool. He hadn't bought an afternoon paper, so he read the advertisements—for stockings, chocolate, canned soups, "dignified" burials. The train sped into a narrow tunnel. Even the bright lights of the car did not keep out the stony darkness. At each station new clusters of passengers pushed their way in. The smell of perfume and perspiration mingled in the air. Makeup melted on the women's faces; their mascara streaked and caked.

Gradually the crowd thinned; the train now rode aboveground, on the El. Through factory windows Herman could see white and black women moving briskly around machines. In a hall with a low metal ceiling, half-naked youths were playing pool. A girl in a bathing suit lay on a folding cot on a flat roof, taking a sunbath in the setting sun. A bird flew through the pale-blue sky. Even though the buildings didn't seem old, an air of age and decay hovered over the city. A dusty mist, golden and fiery, hovered above everything, as if the earth had entered the tail of a comet.

The El stopped, and Herman bolted out through the door. He ran down the iron steps and walked on into a park. Trees and grass grew there, just as they would in the middle of a field; birds hopped about and chirped in the branches. In the evening, the park benches would be full, but now only a few elderly people occupied them. One old man was reading a Yiddish newspaper through a pair of blue spectacles and a magnifying glass. Another had rolled his trouser leg up to the knee and was warming his rheumatic leg. An old woman was knitting a jacket from coarse gray wool.

Herman turned left onto the street where Masha lived with Shifrah Puah. It had only a few houses, separated by empty lots overgrown with weeds. There was an old warehouse, with bricked-up windows and a gate that was always shut. In one dilapidated house, a carpenter was making furniture that he sold "unfinished." A "For Sale" sign hung on an empty house whose windows had been knocked out. It seemed to Herman that the street couldn't make up its mind whether to remain part of the neighborhood or to give up and disappear.

Shifrah Puah and Masha lived on the third floor of a house with a broken porch and a vacant ground floor, the windows of which were covered with boards and tin. A shaky stoop led to the entrance.

Herman climbed up two flights and stopped—not because he was tired, but because he needed time to complete a fantasy. What would happen if the earth were to split into two parts, exactly between the Bronx and Brooklyn? He would have to remain here. The half with Yadwiga would be drawn into a different constellation by another star. What would happen then? If Nietszche's theory about the eternal return was true, perhaps this had already occurred a quadrillion years ago. God does everything that he is capable of doing, Spinoza wrote somewhere.

Herman knocked on the kitchen door and Masha

opened it immediately. She wasn't tall, but her slenderness and the way she held her head gave the impression that she was. Her hair was dark with a reddish cast. Herman liked to say that it was fire and pitch. Her complexion was dazzlingly white, her eyes light blue with flecks of green, her nose thin, her chin pointed. She had high cheekbones and hollow cheeks. A cigarette dangled between her full lips. Her face reflected the strength of those who have survived peril. Masha now weighed one hundred and ten pounds, but at the time of the liberation she had weighed seventy-two.

"Where's your mother?" Herman asked.

"In her room. She'll be out soon. Sit down."

"Here, I've brought you a present." Herman handed her a package.

"A present? You mustn't bring me presents all the time. What is it?"

"It's a box for holding stamps."

"Stamps? That will come in handy. Are there stamps already in it? There are. I have about a hundred letters to write, but weeks pass and I can't seem to pick up a pen. The excuse I give myself is that there are no stamps in the house. Now I won't have any excuse left. Thanks, dear, thanks. You shouldn't have spent the money. Well, let's eat. I've cooked something you like—stewed meat and groats."

"You promised me not to cook meat any more."

"I promised myself, too, but without meat there's nothing to cook. God himself eats meat—human flesh. There are no vegetarians—none. If you had seen what I have seen, you would know that God approves of slaughter."

"You don't have to do everything God wants."

"You do, you do."

The door from the other room opened and Shifrah

Puah came in—taller than Masha, a brunette with dark
eyes, black hair streaked with gray, which she wore pulled
back in a bun, a sharp nose, and eyebrows that grew together. She had a mole on her upper lip; hairs grew on
her chin. There was a scar on her left cheek, made by a
Nazi bayonet in the first weeks of the Hitler invasion.

It was easy to see that she had once been an attractive
woman. Meyer Bloch had fallen in love with her, had
written Hebrew songs to her. But the camps and illness
had ruined her. Shifrah Puah always wore black. She still
mourned for her husband, her parents, sisters, and
brothers—all exterminated in the ghettos and camps.
Now she squinted like someone who suddenly comes out of
the dark into the light. She raised her small, long-fingered
hands, as if to smooth her hair, and said, "Oh, Herman! I
hardly recognized you. I've got into the habit of sitting
down and falling off to sleep. At night I lie wide awake
till morning, thinking. During the day my eyes yearn for
sleep. Did I sleep long?"

"Who knows? I didn't even know you were asleep,"
Masha said. "She walks around the house as quiet as a
mouse. There are real mice here, and I can't tell the difference any more. She walks around all night and doesn't
even bother to turn on the light. One of these days, you'll
fall in the dark and break a leg. Mark my words."

"You're beginning again. I don't really sleep, but a cur-
tain seems to fall over my face and my mind turns blank.
It shouldn't happen to you. What do I smell? Is something burning?"

"Nothing's burning, Mama, nothing's burning. My
mother has a peculiar habit—everything she does herself
she blames on me. She burns everything she cooks, and as
soon as I make something, she smells it burning. If she
pours herself a glass of milk, she lets it run over, and she

warns me to be careful. It must be a Hitler sickness. In our camp, there was a woman who informed on others—she accused them of the very things she had done herself. It was pathological and funny, too. There are no crazy people; the mad only pretend to be crazy."

"Everyone's sane—only your mother is crazy," Shifrah Puah grumbled.

"I didn't mean that, Mama. Don't put words in my mouth. Sit down, Herman, sit down. He brought me a little box to keep stamps in. Now I'll have to write letters. I should have cleaned your room today, Herman, but I got involved in a thousand other things. I've told you: be a boarder like all other boarders—if you don't demand that your room be kept neat and clean, you'll live in dirt. The Nazis forced me to do things for so long that I can't do anything of my own free will any more. If I want to do something, I have to imagine that a German is standing over me with a gun. Here in America, I've come to realize that slavery isn't such a tragedy after all—for getting things done, there's nothing better than a whip."

"Listen to her carrying on. Ask her what she's talking about," Shifrah Puah complained. "She has to say something contrary, that's all. She inherited it from her father's family—he should rest in the Garden of Eden. They all loved to argue. My father—may he rest in peace—your grandfather, once said, 'Their Talmudic arguments are brilliant, but somehow they end up proving that one is allowed to eat bread on Passover.' "

"How did bread on Passover get into this? Do me a favor, Mama, and sit down. I can't bear to see you standing up. She's so shaky I imagine she's going to fall any minute. And she does fall. A day doesn't pass without her falling."

"What will you think up about me next? I was lying in

the hospital in Lublin and was at death's door. I was at peace at last. Suddenly she appears and calls me back from the other world. What did you need me for if you keep making up lies about me? It's good to die, it's a pleasure. Whoever has tasted death has no more use for life. I thought she was dead too. Suddenly I find out she's alive and has come looking for me. One day she finds me, and the next day she's already talking back to me and pricking me with a thousand needles. If I should tell it all, anyone listening would think I was out of my mind."

"You are, Mama, you are. I would need a barrel of ink to describe the condition she was in when I brought her out of Poland. But one thing I can say with a clear conscience: no one has ever tormented me the way she does."

"What have I done to you, daughter, to make you talk like this? You were healthy even then—may no evil eye befall you—and I was dead. I told her openly, 'I don't want to live any more. I've had enough.' But she pulled me back to life with a fury. You can destroy a person with anger, but you can bring him back to life with it too. Why did you need me? It suited her fancy to have a mother, that's all. And that husband of hers, Leon, didn't appeal to me from the beginning. I took one look at him and I said, 'Daughter, he's a charlatan.' Everything is written on a person's forehead, they say, if you know how to read. My daughter can read the most difficult books, but when it comes to people, she doesn't know her hands from her feet. Now she's been left sitting here, a deserted wife, a grass widow forever."

"If I want to get married, I won't wait for a divorce."

"What! We're still Jews, not Gentiles. What's happening to the stew? How long does a stew have to sit on the fire? The meat will dissolve. Just let me look at it. Oh, my God! There's not a drop of water in the pot. Oh, you can't depend on her! I smelled it burning. They made a cripple out of me, those fiends, but I still have my sense of smell. Where are your eyes? You've read too many ridiculous books, God pity me!"

3

MASHA smoked while she ate. She alternated between a bite of food and a puff on her cigarette. She tasted a bit of each dish and pushed the plate away, but she kept passing food to Herman, urging him to eat. "Imagine you're in the hayloft in Lipsk and your peasant has served you a piece of pork. How do we know what tomorrow will bring? It can happen again. Slaughtering Jews is part of nature. Jews must be slaughtered—that's what God wants."

"Daughter, you're breaking my heart."

"It's the truth. Papa always said that everything comes from God. You say it, too, Mama. But if God could allow the Jews of Europe to be killed, what reason is there to think He would prevent the extermination of Jews of America? God doesn't care. That's how God is. Right, Herman?"

"Who knows?"

"You have the same answer for everything: 'Who knows?' Someone must know! If God is almighty and omnipotent, He ought to be able to stand up for His beloved people. If He sits in heaven and stays silent, that means it must bother Him as much as last year's frost."

"Daughter, are you going to leave Herman in peace or aren't you? First you burn the meat, then you pester him with questions while he's trying to eat."

"It doesn't matter," Herman said. "I wish I knew the answer. It could be that suffering is an attribute of God. If one agrees that everything is God, then we are God too, and if I beat you, it means that God has been beaten."

"Why should God beat Himself? Eat up. Don't leave anything on your plate. Is that your philosophy? If the Jew is God and the Nazi is God, then there's nothing to talk about. Mama baked a kuchen. I'll bring you a piece."

"Daughter, first he has to eat the compote."

"What's the difference what he eats first? It all gets mixed up in the stomach anyway. You're a dictator, Mama, that's what you are. All right, bring him the compote."

"I beg you, don't quarrel on my account. What I eat first is of no importance. If you two can't live together peacefully, how can there ever be peace? The last two people on earth will kill each other."

"Do you doubt it?" Masha asked. "I don't. They'll stand opposite one another with atomic bombs and starve to death, because neither will give the other a chance to eat. If one were to take time out to eat, the other would throw the bomb. Papa always took me with him to the movies. She hates movies"—Masha nodded toward her mother—"but Papa was crazy about them. He used to say that when he was at the movies, he forgot all his troubles. I'm not interested in them now, but then I loved them too. I used to sit with him and he would let me hold his cane. When Papa left Warsaw, that day when all the men went away across the Praga bridge, he pointed to his cane and said, 'As long as I have this, I'm not lost.' Why am I bringing this up? Oh, yes! In one movie, they showed two deer—bucks—fighting over a female. They locked antlers and thrashed about till one of them fell dead. The survivor was half dead himself. The whole time, the female

stood by chewing grass as if she wasn't involved at all. I
was a child—in the second year of high school. I thought
then, if God can instill such violence in innocent beasts,
there is no hope. I often thought of that film in the
camps. It made me hate God."

"Daughter, you shouldn't talk that way."

"I do many things I shouldn't do. Bring the compote!"

"How can we understand God?" Sifrah Puah went to
the stove.

"Really, you shouldn't argue with her so much," Herman said quietly. "What can you accomplish by it? If my
mother were alive now, I wouldn't talk back to her."

"You're teaching me how to act? I have to live with her
—not you. Five days out of the week, you stay with your
peasant, and when you finally come here, you start preach-
ing. She infuriates me with her piety and narrow-minded-
ness. If God is so right, why does she raise such a fuss because the soup isn't ready as fast as she wants it to be? If
you want my opinion, she's more devoted to material
things than any atheist. First, she urged me to marry Leon
Tortshiner because he used to bring her little cakes.
Later, she started to find fault with him—God knows
why. What difference was it to me who I married? After
all I'd been through, how could it matter? But tell me,
how is your little peasant? Did you tell her you were
going on a book-selling trip again?"

"What else?"

"Where are you today?"

"In Philadelphia."

"What happens if she finds out about us?"

"She'll never find out."

"There's always the possibility."

"You may be sure she will never separate us."

"I'm not so sure. If you can spend so much time with

an illiterate goose, then you certainly don't have a need
for anything better. And what sense is there in doing the
dirty work for a swindler of a rabbi? At least become a
rabbi and swindle in your own name."

"I can't do that."

"You're still hiding in your hayloft. That's the truth!"

"Yes, it's the truth. There are soldiers who can drop a
bomb on a city and kill a thousand people, but they can't
bring themselves to slaughter a hen. As long as I don't see
the reader I deceive and he doesn't see me, I can stand it.
Besides, what I write for the rabbi doesn't do any harm.
On the contrary."

"Does that mean you're not a fraud?"

"I am and let's stop talking about it!"

Shifrah Puah returned. "Here's the compote. Wait, let
it cool. What's she saying about me, my daughter? What is
she saying? You would think I was her worst enemy, the
way she talks."

"Mama, you know the proverb: 'God protect me from
my friends, I'll protect myself from my enemies.' "

"I saw how you protected yourself from them. Oh well,
since I'm still alive after they butchered my family and my
people, you are right. You alone, Masha, are responsible. I
would have been at rest now if it hadn't been for you."

4

AFTER supper, Herman went to his room. It was a tiny
room with a single window overlooking a small yard.
Below there was grass growing and a crooked tree. The
bed was rumpled. Books, manuscripts, and scraps of paper
covered with Herman's doodles lay scattered about.

Just as Masha always had to hold a cigarette between her fingers, so Herman had to hold a pen or a pencil. He wrote and made notes even in the hayloft in Lipsk, whenever there was enough light coming through the cracks in the roof. He practiced an ornate calligraphy, elaborating the letters with flourishes. He drew pictures of outlandish creatures with protruding ears, long beaks, and round eyes, and surrounded them with trumpets, horns, and adders. He even wrote in his dreams—on yellowish paper in Rashi script, a combination of a story book, cabalistic revelations, and scientific discoveries. He sometimes woke up with a cramp in his wrist from too much writing.

Herman's room was under the roof, and during the summer it was always hot, except early in the morning before the sun rose. Heavy soot sifted in through the open window. Although Masha changed the sheets and pillow cases frequently, the bedding always looked grimy. There were holes in the floor, and at night mice could be heard scratching underneath. Several times Masha set a trap, but the sound of the trapped creatures in agony was too much for Herman. He would get up in the middle of the night and free them.

As soon as he came into his room, Herman stretched out on the bed. His body was racked by pain. He suffered from rheumatism and sciatica; sometimes he thought he was walking around with a spinal tumor. He had neither the patience to go to doctors nor confidence in them. The years of Hitlerism had left him with a fatigue he never quite got rid of except when he made love to Masha. After eating, his stomach ached. Every little draft clogged his nose. Often his throat was sore, and he grew hoarse. Something in his ear pained him—an abscess, a growth? The one thing his organism escaped was fever.

It was evening, but the sky was still light. A single star

shone brightly, blue and green, near and far, with a glow
and substantiality that baffled him. A straight line led
from its height in the universe directly to Herman's eye.
This heavenly body (if it was a body) twinkled with
cosmic joy; it laughed at the physical and spiritual small-
ness of a being that possessed only a talent for suffering.

The door opened and Masha came in. In the twilight
her face was a mosaic of shadows. Her eyes seemed to gen-
erate their own light. She had a cigarette between her lips.
Herman repeatedly warned her that one day she would
start a fire with her cigarettes. "Sooner or later I will
burn," she always replied. Now she stood at the door, inhaling. The glow of the cigarette made her face seem fiery
and fantastic for a moment. Then she removed a book
and magazine from a chair and sat down. She said, "God
in heaven, it's hot as hell here."

Despite the heat, Masha would not undress as long as
her mother was awake. For appearance's sake, she had put
bedding on the sofa in the living room.

Meyer Bloch, Masha's father, had considered himself an
unbeliever, but Shifrah Puah remained devout and maintained a strictly kosher kitchen. She even wore a wig on
the High Holy Days when she went to pray. On the Sabbath, she insisted that Meyer Bloch perform the sanctification ceremony and sing the Sabbath hymns, although after
the meal he would lock himself in his study and write poetry in Hebrew.

The ghetto, the concentration camps, the dis-
placed-person camps, had unsettled the traditions of both
mother and daughter. In the German camp where Shifrah Puah had lived with Masha after the war, couples cop-
ulated openly. When Masha married Leon Tortshiner,
Shifrah Puah slept in one room with her daughter and
son-in-law, separated only by a screen.

Shifrah Puah would say that the soul, like the body, could take so many blows and no more; then it stopped feeling pain. In America, her piety intensified. She prayed three times a day and often went around with a cloth covering her hair, imposing restrictions upon herself that she hadn't observed even in Warsaw. She continued to live in spirit with those who had been gassed and tortured. She was always lighting paraffin-filled glasses—memorial candles for friends and relatives. In the Yiddish newspapers she read nothing but the accounts of those who had survived the ghettos and concentration camps. She saved money from her food budget to buy books about Majdanek, Treblinka, Auschwitz.

Other refugees used to say that with time one forgets, but neither Shifrah Puah nor Masha would ever forget. On the contrary, the further removed they were from the holocaust, the closer it seemed to become. Masha would attack her mother for grieving so much for the dead victims, but when her mother was silent, Masha would take over. When she talked of German atrocities, she would run to the mezuzah on the door and spit on it.

Shifrah Puah would pinch her own cheeks. "Spit, daughter, blaspheme! We've had one catastrophe here, and we'll have another one there!" And she would point to the sky.

Masha's separation from Leon Tortshiner and the affair she was carrying on with Herman Broder, the husband of a Gentile woman, were to Shifrah Puah a continuation of the horrors that had begun in 1939; it seemed they would never cease. But, nevertheless, Shifrah Puah felt close to Herman and called him "my child." She was impressed by his knowledge of Judaism.

Every day in her prayers, she implored the Almighty to make Leon Tortshiner agree to divorce Masha, and Her-

man separate from his Gentile wife, and let her, Shifrah
Puah, live to have the joy of leading her daughter to the
wedding canopy. But it appeared that such rewards were
not to be hers. Shifrah Puah blamed herself: she had re-
belled against her parents, she treated Meyer badly, she
had paid too little attention to Masha when she was growing up, when it would have been possible to instill the
fear of God in her. And the greatest sin she had committed was to have remained alive when so many innocent
men and women had been martyred.

Shifrah Puah was in the kitchen, washing the dishes
and mumbling to herself. She seemed to be arguing with
an unseen person. She turned off the light and turned it
on again. She recited the prayer to be said before retiring,
took a sleeping pill, filled the hot-water bottle. Shifrah
Puah suffered from heart, liver, kidney, and lung ail-
ments. Every few months she would fall into a coma and
the doctors would give her up, but each time she gradually recovered. Masha listened to every move her mother
made, always on the alert should help be needed. Mother
and daughter loved one another, yet held innumerable
grudges against each other. Their grievances dated back to
the time when Meyer Bloch was still alive. He had carried
on an allegedly platonic love affair with a Hebrew poetess,
a teacher of Masha's. Masha would say jestingly that the
love affair had started with a discussion about some rule
in Hebrew grammar and had never gone any further. But
Shifrah Puah had not forgiven Meyer even this small un-
faithfulness.

Shifrah Puah's room was dark now, and still Masha sat
on the chair in Herman's room, smoking one cigarette
after another. Herman knew that she was preparing some
unusual story for their love play. Masha compared herself

to Scheherazade. The kissing, the fondling, the passionate love-making was always accompanied by stories from the ghettos, the camps, her own wandering through the ruins of Poland. Through them all, men pursued her: in bunkers, in the forest, in the hospital where she had worked as a nurse.

Masha had collected scores of adventures. Sometimes it seemed she must be making them up, but Herman knew she was not a liar. Her most complicated experiences had come after the liberation. The moral of all her tales was that if it had been God's purpose to improve His chosen people by Hitler's persecution, He had failed. The religious Jews had been practically wiped out. The worldly Jews who managed to escape had, with few exceptions, learned nothing from all the terror. Masha boasted and confessed at the same time. Herman would warn her not to smoke in bed, but she would kiss him and blow smoke rings at him. Sparks from her cigarettes would land on the sheet. She would chew gum, munch chocolates, drink Coca-Cola. She would bring Herman food from the kitchen. Their love-making was not merely a matter of a man and a woman having intercourse, but a ritual that often lasted till daybreak. It reminded Herman of the ancients, who would relate the miracle of the exodus from Egypt until the morning star rose.

Many of the heroes and heroines that peopled Masha's dramas had been killed, had died in epidemics, or were trapped in Soviet Russia. Others had settled in Canada, Israel, in New York. Once Masha had gone into a bakery to buy a cake and the baker had turned out to be a former Capo. Refugees recognized her in the cafeteria on Tremont Avenue, where she was a cashier. Some had become rich in America—had opened factories, hotels, supermarkets. The widowers had taken new wives, the widows new husbands. Women who had lost their children and were still young had other children in new marriages. Men who had been smugglers in Nazi Germany and dealt in black-market goods had married German girls, sometimes the daughters and sisters of Nazis. No one had repented his sins—neither the aggressor nor the victim. Take Leon Tortshiner, for example.

Masha never tired of talking about Leon Tortshiner and his trickery. He was everything at once: a pathological liar, a drunkard, a braggart, a sex maniac, a gambler who would wager the shirt on his back. He invited his mistress to the wedding banquet that Masha and her mother had paid for with their last pfennigs. He dyed his hair; he assumed the title of Doctor, to which he had no right; he had been accused of plagiarism. He belonged at one and the same time to the Zionist Revisionist Party and to the Communist Party. The New York judge who had granted Masha a legal separation had allotted her fifteen dollars a week alimony, but Leon Tortshiner had yet to pay one cent. On the contrary, he used every device to get money out of her. He still telephoned her, wrote her letters, and begged her to return to him.

More than once, Herman had made Masha promise not to stay up late. They both needed to get up in the morning to go to work. But Masha seemed hardly to require sleep. She could doze off and wake up refreshed a few minutes later. Her dreams plagued her. She would shout in her sleep, talk German, Russian, Polish. The dead revealed themselves to her. She would use a flashlight and show Herman the scars the dead had left on her arms, her breasts, her thighs. Her father appeared to her in a dream and read her verses he had written in the other world. A stanza had remained in her mind and she had recited it to Herman.

Even though Masha had had love affairs of her own in the past, she could never forgive Herman his former relationships with women—not even with those who had died. Had he ever loved Tamara, the mother of his children? Had her body been more attractive to him than Masha's? In what way? Well, and what about that student of romance languages, the girl with the long braids? And Yadwiga? Was she really as cold as he said she was? And what would happen if Yadwiga were suddenly to die—if she were to commit suicide? If Masha were to die—how long would he remember her? How long would he wait before finding someone else? If he would just once be honest with her!

"How long would *you* wait?" Herman asked.

"I would never have anyone again."

"Is that the truth?"

"Yes, you devil, it's the holy truth." And she kissed him long and passionately. It became so still in the room that the scratching of a mouse could be heard under the flooring.

Masha possessed the suppleness of an acrobat. She aroused in him desires and powers he didn't know he had. In some mystical way she could temporarily stop the bleeding during her period. Even though neither Masha nor Herman was perverse, they talked endlessly to each other of unusual sexual behavior and perversions. Would she enjoy torturing a Nazi murderer? Would she make love to women if there were no men left on earth? Could Herman turn homosexual? Would he copulate with an animal if all humans had perished? It was only since his affair with Masha that Herman had begun to understand why union, the joining of male and female, was so important in the Cabala.

At moments when Herman fantasized about a new

metaphysic, or even a new religion, he based everything on the attraction of the sexes. In the beginning was lust. The godly, as well as the human, principle is desire. Gravity, light, magnetism, thought may be aspects of the same universal longing. Suffering, emptiness, darkness are nothing more than interruptions of a cosmic orgasm that grows forever in intensity . . .

5

TODAY Masha had morning hours at the cafeteria. Herman had slept late; it was a quarter to eleven when he awoke. The sun was shining, and the sound of birds and the rumble of a delivery truck came through the open window. In the other room, Shifrah Puah was reading the Yiddish newspaper, occasionally heaving a deep sigh over the troubles of the Jews and human cruelty in general. Herman went into the bathroom, shaved, and bathed. His clothing was in the Coney Island apartment, but he kept some shirts, handkerchiefs, and underwear here in the Bronx. Shifrah Puah had washed and ironed a fresh shirt for him. She behaved toward him like a mother-in-law. Even before he was dressed, she had started to make his omelet; she had bought strawberries especially for him. Herman felt catered to and at the same time embarrassed when he ate breakfast with Shifrah Puah. She insisted that he wash his hands from a pitcher, according to the Orthodox ritual. Now that Masha wasn't at home, she gave him his hat to wear when he recited the prayer over the hand-washing and later for the benediction. She sat opposite him at the table, nodding and muttering. Herman knew what she was thinking: in the camps one hadn't allowed oneself to so much as imagine a feast like this. There a person would have risked his life for a piece of bread, a potato. Shifrah Puah picked up a slice of bread as if she were touching a sacred object. She bit into it carefully. Guilt stared out of her dark eyes. Could she permit herself to enjoy God's bounty when so many God-fearing Jews had died of starvation? Shifrah Puah often maintained that she had been permitted to survive only because of her sins. The blessed souls, the pious Jews, God had taken to Himself.

"Eat up everything, Herman. It's forbidden to leave anything."

"Thanks. The omelet is excellent."

"How can it be bad? Fresh eggs, fresh butter. America —long may it prosper—is full of good things. Let's hope we don't lose it through sinfulness. Wait, I'll bring the coffee."

In the kitchen, while she poured out the coffee, Shifrah Puah broke a glass. Breaking dishes was one of her failings. Masha often scolded her because of this and Shifrah Puah was ashamed of her weakness. Her vision wasn't what it should be. In the past, she assured Herman, she had never broken a thing, but she had come out of the camps a bundle of nerves. Only God in heaven knew how much she suffered, how tortured she was by nightmares. How can one stay alive remembering all she remembered? That very moment, as she stood at the stove, she had seen in her mind's eye a young Jewish girl stripped naked and balancing on a log over a pit of excrement. All around her stood groups of Germans, Ukrainians, Lithuanians, taking bets on how long she would be able to stand there. They shouted insults at her and at the Jews; half drunk, they watched until this eighteen-year-old beauty, this daughter of rabbis and esteemed Jews, slipped and fell into offal.

Shifrah Puah recalled a hundred such incidents to Herman. It was this memory that had caused her to drop the glass. Herman went to help her pick up the pieces, but she wouldn't let him. He might—God forbid—cut his fingers. She swept up the slivers of glass with a brush and dustpan and then carried in his coffee. He often had the feeling that whatever she touched became holy. He drank his coffee and ate a piece of cake she had baked especially for him (the doctor had put her on a strict diet). He was sunk in thoughts so old and familiar that they were no longer expressible in words.

Herman didn't have to go to his office. Masha was through at noon and he went to the cafeteria to meet her. She was to get her first vacation this summer—one week. She was anxious to go somewhere with him, but where? Herman walked down Tremont Avenue toward the cafeteria. He passed shops selling fancy goods, ladies' wear, stationery. Salesmen and saleswomen sat and waited for customers just as in Tzivkev. Chain stores had driven many of the small businesses into bankruptcy. Here and there a for-rent sign hung on the door. There was always someone ready to try his luck again.

Herman entered the cafeteria through the revolving door and saw Masha. There she stood, the daughter of Meyer Bloch and Shifrah Puah, accepting checks, counting money, selling chewing gum and cigarettes. She caught sight of him and smiled. According to the cafeteria clock, Masha had twenty minutes more to work, so Herman sat down at a table. He preferred a table next to the wall or, if possible, in a corner between two walls, so that no one could come up behind him. Despite the big meal he had just eaten, he bought a cup of coffee and some rice pudding at the counter. It seemed impossible for him to put on weight. It was as if a fire in him consumed everything. From a distance, he watched Masha. Although the sun shone in through the windows, the electric lights were on. At neighboring tables men were openly reading Yiddish newspapers. They didn't need to hide from anyone. It always seemed like a miracle to Herman. "How long can this last?" he would ask himself.

One of the customers was reading a Communist paper. He probably felt dissatisfied with America, hoped for a revolution, for the masses to swarm into the street, to break the store windows Herman had just passed, and drag the salespeople off to prison or to slave-labor camps.

Herman sat quietly, preoccupied with the complexities of his situation. He had remained in the Bronx for three days. He had telephoned Yadwiga and told her that he had had to go on from Philadelphia to Baltimore, and had promised to be back this evening. But he wasn't sure that Masha would let him go; they had talked of going to a film together. She used every device to keep him with her, and made things as difficult as she could. Her hatred of Yadwiga approached the irrational. If Herman had a stain on his clothing or a button was missing from his coat, Masha would accuse Yadwiga of being indifferent to him, of living with him only because he was supporting her. Masha was the best argument Herman knew for Schopenhauer's thesis that intelligence is nothing more than a servant of blind will.

Masha finished her work at the cash register, gave the money and the checks to the cashier who was relieving her, and came over to Herman's table with her lunch on a tray. She had slept very little the night before and had awakened early, but she didn't look tired. The usual cigarette hung between her lips, and she had already had

quite a few cups of coffee. She loved spicy food—
sauerkraut, dill pickles, mustard; she added salt and pep-
per to everything she ate, drank her coffee black without
sugar. She took a sip of coffee and drew deeply on her cigarette. She left three-fourths of the meal uneaten.

"Well, how is my mother?" she asked.

"Everything's all right."

"All right? I have to take her to the doctor tomorrow."

"When is your vacation?"

"I'm not sure yet. Come, let's get out of here! You
promised to take me to the zoo."

Both Masha and Herman could walk for miles. Masha
stopped often at store windows. She belittled American
luxuries, but she had a keen interest in bargains. Businesses that were closing down might be selling goods at
great reductions—sometimes less than half price. For pennies Masha would buy remnants of fabric from which she
made clothes for herself and her mother. She also sewed
bedspreads, curtains, even slip covers for the furniture.
But who came to visit her? And where did she go? She
had alienated her refugee friends—first, to avoid Leon
Tortshiner, who was in their circle, and second, because
of her life with Herman. There was always the danger
that he might meet someone who knew him from Coney
Island.

They stopped at the Botanical Gardens to look at the
flowers, palms, cactuses, the innumerable plants grown in
the synthetic climate of hothouses. The thought occurred
to Herman that Jewry was a hothouse growth—it was
kept thriving in an alien environment nourished by the
belief in a Messiah, the hope of justice to come, the promises of the Bible—the Book that had hypnotized them forever.

After a while Herman and Masha continued on to the Bronx Zoo. Its reputation had reached them even in Warsaw. Two polar bears dozed in the shadow of an overhanging ledge by a pool of water, undoubtedly dreaming of snow and icebergs. Each animal and bird conveyed something in its own wordless language, a story handed down from prehistoric times, both revealing and concealing the patterns of continuous creation. The lion slept, and from time to time lazily opened his golden eyes, which expressed the despondency of those who are allowed neither to live nor to die, and with his mighty tail swept away the flies. The wolf paced to and fro, circling his own madness. The tiger sniffed at the flooring, seeking a spot on which to lie down. Two camels stood immobile and proud, a pair of Oriental princes. Herman often compared the zoo to a concentration camp. The air here was full of longing —for deserts, hills, valleys, dens, families. Like the Jews, the animals had been dragged here from all parts of the world, condemned to isolation and boredom. Some of them cried out their woes; others remained mute. Parrots demanded their rights with raucous screeching. A bird with a banana-shaped beak turned its head from right to left as if looking for the culprit who had played this trick on him. Chance? Darwinism? No, there was a plan—or at least a game played by conscious powers. Herman was reminded of Masha's words about the Nazis in heaven. Wasn't it possible that a Hitler presided on high and inflicted suffering on imprisoned souls? He had equipped them with flesh, blood, teeth, claws, horns, anger. They had either to commit evil or to perish.

Masha threw her cigarette away. "What are you thinking about—which came first, the chicken or the egg? Come, buy me some ice cream."

· CHAPTER THREE ·

1

HERMAN spent two days with Yadwiga. Since he planned to go away with Masha for her week's vacation, he was careful to tell Yadwiga beforehand about a trip he would have to take to faraway Chicago. To make it up to her in advance, he took her on a one-day outing. Right after breakfast, they walked to the Boardwalk and he bought rides on a carousel. Yadwiga almost screamed when Herman sat her on a lion—he mounted a tiger. With one hand she held on to the lion's mane and with the other she held an ice-cream cone. Next they rode on the Wonder Wheel and the little car in which they sat hurtled back and forth. Yadwiga fell over Herman and laughed with fright and glee. After a lunch of knishes, stuffed derma, and coffee, they strolled over to Sheepshead Bay, where they took a boat to Breezy Point. Yadwiga was afraid she might become seasick, but the water stayed calm; the waves, a mixture of green and gold, barely moved. The breeze had tousled Yadwiga's hair and she tied it back with a kerchief. Music was playing at the pier where the boat stopped, and Yadwiga drank lemonade. In the evening, after a fish dinner, Herman took her to a musical film full of dancing, singing, beautiful women, and magnificent palaces. He translated for her so that she would know what was happening. Yadwiga snuggled up close to him, held his hand, and from time to time raised it to her lips. "I'm so happy . . . so lucky," she whispered. "God himself has sent you to me!"

That night, after a few hours of sleep, Yadwiga awakened, filled with desire. She begged him, as she had so many times before, to give her a child, to arrange for her conversion to Judaism. He promised her everything she asked.

In the morning, Masha telephoned Herman to say that her vacation had been postponed for a few days, because the cashier who was to substitute for her was ill. Herman told Yadwiga that the Chicago trip, on which he had hoped to sell a lot of books, had to be put off and instead he was going to Trenton, close by. He made a brief stop at the rabbi's office on Twenty-third Street, then he took the subway to Masha's house. He should have been content, but he was tormented by the foreboding of some catastrophe. What would it be—would he be taken sick? Would some misfortune befall Masha or Yadwiga, God forbid? Would he be arrested or deported for failing to pay taxes? True, he probably didn't earn enough, but still he should have filled out the form; it was possible he owed the federal government or the state a few dollars. Herman was aware that some of his fellow countrymen from Tzivkev knew he was in America and made efforts to get in touch with him, but he preferred to keep his distance. Every human contact was a potential danger to him. He even knew he had distant relatives somewhere in America but he neither asked nor wanted to know where they were.

That evening Herman spent with Masha. They quarreled, made up, quarreled again. As always, their conversation abounded with promises they both knew would never be kept, with fantasies of pleasures not to be achieved, with questions asked as a spur to their mutual excitement. Masha wondered if she would have allowed him to sleep with her sister, if she had had one. Would she enjoy sharing Herman and his brother, if he had had a brother? What would she do if her father were still alive and had developed an incestuous passion for her? Would Herman still find her desirable if she decided to go back to Leon Tortshiner, or marry some rich man for his money? If her mother were dead, would Masha move in with Herman and Yadwiga? Would she leave him if he became impotent? Often their conversations culminated in talk of death. They both believed they would die young. Masha urged Herman again and again to acquire a cemetery plot for the two of them so that they could be buried together. In her passion, Masha assured Herman that she would visit him in his grave and they would make love. How could it be otherwise?

Masha had to leave for the cafeteria early in the morning, and Herman remained in bed. As usual, he was behind in his work for Rabbi Lampert, and he resolved to finish the manuscript that had been promised. He had given the rabbi a false address at which to have a telephone installed, but it seemed the rabbi had forgotten all about it. Thank God, he was too preoccupied with his own business to remember. The rabbi made notes, but he never consulted them. None of the old philosophers and thinkers could have foreseen an epoch such as this one: the helter-skelter epoch. Work in haste, eat in haste, speak in haste, even die in haste. Perhaps rushing was one of God's attributes. Judging by the swiftness of electromagnetic flow and the momentum with which the galaxies

move outward from the center of the universe, one might
conclude that God is impatient. He prods the angel Metatron; Metatron pushes the angel Sandalphon, the sera-
phim, cherubim, Ophanim, Erelim. Molecules, atoms, and
electrons move with mad speed. Time itself is pressed for
time in which to carry out the tasks it has taken upon itself in endless space, in infinite dimensions.

Herman fell asleep again. His dreams too were hurried,
running into one another, wiping out the law of identity,
negating the categories of reason. He dreamed that while
he was having intercourse with Masha, the upper part of
her body had become separated from the lower part and
was standing before a mirror chiding him and pointing
out that he was copulating with only half a woman. Herman opened his eyes. It was fifteen minutes past ten.
Shifrah Puah was saying her morning prayers in the
other room—slowly, syllable by syllable. He dressed and
went into the kitchen, where, as always, she had breakfast ready for him. A Yiddish newspaper lay on the table.

Herman leafed through it while he drank his coffee.
Suddenly he saw his own name. It was in the "Personals"
section: "Mr. Herman Broder of Tzivkev, please contact
Reb Abraham Nissen Yaroslaver." There was an address
on East Broadway, as well as a telephone number. Herman sat rigid. It was pure chance that he had seen it. Generally he contented himself with skimming the headlines
on the front page. He knew who Reb Abraham Nissen Yaroslaver was—an uncle of his dead wife, Tamara, a
learned man, an Alexandrover Hasid. When Herman first
arrived in America, he had visited him and promised that
he would come again. Even though his niece was no
longer alive, Reb Abraham Nissen wanted to help Herman, but Herman avoided him because he didn't want
him to know that he was married to a Gentile woman.

And here was Reb Abraham Nissen looking for him in the newspaper!

"What can this mean?" Herman asked himself. He was frightened of this man who was involved with the Tzivkev Landsleit. I'll pretend I didn't see it, he decided. But he sat a long time, staring at the notice. The telephone rang and Shifrah Puah answered it. She said, "Herman, it's for you. Masha."

Masha called to say that she had to work an extra hour and would meet Herman at four. While they talked, Shifrah Puah picked up the paper. She saw his name and turned her head toward him in surprise, pointing to the paper with her finger. As soon as Herman hung up, Shifrah Puah said, "They're looking for you in the newspaper. Here."

"Yes, I saw it."

"Call up. They give a phone number. Who is it?"

"Who knows? Probably someone from the old country."

"Call them up. If they put it in the paper, it must be important."

"Not for me."

Shifrah Puah raised her eyebrows. Herman remained at the table. After a while he tore out the notice. He showed her that there was nothing on the back of it but another advertisement and that no text would be missing that she might want to read. Then he said, "They want to drag me into the Landsmanscaft, but I neither have the time for it nor the patience."

"Maybe some relative has turned up."

"There is no one left."

"Nowadays if someone is looked for, it's no small matter."

Herman had determined earlier to go back to his room and put in a few hours' work. Instead, he said goodbye to

Shifrah Puah and went out. With slow steps he walked toward Tremont Avenue. He thought he would go to the park, sit on a bench, and go over the manuscript, but his legs carried him to a phone booth. He felt depressed, and he realized that the premonition that had nagged him for the past few days must have to do with this advertisement. There was such a thing as telepathy, clairvoyance— whatever it might be called.

He turned into Tremont Avenue and went into a drugstore. He dialed the number given in the newspaper. "I'm getting myself into a mess," he thought. He could hear the telephone ringing, but there was no answer.

"Well, it's better this way," he decided. "I won't call again."

At that moment Reb Abraham Nissen's voice asked, "Who is it? Hello?" The voice sounded old, cracked, and familiar, even though Herman had only spoken to the man once, and then not on the telephone.

Herman cleared his throat. "This is Herman," he said. "Herman Broder."

There was a silence, as if Reb Abraham Nissen had been caught by surprise. After a moment he seemed to collect himself; his voice became louder and clearer. "Herman? You saw the notice in the newspaper? I have news for you, but don't be frightened. It isn't—God forbid— bad news. On the contrary. Don't get nervous."

"What is it?"

"I have information about Tamar Rachel—Tamara. She's alive."

Herman didn't answer. Apparently somewhere in his mind he had allowed for the possibility that this might happen, because he was not as shocked as he might have been. "And the children?" he asked.

"The children are gone."

Herman said nothing for a long time. The quirks of his own fate had been so extraordinary that nothing could surprise him any more. He heard himself saying, "How can this be? A witness saw her being shot—what was his name? I can't think of it."

"Yes, it's true, she was shot, but she remained alive. She escaped to a friendly Gentile's house. Later she made her way to Russia."

"Where is she now?"

"Here in my house."

Again the silence between the two men was long. Then Herman asked, "When did she arrive?"

"She's been here since Friday. She just knocked at the door and came in. We've been looking all over New York for you. Just a minute, I'll call her to the phone."

"No, I'll come right over."

"What? Well—"

"I'll come right over," Herman repeated. He tried to hang up the receiver, but it fell from his hand and dangled at the end of the cord. He thought he heard Reb Abraham Nissen's voice still coming from it. He opened the door of the booth. He stared at a counter opposite him where a woman was sitting on a stool sipping a drink through a straw while a man served her some cookies. She was flirting with the man and all the wrinkles in her rouged face smiled imploringly, with the humility of those who can no longer demand but only beg. Herman replaced the receiver, left the booth, and walked to the door.

Masha often accused him of being a "mechanical man" and at this moment he agreed with her. His feelings were dammed up and his mind was calculating coldly. He was to meet Masha at four o'clock. He had promised Yadwiga he would be home in the evening. He still had the rabbi's

manuscript to finish. As he stood in the doorway of the
drugstore, customers going in and out bumped into him.
He was reminded of Spinoza's definition of wonder:
"When the mind is without motion because the imagination of this particular thing has no connection with the
rest . . ."

Herman started to walk, but he could not remember in
which direction the cafeteria was located. He stopped in
front of a mailbox.

"Tamara, alive!" He said the words out loud. This hysterical woman, who had tormented him and whom he had
been about to divorce when the war broke out, had risen
from the dead. He wanted to laugh. His metaphysical
joker had played him a fatal trick.

Herman knew that every minute was precious, but he
was unable to move. He leaned against the mailbox. A
woman dropped a letter into it and eyed him suspiciously.
Run away? Where to? With whom? Masha couldn't leave
her mother. He had no money. Yesterday he had changed
a ten-dollar bill and until the rabbi gave him a check he
was left with four dollars and some change. And what
would he say to Masha? Her mother would certainly tell
her about the notice.

He concentrated on his watch. The small hand pointed
to the eleven and the big one to the three, but their meaning didn't register. He became absorbed in the watch face
as if some mental exertion were required to read the time.

"If only I were wearing my good suit!" For the first
time Herman felt the common ambition of the refugee: to
show that he had achieved a degree of success in America.
At the same time, something in him mocked this trite desire.

2

HERMAN walked to the El and climbed the steps. Except for its impact on him, Tamara's return had changed nothing. The passengers read their newspapers and chewed gum as always. The train's fans made the same rumbling noise. Herman picked up a discarded newspaper from the floor and tried to read it. It was a horse-racing sheet. He turned the page, read a joke, and smiled. Along with the subjectivity of appearances, there is a mystic objectivity.

Herman pulled his hat brim down to keep the light from shining through his eyelids. "Bigamy? Yes, bigamy." In a sense, he could be accused of polygamy. During the years he believed Tamara dead, he had tried to remember her good qualities. She had loved him. She was essentially a spiritual person. He had often spoken to her soul, begged her forgiveness. At the same time, he knew that her death had spared him misery. Even the years wasted in the hayloft in Lipsk had sometimes seemed a respite when set against the trouble Tamara had caused him during their years together.

Herman no longer remembered exactly why he had quarreled so bitterly with her, why he had left her and neglected their children. The conflict between husband and wife had become an endless haggle in which one party was never able to convince the other. Tamara talked incessantly of the redemption of humanity, the plight of the Jews, the role of woman in society. She praised books which Herman considered little better than pulp, was enthusiastic about plays that revolted him, sang the current song hits with gusto, and attended the lectures of all the party demagogues. When she was a Communist, she wore a leather jacket à la Cheka; when she became a Zionist, she wore a Star of David around her neck. She was constantly celebrating, protesting, signing petitions, and raising funds for all kinds of party purposes. In the late thirties, when the Nazi leaders visited Poland and nationalist students beat up Jews and forced Jewish students to stand during the lectures at the university, Tamara, like many others, had turned to religion. She began to light candles on Friday night and to keep a kosher household. She seemed to Herman to be the incarnation of the masses, always following some leader, hypnotized by slogans, never really having an opinion of her own.

In his irritation he had overlooked her devotion to him and the children, the fact that she was always there to help him and others. Even when he had moved out of the house and lived in a furnished room, she would come and clean it for him and bring him food. She nursed him when he was sick, mended his clothes, and washed his linen. She even typed his dissertation, although in her opinion it was anti-humanistic, anti-feminist, and depressing in outlook.

"Could she possibly have calmed down?" Herman asked himself. "Let's see, how old would she be?" He couldn't figure out her age exactly, but she was older than he. Herman tried to bring events into some order, to piece together what must have happened. The children had been taken from her. She had been shot; with the bullet lodged in her body, she had found refuge in a Gentile home. Her wound had healed; she had been smuggled into Russia. It must have happened before 1941. Well, and where had she been all those years? Why hadn't he heard from her since 1945? True, Herman hadn't searched for her. He had never looked through the lists that were published in the Yiddish newspapers for those seeking lost relatives. Had anyone ever been in such a predicament? Herman asked himself. No. Trillions, quadrillions of years would have to pass before this combination of circumstances repeated itself. Again Herman felt like laughing. Some heavenly intelligence was conducting experiments on him, similar to those the German doctors had carried out on the Jews.

The train stopped and Herman jumped up—Fourteenth Street! He climbed the stairs to the street, turned east, and walked to the bus stop to wait for an eastbound bus. The morning had been cool, but it was becoming hotter by the minute. Herman's shirt clung to his back. Some article of clothing was making him uncomfortable, but he was unable to identify it. Was it his collar, the elastic waistband of his underwear, perhaps his shoes? He passed a mirror and saw his reflection: lean and wasted, a bit stooped, wearing a battered hat and rumpled trousers. His tie was twisted. Herman had shaved just a few hours ago, but his beard already made a shadow on his face. "I can't go there looking like this!" he said to himself in alarm. He slowed his pace. He looked into the store windows. Perhaps he could pick up a cheap shirt. Maybe there was a place nearby where he could get his suit pressed. At least he could get his shoes shined. He stopped at a shoeshine stand and a young black boy started to smear shoe polish on his shoes with his fingers, tickling Herman's toes through the leather. The warm air, filled with dust, gasoline fumes, odors of asphalt and sweat, was nauseating. "How long can the lungs endure it?" he wondered. "How long can such a suicidal civilization last? They'll all suffocate—first they'll go mad, then choke."

The black boy started to say something about Herman's shoes, but Herman didn't understand his English. Only the first syllable of each word reached his ears. The boy was half naked. His square-shaped head was sweating.

"How's business?" Herman asked, trying to make conversation, and he answered, "Pretty good."

3

HERMAN sat on the bus that went from Union Square to East Broadway and looked out the window. The neighborhood had changed since his arrival in America. Now many Puerto Ricans lived there. Whole blocks of buildings had been torn down. Nevertheless, one still occasionally saw a sign in Yiddish and, here and there, a synagogue, a yeshiva, a home for the aged. Somewhere in the area was the headquarters of the Tzivkev Landsleit Society that Herman was so anxious to avoid. The bus passed kosher restaurants, a Yiddish film-theater, a ritual bath, a hall that could be rented for weddings or bar mitzvahs, and a Jewish funeral parlor. Herman saw young boys with earlocks longer than any he had seen in Warsaw, their heads covered by broad-brimmed velvet hats. It was in this section and on the other side of the bridge in Williamsburg that the Hungarian Hasidim, followers of the rabbis of Sącz, Belz, and Bobow, had settled, continuing the old feuds. Some of the extremist Hasidim even refused to recognize the land of Israel.

On East Broadway, where Herman got off the bus, he glimpsed through a basement window a group of white-bearded men studying the Talmud. Their eyes under heavy brows expressed scholarly sharpness. The wrinkles on their high foreheads reminded Herman of the ruled lines of parchment scrolls used by scribes to guide their letters. The faces of the old men reflected a stubborn grief as ancient as the books they studied. For an instant Herman toyed with the idea of joining them. How long would it be before he too was a graybeard?

Herman recalled what he had learned from a landsman about the circumstances of Reb Abraham Nissen Yaroslaver's coming to America a few weeks before Hitler's invasion of Poland. In Lublin he had owned a small establishment that published rare religious books. He had traveled to Oxford to copy an old manuscript that had been discovered there. In 1939 he had come to New York to enlist prenumerants for printing this manuscript, and was prevented from returning by the Nazi invasion. He lost his wife, but in New York had married the widow of a rabbi. He had given up his plan to publish the Oxford manuscript and instead had begun work on an anthology of the writings of the rabbis who had perished at the hands of the Nazis. His present wife, Sheva Haddas, helped him. Both of them had taken it upon themselves to observe mourning one day a week—Monday—for the martyrs in Europe. On that day, they fasted, sat in their stocking feet on low stools, and observed all the rules of shiva.

Herman approached the house on East Broadway and glanced up at the windows of Reb Abraham Nissen's ground-floor apartment. They were hung with half curtains, like those used in the old country. He climbed the short flight of stairs and rang the doorbell. There was no response at first. He thought he heard whispering behind the door, as if those inside were debating whether or not to let him in. The door opened slowly and an old woman,

obviously Sheva Haddas, stood on the threshold. She was
short, thin, had wrinkled cheeks and a sunken mouth, and
wore a pair of spectacles on her hooked nose. In her high-
collar dress and bonnet, she looked exactly like the pious
women in Poland. There was no trace of America in her
appearance, or any indication of hurry or excitement;
from her manner, it would seem that such a reunion between husband and wife was an everyday occurrence.

Herman greeted her and she nodded. They walked
down a long foyer without speaking. Reb Abraham Nissen stood in the living room—short, stocky, stooped, with
a pale face, a full yellow-and-gray beard, and disheveled side-
locks. He had a high forehead, a flattened skullcap sat
on his head. The brown eyes under the gray-yellow eyebrows expressed both confidence and sorrow. A broad,
fringed garment could be seen beneath his unbuttoned
robe. Even the house smell seemed to belong to the past
—fried onions, garlic, chicory, wax. Reb Abraham Nissen
looked at Herman and his gaze seemed to say, "Words are
superfluous." He glanced at a door that led to another
room.

"Call her in," he ordered his wife. Calmly, the old
woman left the room.

Reb Abraham Nissen said, "A miracle from heaven!"

It seemed to take a long time. Again, Herman imagined
he heard a whispered argument. The door opened and
Sheva Haddas led Tamara into the room as if she were
leading a bride to the canopy.

Herman took everything in at once. Tamara had aged a
little, but she appeared surprisingly young. She was wearing American clothes and had obviously visited a beauty
parlor. Her hair was jet black and had the artificial sheen
of fresh dye, her cheeks were rouged, her eyebrows
plucked, her fingernails red. She made Herman think of a

stale loaf of bread put into a hot oven to be freshened up. Her hazel eyes seemed to look at him sideways. Until this moment, Herman would have sworn that he remembered Tamara's features perfectly. But now he noticed something that he had entirely forgotten: a crease at the corner of her mouth that had always been there and that gave her an expression combining vexation, suspicion, and irony. He stared at her: the same nose, the same cheekbones, the same set of the mouth, the same chin, lips, ears. He heard himself saying, "I hope you recognize me."

"Yes, I recognize you," she answered, and it was Tamara's voice, although it was somewhat changed—perhaps because of its guarded tone.

Reb Abraham Nissen motioned to his wife and they both left the room. Herman and Tamara remained silent a long time.

"Why is she wearing pink?" Herman thought. His embarrassment had subsided and he experienced a feeling of irritation that the woman who had seen their children taken away to be killed allowed herself to be dressed in this fashion. Now he was glad that he hadn't changed into his good clothes. He again became the Herman he used to be—the man who didn't get along with his wife, the husband who had turned away from her. "I didn't know you were alive," he said. And he was ashamed of his own words.

"That's something you *never* knew," Tamara retorted sharply in her old way.

"Well, sit down—here on the sofa."

Tamara sat. She was wearing nylon stockings. She pulled down her dress, which had risen above her knees. In silence, Herman stood across the room from her. It occurred to him that the spirits of the newly dead encountered one another in this way, speaking the words of the living, not yet knowing the language of the dead. "How did you come here—by boat?" he asked.

"No, by plane."

"From Germany?"

"No, from Stockholm."

"Where were you all this time? In Russia?"

Tamara seemed to be mulling over his question. Then she said, "Yes, in Russia."

"I didn't know you were alive until this morning. An eyewitness came to me and told me that he had seen you being shot."

"Who was he? Nobody came out alive. Unless he was a Nazi."

"He was a Jew."

"It can't be. They shot two bullets into me. One is in my body to this day," Tamara said, indicating her left hip.

"Can't it be removed?"

"Perhaps here in America."

"It's as if you've risen from the dead."

"Yes."

"Where did it happen? In Nalenczew?"

"In a field on the outskirts. I managed to get away at night, though my wounds were bleeding. It was raining, or else the Nazis would have seen me."

"Who was the Gentile?"

"Pawel Czechonski. My father had done business with him. I went to him, thinking, 'What could possibly happen now? At the worst, he'll report me.' "

"He saved your life?"

"I stayed there four months. They couldn't trust a doctor. He was my doctor. He and his wife."

"Have you heard from them since?"

"They're no longer alive."

They were both silent. Then Tamara asked, "How is it that my uncle didn't know your address? We had to put an advertisement in the paper."

"I don't have my own apartment. I live with someone else."

"You could have left him your address."

"What for? I don't see anyone."

"Why don't you?"

He wanted to reply, but the words wouldn't come. He pulled a chair from the table and sat down on the edge of it. He knew that he should ask her about the children, but he was unable to do so. Even when he heard people talking about children who were alive and healthy, he felt something akin to panic. Every time Yadwiga or Masha expressed the wish to have a child by him, he would change the subject. Somewhere among his papers there were photographs of little Yocheved and David, but he never dared to look at them. Herman had not behaved toward them as a father should. At one time he had even denied their existence and played the role of a bachelor. And here was Tamara—the witness of his crime. He was afraid that she would begin to cry, but she retained her composure.

"When did you find out that I was alive?" he asked.

"When? After the war. By an extraordinary coincidence. An acquaintance of mine—actually, a close friend—was wrapping a package in a Yiddish newspaper from Munich and happened to see your name in it."

"Where were you then? Still in Russia?"

Tamara didn't answer, and he didn't repeat his question. From his own experience with Masha and other survivors of the German camps, he knew that the whole truth would never be learned from those who had survived the concentration camps or the wandering through Russia—not because they lied but because it was impossible for them to tell it all.

"Where do you live?" Tamara asked. "What do you do?" In the bus Herman had imagined that Tamara would ask these questions. Nevertheless, he sat in stunned silence.

"I didn't know you were alive and—"

Tamara smiled wryly. "Who is the lucky woman who has taken my place?"

"She isn't Jewish. She's the daughter of the Pole in whose house I hid."

Tamara considered his reply. "A peasant?"

"Yes."

"Was that how you repaid her?"

"You might say it was that."

Tamara looked at him but didn't answer. She had the absent expression of someone who is saying one thing and thinking another.

"What kind of work do you do?" she repeated.

"I work for a rabbi—an American rabbi."

"What do you do for the rabbi? Answer questions on ritual law?"

"I write books for him."

"And what does he do? Dance with shiksehs?"

"That's not as far from the truth as you might think. I see you've already learned a great deal in this country."

"There was an American woman in our camp. She had come to Russia looking for social justice and was immediately packed off to a camp, the camp I was in. She died there of diarrhea and starvation. I have the address of her sister somewhere. She held my hand before she died and made me promise to locate her relatives and tell them the truth."

"Her family is also Communist?"

"It would seem so."

"They won't believe you. They're all hypnotized."

"There were mass deportations to the camps. They took men, starved them, and made them do work that would destroy even the strongest within a year. I witnessed it myself. If I hadn't seen it, I wouldn't believe it either."

"What happened to you?"

Tamara bit her lower lip. She shook her head as if to indicate the futility of relating what was beyond belief. This was not the garrulous Tamara he had known but a different person. The odd thought occurred to him that perhaps this wasn't Tamara but her sister. Then suddenly she began to speak.

"What happened to me can never be fully told. The truth is, I don't really know myself. So much happened that I sometimes imagine nothing happened. I have completely forgotten many things, even about our life together. I remember lying on a wooden plank in Kazakhstan, trying to recall why, during the summer of 1939, I took the children on a visit to my father, but I simply couldn't find any sense or reason for what I had done.

"We sawed logs in the forest—twelve and fourteen hours a day. At night it was so cold I couldn't sleep at all. It stank so, I couldn't breathe. Many of the people suffered from beriberi. One minute a person would be talking to you, making plans, and suddenly he would be silent. You spoke to him and he didn't answer. You moved closer and saw that he was dead.

"So I lay there and asked myself, 'Why didn't I go with Herman to Tzivkev?' But I couldn't recall a thing. This, they tell me, is a psychological illness. I suffer from it. Sometimes I remember everything and sometimes nothing. The Bolsheviks taught us to be atheists, but I still be-

lieve everything is predestined. It was fated that I had to
stand by and watch those monsters rip out my father's
beard and a piece of his cheek as well. Anyone who did
not see my father at that moment doesn't know what it
means to be a Jew. I never knew it myself or I would have
followed in his footsteps.

"My mother fell at their feet and they trampled on her
with their boots and spat at her. They would have raped
me, but I was having my period and you know how I
bleed. Oh, later it stopped, it stopped all right. Where
does one get blood if one doesn't have bread? You ask
what happened to me? A speck of dust blown by the wind
across land and desert can't tell where it's been. Who was
the Gentile who hid you?"

"It was our servant. You knew her—Yadwiga."

"You married *her?*" Tamara looked as if she were about
to laugh.

"Yes."

"Forgive me, but wasn't she simple-minded? Your
mother used to make fun of her. She didn't even know
how to put on a pair of shoes. I remember your mother
telling me how she tried to put the left shoe on the right
foot. If she was given money to buy something, she would
lose it."

"She saved my life."

"Yes, I suppose one's life is worth more than anything
else. Where did you marry her—in Poland?"

"In Germany."

"Was there no other way to repay her? Well, I'd better
not ask."

"There isn't anything to ask. That's the way it is."

Tamara stared at her leg. She raised her dress a bit and
scratched her knee, then quickly pulled her skirt down
over it. "Where do you live? Here in New York?"

"In Brooklyn. It's part of New York."

"I know. I was given an address there. I have a book full of addresses. I would need a whole year just to go around telling relatives how this one died, how that one died. I've already been to Brooklyn. My aunt explained the way, and I went alone by subway. I came to a house and no one there knew a word of Yiddish. I tried to speak in Russian, Polish, German, but they knew only English. I tried sign language to indicate to them that their aunt had died. The children simply laughed at me. The mother looked like a fine woman, but without a trace of Jewishness in her. People know a little, a drop in the ocean, about what the Nazis did. But the world knows nothing about what Stalin did and is still doing. Not even those who live in Russia know the whole story. What did you say your job was—a writer for a rabbi?"

Herman nodded. "Yes, in a way. I am also a book salesman." He found himself lying out of habit.

"You do that in addition? What kind of books do you sell? Yiddish books?"

"Yiddish, English, Hebrew. I am a so-called traveling salesman."

"Where do you travel?"

"Different cities."

"And what does your wife do when you go away?"

"What do other wives do when their husbands travel? Here in America, selling is an important profession."

"Do you have any children by her?"

"Children? No!"

"It wouldn't shock me if you did have. I met young Jews who married former Nazis, and when it comes to talking about what some girls did to save their skins, I'd better be quiet. People became totally depraved. In a bed next to mine, a brother and sister were carrying on. They couldn't even wait till it grew dark. So what can surprise me any more? Where did she hide you?"

"I told you, in a hayloft."

"And her parents didn't know?"

"She has a mother and a sister. No father. They didn't know."

"Of course they knew. Peasants are crafty. They figured out that after the war you would marry her and take her to America. I assume you crawled into bed with her even when you were with me."

"I didn't crawl into her bed. You're talking nonsense. How could they know that I would get a visa to America? As a matter of fact, I had intended to go to Palestine."

"They knew, they knew. Yadwiga may be an idiot, but her mother talked it over with other peasants and they helped her figure it out. Everyone wants to come to America. The whole world is dying to come to America. If the quotas were opened, America would become so jammed there wouldn't be room for as much as another pin. Don't think I'm angry at you. In the first place, I'm not angry at anyone any more. In the second place, you didn't know I was alive. You deceived me while we lived together. You ran away from the children. You didn't even write me a letter during those last few weeks, knowing that the war was about to break out at any moment. I know of fathers who risked their lives crossing frontiers in order to be with their children. Men who had managed to escape to Russia turned themselves over to the Nazis out of longing for their families. But you remained in Tzivkev and crept into a hayloft with your lover. How can I even pretend to have any claims on such a person? Well, why don't you have any children by her?"

"I don't and that's that."

"Why look at me like that? *You* married her. Since my father's grandchildren weren't good enough for you and you were as ashamed of them as if they were scabs on your scalp, why shouldn't you have other children by Yadwiga? Her father was certainly a finer man than mine."

"Well, for a moment I thought you had changed, but I see you're still the same."

"No, not the same. You are looking at a different woman. Tamara who left her murdered children and fled to Skiba—that's the name of the village—is another Tamara. I am dead, and when his wife is dead, the husband may do as he pleases. It's true, this body of mine is still dragging itself about. It has even dragged itself to New York. They put nylon stockings on me, dyed my hair, and polished my fingernails, God help me, but Gentiles have always prettied up their corpses, and Jews nowadays are Gentiles. So I bear no grudges against anyone, nor am I dependent on anyone. I wouldn't have been surprised to hear that you married a Nazi, one of those who danced on corpses and ground her heels into the eyes of Jewish daughters. How can you possibly know what happened? I just hope you're not playing the same tricks on your new wife that you played on me."

Footsteps and voices could be heard from behind the door that led to the foyer and the kitchen. Reb Abraham Nissen Yaroslaver came in, followed by Sheva Haddas. Both husband and wife shuffled rather than walked. Reb Abraham Nissen addressed Herman.

"You probably don't have an apartment as yet. You may stay with us till you find one. Hospitality is an act of charity, and besides, you are relatives. As the Holy Book says, 'And thou shalt not hide thyself from thine own flesh.' "

Tamara interrupted. "Uncle, he has another wife."

Sheva Haddas clasped her hands. Reb Abraham Nissen looked baffled.

"Well, that's another story—"

"There was an eyewitness who testified that he saw how they were—" Herman stopped himself. He had neglected to warn Tamara not to tell them that his wife was a Gentile. He looked toward Tamara and shook his head. He had a childish impulse to leave the room before being disgraced. He moved toward the door, hardly aware of what he was doing.

"Don't run away. I won't force you into anything," Tamara said.

"Truly it's something one only reads about in the newspaper," Sheva Haddas said.

"You haven't, God forbid, committed any sin," Abraham Nissen said. "Had you known she was alive, it would have meant you were living illegally with a woman. But in this case, Rabbi Gershom's interdiction does not apply to you. One thing is definite: you'll have to divorce your present wife. Why didn't you tell us?"

"I didn't want to trouble you."

Herman signaled to Tamara, this time with his finger on his lips. Reb Abraham Nissen grasped his beard. Sheva Haddas's eyes expressed a motherly grief. Her head, covered by its bonnet, nodded submission to the ancient prerogative of masculine infidelity, the passion for new embraces that even the most righteous man could not resist. It has always been this way and so it will remain, she seemed to be thinking.

"These are issues a man and wife must discuss alone," she said. "Meanwhile, I'll make something to eat." She turned toward the door.

"I've just eaten, thank you," Herman said quickly.

"His wife is a good cook. She has undoubtedly prepared some greasy soup for his supper." Tamara grimaced with derision in the way Orthodox Jews sometimes do when they mention pork.

"A glass of tea with a cookie?" Sheva Haddas asked.

"No, nothing, really."

"Perhaps you should go into the other room and talk it over," Reb Abraham Nissen said. "As they say, 'These are matters between him and her alone.' If I can help you, I will certainly do so." In a changed tone, the old man continued, "This is a time of moral chaos. The guilty ones are the wicked murderers. Do not take the blame on yourself. There was no choice."

"Uncle, there is no lack of wicked people among the Jews. Who do you think dragged us away to that meadow? Jewish police. Before dawn they broke down all the doors, searched in cellars and attics. If they found people hiding, they beat them with rubber clubs. They corraled us with ropes as if we were cattle going to slaughter. I said a word to one of them and he kicked me so hard I'll never forget it. They didn't know, the fools, that they wouldn't be spared either."

"As it is said, 'Ignorance is the root of all evil.' "

"The GPU in Russia were no better than the Nazis."

"Well, the prophet Isaiah said, 'And man is bowed down and man is humbled.' When people stop believing in the Creator, anarchy prevails."

"It's the human species," Herman said, as if to himself.

"The Torah says, 'For the imagination of man's heart is evil from his youth.' But that's why there is a Torah. Yes, go in there and talk it over together."

Reb Abraham Nissen opened the door to a bedroom. There were two beds in it, covered with European spreads and placed lengthwise, head to head, as in the old coun-

try. Tamara shrugged her shoulders and went in first;
Herman followed. It reminded him of the bridal chambers into which, years ago, brides and grooms were escorted on their wedding night.

New York hurried along outside, but here behind the
half curtains a part of Nalenczew or Tzivkev survived. Everything re-created a picture of bygone years: the faded
yellow of the walls, the high ceiling, the floorboards, even
the style of the chest of drawers and the upholstery of the
armchair. An experienced stage director couldn't have se-
lected a more suitable setting, Herman thought. He
smelled the odor of snuff. He sat down in the armchair
and Tamara seated herself on the edge of the bed.

Herman said, "You needn't tell me, but—if you assumed I was dead, then you must surely have—with
others—"

He couldn't go on. His shirt was wet again.

Tamara examined him, slyly.

"You want to know? Everything at once?"

"You don't have to tell me. But I've been honest with
you and deserve—"

"Did you have any choice? You had to tell me the truth.
According to the law, I'm your wife, which means that
you have two wives. They're strict about such things in
America. No matter what I did, I want you to know one
thing: love is no sport for me."

"I didn't say it was a sport."

"You made a caricature of our marriage. I came to you
an innocent girl and—"

"Stop it!"

"The fact is that no matter how much we suffered,
never knowing whether we would live another day or
even another hour, we needed love. We craved it more
than when things were normal. People lay in bunkers or

in attics, hungry and lousy, but they kissed and held hands. I would never have guessed that people could be so passionate in such circumstances. To you I was less than nothing, but men devoured me with their eyes. God help me! My children had been murdered and men wanted me to carry on affairs with them. They offered me a loaf of bread, a bit of fat, or some privilege at work. Don't imagine these were small matters. A crust of bread was a dream. A few potatoes were a fortune. There was business going on in the camps all the time, deals being made a few steps away from the gas chamber. The total merchandise could fit into a shoe, but that's how desperate people were to save their lives. Handsome men, younger than I, husbands of attractive wives, ran after me and promised me the moon.

"It didn't occur to me that you might be alive, but even if you were, I owed you no loyalty. On the contrary, I wanted to forget you. But wanting is one thing and being able to do it is something else again. I have to love a man or sex is disgusting to me. I used to envy those women for whom love was a game. What then is it, after all, if not a game? But there is something in me, the accursed blood of my God-fearing grandmothers, that stopped me.

"I told myself that I was a damned fool, but when a man touched me I had to pull away. They thought I was crazy and they were right too. They called me hypocrite. People became rough. One highly esteemed man tried to rape me. In the middle of all this, my camp mates in Jambul set about arranging a match for me. They all said the same thing: 'You are young and must get married.' But you are the one who got married, not I. One thing I know, the merciful God in whom we believed does not exist."

"Then there was no one?"

"You sound disappointed. No, I had no one and will never have anyone again. I want to stand pure before the souls of my children."

"I thought you said God does not exist."

"If God was able to watch all this horror and remain silent, then He's no God. I talked to devout Jews, even rabbis. There was a young man in our camp—he had been a rabbi in Old Dzikow. He was so pious—there aren't any left like him. He had to work in the forest, though he didn't have the strength for it. Those Reds knew well enough that his work was worthless, but torturing a rabbi was considered a good deed. On Saturdays, he wouldn't take his portion of bread, because of the law against carrying anything on the Sabbath. His mother, the old rabbi's wife, was a holy person. Only God in heaven knows how she comforted others and how she gave away the last of what she owned to help. She became blind as a result of the conditions in the camp. But she knew all the prayers by heart and recited them up to her last moment.

"Once I asked the son, 'How can God allow such tragedies?' He tried to give me all kinds of excuses. 'We don't know God's ways,' and all the rest of it. I didn't argue with him, but I felt bitter. I told him about our children and he turned pale as chalk and looked ashamed—as if he himself had been responsible. Finally, he said, 'I beg of you, don't speak any more.' "

"Yes, yes."

"You don't even ask about the children."

Herman waited a minute. "What is there to ask?"

"No, don't ask. I knew that there were great people among adults, but that children—small children—can become great, I would never have believed. They grew up overnight. I tried to give them some of my rations, but they refused to eat any of my share. They went to their deaths like saints. Souls exist; it's God who doesn't. Don't try to contradict me. That's my conviction. I want you to know that our little David and Yocheved come to me. Not in my dreams, but when I am awake. Naturally, you think I'm crazy, but that doesn't bother me in the least."

"What do they say to you?"

"Oh, different things. Where they are they are children again. What do you want to do? Divorce me?"

"No."

"Then what shall I do? Move in with your wife?"

"First of all, you must get yourself an apartment."

"Yes. I can't stay here."

· CHAPTER FOUR ·

1

"WELL, the impossible is possible," Herman said to himself. "It's really happened."

He walked along Fourteenth Street, muttering. He had left Tamara at her uncle's house and was on his way to Masha, having phoned her from a cafeteria on East Broadway to tell her that a distant relative of his from Tzivkev had turned up. Sardonically he had given the relative a name—Feivl Lemberger—and had described him as a Talmudic scholar, a man in his sixties. "Are you sure it isn't Eva Kracover, a former girl friend of yours in her thirties?" Masha had asked.

"If you like, I'll introduce you to him," Herman had replied.

Now Herman stopped at a drugstore to phone Yadwiga. All the phone booths were occupied and he had to wait. What was so bewildering was not so much the event itself, but the fact that in all his fantasies and imaginings the possibility that Tamara was alive had not occurred to him. Perhaps his children too would rise up from the dead? The scroll of life would roll back and all that had been would be once again. As long as the Powers were

[*85*]

playing with him, they undoubtedly had something more in store. Had they not created a Hitler and a Stalin? One could rely on their ingenuity.

After ten minutes all five telephone booths were still occupied. One man gesticulated as he talked, as if the party at the other end of the line could see him. A second moved his lips in an uninterrupted monologue. A third talked and smoked while lining up the change he needed to prolong the conversation. A girl laughed and kept looking at the red fingernails of her left hand, as if the dialogue with her telephone partner concerned those nails, their shape and color. Each of the talkers was apparently involved in a situation that demanded explanations, apologies, subterfuge. Their faces expressed deceit, curiosity, worry.

At last a booth became vacant and Herman entered, breathing the odor and warmth of another man. He dialed the number and Yadwiga answered at once, as if she had been standing by the phone, waiting.

"Yadzia darling, it's me."

"Oh, yes!"

"How are you?"

"Where are you calling from?"

"From Baltimore."

Yadwiga paused a second. "Where is that? Well, it makes no difference."

"A few hundred miles from New York. Can you hear me clearly?"

"Yes. Very well."

"I'm trying to sell books."

"Are they buying?"

"It's hard work, but they're buying. They're the ones who pay our rent. How did the day go for you?"

"Oh, I did the laundry—things get so grimy here," Yadwiga said, unaware that she always said the same things. "The laundries here tear the clothes to shreds."

"How are the birds?"

"They're chattering. They're together all day and they kiss each other."

"Lucky creatures. I'll spend the night here in Baltimore. Tomorrow I'm going to Washington, which is even farther away, but I'll speak to you on the phone. The telephone doesn't care about distances. Electricity carries the voice a hundred and eighty thousand miles a second," Herman said, not knowing why he was giving her this information. Perhaps he wanted to impress upon her how far away he was, so that she would not expect him to return home soon. He could hear the chirping of the birds. "Has anyone been to see you? I mean, one of the neighbors?" he asked.

"No. But the doorbell rang. I opened the door with the chain on and a man was standing there with a machine that sucked up dust. He wanted to show me how it worked, but I said that I couldn't let anyone in without you."

"You did the right thing. He was probably a vacuum-cleaner salesman, but he might also have been a thief or a murderer."

"I didn't let him in."

"What will you do tonight?"

"Oh, I'll wash dishes. Then your shirts need ironing."

"They can do without it."

"When will you call?"

"Tomorrow."

"Where will you eat supper?"

"Philadelphia, I mean Baltimore, is full of restaurants."

"Don't eat any meat. You'll ruin your stomach."

"Everything is ruined anyhow."

"Go to bed early."

"Yes. I love you."

"When will you come home?"

"Not before the day after tomorrow."

"Come soon, it's lonesome without you."

"I miss you too. I'll bring you a gift."

And Herman hung up the receiver.

"A gentle soul," Herman said to himself. "How is it that such goodness survives in this corrupt world? That is a mystery—unless one believes in the transmigration of souls." Herman remembered Masha's insinuation that Yadwiga too might have a lover. "It's not true," he thought, becoming angry. "She is truth itself." Nevertheless, he let himself imagine a Pole standing close to Yadwiga while she spoke to Herman on the phone. The Pole was playing the very same tricks that were so familiar to Herman. "Well, one can be certain of only one thing—death."

Herman thought of Rabbi Lampert. If he didn't deliver the promised chapter that day, the rabbi might fire him once and for all. It was rent time again, in the Bronx and in Brooklyn. "I'll run away! It's simply too much. It will be the end of me."

When he reached a station, he went down the steps to the subway. Such heat and humidity! Young blacks ran quickly, shouting in tones as much African as New York. Women whose dresses were wet under the armpits jostled each other with their packages and purses, their eyes glinting in fury. Herman put his hand into his trousers pocket for a handkerchief, but it was wet. On the platform, a dense crowd was waiting, bodies pushed against one another. The train rode into the station with a shrill whistling, as if it would fly right past the platform, the cars already packed. The crowd on the platform lurched toward the opening doors before the passengers inside could make their way out. An irresistible force shoved Herman into the car. Hips, breasts, elbows pressed against him. Here, at least, the illusion of free will had vanished. Here man was tossed about like a pebble or like a meteor in space.

Herman stood trapped in the congestion and envied the tall men, the six-footers, who could catch a breath of cool air from the ventilators. It hadn't been this hot even during the summer in the hayloft. Jews must have been packed together like this in the freight cars that carried them to the gas chambers.

Herman shut his eyes. What should he do now? Where should he begin? Tamara almost certainly had come without money. She would receive some support from the Joint Distribution Committee if she concealed the fact that she had a husband. But she had already said that she had no intention of deceiving the American philanthropists. And now he was a bigamist and had a lover as well. If he were discovered, he could be arrested and deported to Poland.

"I must see a lawyer. I must go to a lawyer right away!" But how could he explain such a situation? American lawyers had simple solutions for everything: "Which one do you love? Divorce the other one. End the affair. Find a job. Go to a psychoanalyst." Herman imagined the judge sentencing him, pointing at him with his index finger: "You have abused American hospitality."

"I want to have all three, that's the shameful truth," he admitted to himself. Tamara's become prettier, calmer, more interesting. She's suffered an even worse hell than Masha. Divorcing her would mean driving her to other men. As for love, these professionals used the word as if it were capable of clear definition—when no one had yet discovered its true meaning.

2

MASHA was at home when Herman arrived. She was apparently in a good mood. She removed the cigarette from her lips and kissed him full on the mouth. From the kitchen he heard the hissing sounds of cooking. He smelled frying meat, garlic, borscht, new potatoes. He heard Shifrah Puah's voice.

Coming to this house always roused his appetite. Mother and daughter were endlessly cooking, baking, handling pots, pans, salting boards, noodle boards. It reminded him of his parents' home in Tzivkev. On the Sabbath, Shifrah Puah and Masha prepared cholent and kugl. Perhaps because he lived with a Gentile, Masha made sure that her Sabbath candles were lighted, the sanctification goblet polished, the table set according to law and custom. Shifrah Puah would often consult Herman on questions of dietary law: she had accidentally washed a dairy spoon together with a meat fork; tallow from a candle had dripped onto a tray; the chicken had no gall. To this last question Herman remembered replying, "Taste the liver and see if it's bitter."

"Yes, it's bitter."

"If it's bitter, it's kosher."

Herman was eating potatoes and schav when Masha asked him about the relative who had gotten in touch with him. He almost choked on the mouthful of food he was eating. He could not remember the name he had given her on the phone. Nevertheless, he began to speak, accustomed as he was to such improvisation.

"Yes, I didn't even know this relative of mine was alive."

"A man or a woman?"

"I told you—a man."

"You say many things. Who is he? Where's he from?"

The name he had invented came back to him—Feivl Lemberger.

"How is he related to you?"

"On my mother's side."

"How?"

"The son of my mother's brother."

"Your mother's maiden name was Lemberger? Seems to me you once mentioned some other name."

"You're mistaken."

"You said on the phone he was a man in his sixties. How can you have such an old cousin?"

"My mother was the youngest. My uncle was twenty years older than she."

"What was your uncle's name?"

"Tuvye."

"Tuvye? How old was your mother when she died?"

"Fifty-one."

"The whole thing sounds fishy. It's an old girl friend. She missed you so badly, she put a notice in the newspaper. Why did you tear it out? You were afraid I'd see the name and phone number. Well, I bought another paper. I'm going to call up right now and find out the truth. This time you've hung yourself with your own belt," Masha said. Hatred and satisfaction were written on her face.

Herman pushed his plate away.

"Why don't you call right now and end this ridiculous cross examination!" he said. "Go ahead, dial the number! I'm bored with your ugly accusations!"

Masha's expression changed. "I'll call when I feel like it. Don't let the potatoes get cold."

"If you haven't any faith in me at all, then our whole relationship is senseless."

"It's senseless all right. Eat the potatoes anyway. If he's your mother's nephew, why did you refer to him as a distant relative?"

"All relatives are distant to me."

"You have your shikseh and you have me, but some bitch from Europe shows up and you leave me to run off and meet her. A whore like that probably has syphilis too."

Shifrah Puah came to the table. "Why don't you let him eat?"

"Mama, don't interfere!" Masha said threateningly.

"I'm not interfering. Are my words worth nothing to you? When a person is eating, don't bother him with complaints. I know of a case where someone, God protect us, choked to death—"

"You have a story for everything! He's a liar, a faker. He's even too stupid to know how to get away with it," Masha said, half to her mother, half to Herman.

Herman picked up a small potato with his spoon; it was round, new, moist with butter, sprinkled with parsley. He was about to put it in his mouth, but stopped himself. He had found his wife but lost his mistress. Was this the joke destiny had in store for him?

Even though he had carefully rehearsed the details of what he would tell Masha about his relative, his memory refused to function. He cut the tender little potato in half with the edge of his spoon. "Should I tell her the truth?"

he asked himself. But no answer came. How strange that despite his distress Herman felt calm. It was the resignation of a criminal caught red-handed who accepted the inevitable punishment.

"Why don't you phone?" he said.

"Eat. I'll bring the dumpling."

He ate the potatoes and each mouthful filled him with energy. He had had no lunch, and he felt drained by the day's events. He thought of himself as a prisoner eating his last meal before execution. Masha would know the truth soon. Rabbi Lampert would surely fire him. He had only two dollars in his pocket. He couldn't apply for government aid—his double life might be exposed. What kind of work could he find? He was even incapable of getting a job as a dishwasher.

Masha served him a pudding and an apple compote with tea. Herman had planned to work on the rabbi's manuscript after supper, but his stomach felt heavy. When he thanked mother and daughter for the meal, Shifrah Puah said, "Why thank us? Thank Him above." She brought Herman a bowl of water in which to wash his fingers and a skullcap so that he might say the benediction. Herman mumbled the first verse of the blessing and retired to his room. Masha filled the sink with water to wash the dishes. It was still light outside, and it seemed to Herman that he heard birds singing in the back-yard tree, but these were not the voices of the sparrows that usually twittered among the branches. Herman played with the thought that they were the spirits of birds of another age, from before the time of Columbus, or even from a prehistoric era, that awakened and sang toward evening. In his room, at night, he had often found beetles so huge and strange that he could not believe they were a product of either this climate or the present time.

The day seemed longer to Herman than any summer day he could recall. He remembered David Hume's words that there was no logical proof the sun would rise the following morning. In that case, neither was there a guarantee that the sun would set this day.

It was hot. He often wondered why the room didn't set itself on fire from the high temperature. On particularly turgid evenings, he imagined flames bursting forth from the ceiling, the walls, the bedding, the books and manuscripts. He stretched out on the bed, alternately dozing and brooding. Tamara had asked for his address and telephone number, but instead he had told her he would call her the following evening. What was it they all wanted? To forget for a while their loneliness and the inevitability of death. Poor and worthless as he was, some people still depended on him. But it was Masha who made it all meaningful. If she were to leave him, then Tamara and Yadwiga would become no more than burdens.

He fell asleep, and when he awoke, it was evening. In the other room, he could hear Masha talking on the telephone. Was she talking to Reb Abraham Nissen Yaroslaver? Or to Tamara? Herman strained to hear. No, she was talking to the other cashier at the cafeteria. After a few minutes, she came into his room. She spoke into the semi-darkness.

"Are you asleep?"

"I've just wakened."

"You lie down and fall right asleep. You must have a clear conscience."

"I haven't murdered anyone."

"One can murder without a knife." Then, in a changed voice, she said, "Herman, I can take my vacation now."

"Starting when?"

"We can leave Sunday morning."

Herman was silent for a moment. "All I have is two dollars and a few pennies."

"Aren't you supposed to get a check from the rabbi?"

"I'm not so sure now."

"You want to stay with your peasant—or perhaps someone else. All year you've promised to take me to the country, but at the last minute you change your mind. I shouldn't say it, but compared to you Leon Tortshiner was an honest man. He lied too, but he bragged harmlessly and thought up silly fantasies. Did you put that notice in the paper yourself? I wouldn't be surprised. All I need to do is dial the number. I'll soon know your tricks."

"Call and find out. For a few cents, you'll know the truth."

"Who did you go to see?"

"My dead wife, Tamara, has risen from the grave. She's polished her nails and come to New York."

"Yes, of course. What happened between you and the rabbi?"

"I'm behind in my work."

"You did it deliberately so that you wouldn't be able to go away with me. I don't need you. Sunday morning I'm going to pack a suitcase and go wherever my eyes lead me. If I don't get out of this city for a few days, I'll lose my mind. I've never been so tired, not even in the camp."

"Why don't you lie down?"

"Thanks for the suggestion; it won't help. I lie there and remember all the savagery, all the humiliations. If I do fall asleep, then I'm back with them immediately. They're dragging me, beating me, chasing me. They come running from all sides, like hounds after a hare. Has anyone ever died from nightmares? Wait, I must get a cigarette."

Masha left the room. Herman got up and looked out

the window. The sky shone pale and dull. The tree below stood motionless. The air smelled of marshes and the tropics. The earth was turning from west to east as it had done from time immemorial. The sun was racing off somewhere with its planets in tow. The Milky Way turned on its axis. In the midst of these cosmic adventures, Herman stood with his handful of reality, with his ridiculous little troubles. It would take only a length of rope, a drop of poison, and they would vanish together with him. "Why doesn't she phone? What is she waiting for?" Herman asked himself. "Maybe she's afraid of the truth."

Masha came back with a cigarette between her lips. "If you want to come with me, I'll pay for you."

"Do you have the money?"

"I'll borrow it from the union."

"You know I don't deserve it."

"No, but if you need a thief, you rescue him from the gallows."

3

HERMAN planned to spend Friday, Saturday, and Sunday in Brooklyn with Yadwiga. Monday he intended to go to the country with Masha.

He had finished the chapter and delivered it to the rabbi, promising solemnly not to be late with his work again. It was his good luck that Rabbi Lampert was always so busy that he never had time to carry out his threats. The rabbi took the manuscript and paid Herman at once. The two telephones on the rabbi's desk kept ringing. He was flying to Detroit that day to give a lecture. When Herman took leave of him, the rabbi shook his head. He seemed to be saying: "Don't think that you're fooling me, greenhorn. I know more than you think." He didn't give Herman his whole hand to shake, only two fingers.

When Herman reached the door, Mrs. Regal, the secretary, called out, "What about your phone?"

"I gave the rabbi the address." And he shut the door behind him.

Each time Herman received a check from Rabbi Lampert, it seemed like a miracle to him. He cashed it as quickly as he could in a bank where the rabbi was known. He himself would have nothing to do with checks. He carried his cash with him in the rear pocket of his trousers even though he was afraid of being robbed. It was Friday, and according to the wall clock of the bank, it was fifteen minutes past eleven. The rabbi had an office on West Fifty-seventh Street, where the bank was also located.

Herman headed in the direction of Broadway. Should he call Tamara? Judging by the way Masha had talked to him from the cafeteria, there could be no doubt that she had already telephoned Reb Abraham Nissen Yaroslaver. She must by now know that Tamara was actually alive. "This time I'll come out of it with every bone broken." Herman realized he was repeating an expression his father had often used.

Herman went into a store to phone and dialed Reb Abraham Nissen Yaroslaver's number. After a few seconds he heard Sheva Haddas's voice.

"Who is this?"

"It's Herman Broder, Tamara's husband." He spoke the words hesitatingly.

"I'll call her."

He couldn't tell how long he waited—a minute, two, five. The fact that Tamara didn't come at once could only mean that Masha had called. At last he heard Tamara's voice—it sounded different from yesterday. Speaking too loudly, she said, "Herman, is that you?"

"Yes, it's me. I still don't believe that what has happened has really happened."

"Well, it really has. I'm looking out of the window and I see a street in New York, full of Jews, God bless them. I can even hear the sounds of fish being chopped."

"You're in a Jewish neighborhood."

"There were Jews in Stockholm, too, good Jews, but here it's a little like Nalenczew."

"Yes, a trace of it has survived. Has anyone phoned you?"

Tamara didn't reply at once. Then she said, "Who should have phoned? I don't know anyone in New York. There are—what are they called?—Landsleit. My uncle was supposed to check on some of them, but—"

"You haven't asked about renting a room yet, have you?"

"Who shall I ask? Monday, I'm going to the organization. Perhaps they will advise me. You promised to phone yesterday evening."

"My promises aren't worth a penny."

"It really is strange. In Russia, things were pretty bad, but at least people were together; whether we were in the camp or in the forest, we were always a group of prisoners. In Stockholm we stayed together too. Here, for the first time, I'm alone. I look out of the window and I feel I don't belong here. Can you come over? My uncle is out and my aunt is going shopping. We could talk."

"All right. I'll come."

"Come. After all, we were once related," Tamara said, and she hung up.

A cab came along just as Herman stepped out into the street. He barely earned enough money for a crust of bread, but he had to hurry now so as not to deprive Yadwiga of the whole day. He sat in the cab and the turmoil within him erupted in laughter. Yes, Tamara was here; it was no hallucination.

The taxi stopped and Herman paid his fare and tipped the driver. He rang the bell and Tamara opened the door. The first thing he observed was that she had removed the red polish from her nails. She was wearing a different dress of a dark color and her hair was slightly disheveled. He even noticed a few white strands. She had sensed his displeasure at seeing her dolled up in American fashion and reverted to her Old World style. She looked older now, and he noticed wrinkles at the corners of her eyes.

"My aunt has just left," she said.

Herman hadn't kissed Tamara at their first meeting. He made a gesture to do so now, but she moved away.

"I'll make some tea."

"Tea? I just had lunch."

"I think I've earned the right to invite you to have a glass of tea with me," she said with Nalenczew coquetry.

He followed her into the living room. The kettle in the kitchen began to whistle, and Tamara left to brew tea. Soon she carried in a tray with tea, lemon, and a plate of cookies—surely baked by Sheva Haddas. They were not uniform in shape, but crooked and twisted like the home-baked cakes in Tzivkev. They smelled of cinnamon and almonds. Herman chewed on a cookie. His tea glass was full and extremely hot and contained a tarnished silver spoon. In some odd way all the mundane characteristics of the Polish-Jewish past, down to the smallest details, had been transplanted to this place.

Tamara seated herself at the table, not too close to Herman and not too far away, just the proper distance for a

woman when sitting with a man who was not her husband, but a relative nevertheless. "I keep looking at you
and I can't believe it really is you," she said. "I can't allow
myself to believe anything. Everything has lost perspective
since I've come here."

"In what way?"

"I've almost forgotten what it was like there. You won't
believe me, Herman, but I lie awake at night and can't remember how we first met or how we grew close. I know
that we quarreled often, but I don't know why. My life
seems to have been peeled away like the skin of an onion.
I'm beginning to forget what happened in Russia and
even more recently in Sweden. We were shunted about
from place to place, God knows why. They gave us papers
and they took them away again. Don't ask me how many
times I had to sign my name those last few weeks! Why
did they need so many signatures? And everything in my
married name—Broder. To the officials, I'm still your
wife, Tamara Broder."

"We can never be strangers."

"You don't mean that, you're only saying it. You consoled yourself very quickly with your mother's maid. But
my children—your children—still come to me. Let's not
talk about it any more! Better, tell me how you live. Is
she a good wife, at least? You had a thousand complaints
about me."

"What can I expect of her? She does the same things she
did when she was our servant."

"Herman, you can tell me everything. In the first place,
we were once together. In the second, as I've told you before, I really no longer think of myself as being part of
this world. Perhaps I can even help you."

"How? When a man hides in an attic for years, he
ceases to be a part of society. The truth is that I'm still

hiding in an attic right here in America. You said so yourself the other day."

"Well, two dead people certainly needn't have any secrets from one another. So long as you've done what
you've done, why don't you find a decent job for yourself?
Writing for a rabbi is no way to spend one's life."

"What else can I do? In order to press pants, you have
to be strong and belong to a union. That's what they call
workers' organizations here, and it's very difficult to get
into one. Other than that—"

"Your children are gone. Why don't you have a child
by her?"

"Perhaps *you* can still have children."

"What for? So that the Gentiles will have someone to
burn? But it's terribly empty here. I've met a woman who
was also in the camps. She lost everyone, but now she has
a new husband, a new set of children. Many people have
started all over again. My uncle kept nagging me until
late in the night to have a talk with you and come to a decision. They are fine people, but a bit too outspoken. He
says you should divorce the other one; if not, you should
divorce me. He even hinted that he intended to leave me
some inheritance. They have one answer for everything:
it's God's will. And because they believe this, they go
through every hell and remain healthy and whole."

"I can't get a Jewish divorce from Yadwiga, because we
weren't married according to Jewish law," Herman said.

"Are you at least faithful to her, or do you have six others?" Tamara asked.

Herman paused. "Do you want me to confess everything?"

"I might as well know the truth."

"The truth is, I have a mistress."

Tamara smiled fleetingly. "I thought so. What can you

talk about with Yadwiga? She's a right shoe on a left foot. Who is your mistress?"

"From over there, from the camps."

"Why didn't you marry her instead of the peasant?"

"She has a husband. They don't live together, but he won't give her a divorce."

"I see, nothing's changed with you. At any rate, you're telling me the truth. Or are you still hiding something?"

"I'm not hiding anything."

"It's all the same to me whether you have one or two, or a dozen. If you were unfaithful to me even though I was young and pretty—at least not ugly—why should you be faithful to a peasant, and an unattractive one at that? Well, and the other one, your sweetheart, does she accept this arrangement?"

"She has no choice. Her husband won't divorce her. And she's in love with me."

"Do you love her too?"

"I can't live without her."

"Well, well, to hear such words from you! Is she beautiful? Intelligent? Charming?"

"She is all three."

"How do you manage it? Do you rush from one to the other?"

"I do the best I can."

"You haven't learned a thing. Absolutely nothing. I might have remained the same myself if I hadn't seen what they did to our children. Everyone tried to console me by telling me that time heals. It's been just the opposite: the further away it is, the more the wound festers. I must get a room somewhere, Herman. I can't live with anyone any more. It was easier with my fellow prisoners. When I didn't want to listen to them, I simply told them to go and bother someone else. But I can't talk that way

to my uncle. He is like a father to me. I don't need a divorce; I will never live with anyone again. Unless, of
course, you want one. In that case—"

"No, Tamara, I don't want a divorce. The feelings I
have for you cannot be taken away by someone else."

"What feelings? You've deceived others—well, you can't
change that—but you're deceiving yourself. I don't want
to preach to you, but no good can come from such a mess.
I looked at you and thought, 'This is the way an animal
looks when it's surrounded by hunters and cannot escape.'
What sort of person is your mistress?"

"A little crazy, but tremendously interesting."

"She hasn't any children?"

"No."

"Is she young enough to have a child?"

"Yes, but she doesn't want children either."

"You're lying, Herman. If a woman loves a man, she
wants to have his child. She wants to be his wife too and
not have him run off to another woman. Why didn't she
get along with her husband?"

"Oh, he's a faker, a parasite, an outcast. He's given himself the title of Doctor and takes money from old women."

"Forgive me, but what did she get in exchange? A man
who has two wives and writes sermons for some fake
rabbi. Have you told your mistress about me?"

"Not yet. But she read the notice in the newspaper and
is suspicious. She may call here at any time. Or has she already?"

"No one has called me. What shall I say if she does ring
up? That I'm your sister? That's what Sarah said to Abimelech about Abraham."

"I told her that a cousin of mine had showed up, a man
called Feivl Lemberger."

"Shall I tell her that I'm Feivl Lemberger?" Tamara

burst into laughter. Her whole appearance was altered. Her eyes lighted up with a gaiety Herman had never noticed before, or had perhaps forgotten. A dimple appeared in her left cheek. For a moment, she looked girlishly mischievous. He rose from his chair and she too stood up.

"Are you going so soon?"

"Tamara, it's not our fault the world went to pieces."

"What do I have to hope for? To be the third wheel on your broken wagon? Let's not spoil the past. We shared many years. With all your carryings on, those were still my happiest years."

They continued to talk, standing in the foyer, near the door. Tamara had heard that the wife of the son of the rebbitzin of Old Dzikow was alive and was about to remarry. But as a religious woman, she would need to be released from the obligation of levirate marriage. There was a brother who was a freethinker, living somewhere in America. "At least I had the privilege of knowing these saints," Tamara said. "Perhaps that was God's purpose in my miserable adventures." Suddenly she moved close to Herman and kissed him on the mouth. It happened so quickly that he didn't even have a chance to return her kiss. He tried to embrace her, but she moved quickly away, indicating that she wanted him to go.

4

FRIDAY in Brooklyn was not unlike Friday in Tzivkev. Although Yadwiga hadn't converted, she tried to observe traditional Judaism. She remembered the Jewish rituals from the time she had worked for Herman's parents. She bought a challah and baked the special little Sabbath cakes. Here in America she didn't have the right oven for making cholent, but a neighbor taught her to cover the gas burners with asbestos pads, so that the food would not burn and would stay hot through Saturday.

On Mermaid Avenue, Yadwiga bought the wine and candles needed for the blessing. She had at some point acquired two brass candlesticks, and although she didn't know how to pronounce the benediction, she would cover her eyes with her fingers for a moment after lighting the Sabbath candles and mumble something, just as she had seen Herman's mother do.

But Herman the Jew ignored the Sabbath. He turned on the lights and shut them off, even though it was forbidden. After the Sabbath meal of fish, rice and beans, chicken and carrot stew, he sat down to write, though this too was proscribed. When Yadwiga asked him why he was breaking God's commandment, he said, "There is no God, do you hear? And even if there were, I would defy Him."

In spite of having been paid, Herman seemed more worried than ever this Friday. Several times he asked Yadwiga whether anyone had telephoned. Between the fish and soup courses, he took a notebook and pen from his breast pocket and jotted something down. Sometimes on Friday evenings, when he was in the mood, he would sing his father's table chants as well as "Sholom Aleichem" and "A Worthy Woman," songs he translated into Polish for Yadwiga. The former was a greeting to the angels who escorted Jews on the Sabbath home from the synagogue. The latter was in praise of the virtuous wife, rarer than a pearl. Once, he had translated for her a hymn about an apple orchard, a loving bridegroom, and a bride bedecked with jewelry. It described caresses that, according to Yadwiga, did not belong in a holy chant. Herman explained that the hymn was written by a cabalist known as the Holy Lion, a miracle worker to whom the prophet Elijah had revealed himself. The wedding of the song took place in the heavenly mansions.

Yadwiga's cheeks would become flushed when he sang these holy songs, and her eyes would become brighter, full of joy in the Sabbath. But tonight he was taciturn and irritable. Yadwiga suspected that he sometimes spent time with other women on his trips. After all, he might occasionally want a woman who could read those tiny letters. Could a man really know what was best for him? How easily men were deluded by a word, a smile, a gesture.

During the week, Yadwiga covered the parakeets' cage as soon as evening came. But on Sabbath eve she let them stay up late. Woytus, the male, would sing along with Herman. The bird would fall into a sort of trance, twitter, trill, and fly around. Tonight Herman wasn't singing, and Woytus perched on the roof of the cage and preened his feathers.

"Has anything happened?" Yadwiga asked.

"Nothing, nothing," Herman said.

Yadwiga left the room and went to turn down the bed. Herman looked out the window. Generally Masha called him on Friday nights. She never used the telephone in her house on the Sabbath, in order not to offend her mother. She would go out for cigarettes and call from a neighborhood store. But tonight the telephone remained silent.

Since Masha had read the notice in the newspaper, he expected the scandal to break at any moment. The lie he had concocted was too obvious. It was inevitable that Masha would soon discover he had not been joking about Tamara's return. Several times yesterday in a tone of jealous triumph, winking ironically, she had repeated the name of his sham cousin, Feivl Lemberger. She was apparently delaying the blow—perhaps so as not to spoil their week's vacation together that was to begin on Monday.

As secure as Herman felt about Yadwiga, he was completely uncertain of Masha. She had never accepted the fact that he lived with another woman. She taunted him by saying that she would go back to Leon Tortshiner. Herman knew that men pursued her. He had often observed them in the cafeteria trying to engage her in conversation, asking for her address and phone number and leaving their cards. The cafeteria personnel, from the proprietor to the Puerto Rican dishwasher, looked her over greedily. Even women admired her graceful figure, long neck, narrow waist, slender legs, the whiteness of her skin. What power did he have that held her? How long would it last? He had tried countless times to prepare himself for the day Masha would break with him.

Now he stood looking out into the dimly lighted street, at the motionless leaves on the trees, at the sky which reflected the lights of Coney Island, at the elderly men and women who had set up chairs around the doorway and were carrying on the long-drawn-out conversations of those with nothing more to hope for.

Yadwiga put her hand on his shoulder. "The bed is ready. The bedding is fresh."

Herman turned off the lights in the living room, leaving the dim glow of the flickering candles. Yadwiga went into the bathroom. From the village, she had brought with her feminine rituals which she never failed to perform. She rinsed her mouth before going to bed, washed herself, and combed her hair. Even in Lipsk she had kept herself immaculate. Here in America, on the Polish radio station, she had picked up all sorts of hygienic advice. Woytus uttered one last protest when it grew dark, and flew into the cage with Marianna. He placed himself firmly next to her on the perch, where they remained motionless till sunup, perhaps getting a taste of the great rest that comes with death, the redeemer of men and animals.

Herman undressed slowly. He imagined Tamara lying awake on the sofa in her uncle's house, her eyes glaring into the darkness. Masha was probably standing near Croton Park or on Tremont Avenue, smoking her cigarettes. Boys who passed by whistled at her. Perhaps a car had stopped and someone was trying to pick her up. Maybe she was actually driving with someone.

The telephone rang and Herman hurried to answer it. One Sabbath candle had gone out, but the other still sputtered. He picked up the receiver and whispered, "Masha!"

There was silence for a moment. Then Masha said, "Are you lying in bed with your peasant?"

"No, I'm not lying in bed with her."

"Where then? Under the bed?"

"Where are you?" Herman asked.

"What difference does it make to you where I am? You could be with me. Instead, you spend your nights with an imbecile from Lipsk. And you have others too. Your cousin Feivl Lemberger is a fat whore, the kind you like. Have you slept with her too?"

"Not yet."

"Who is she? You might just as well tell me the truth."

"I told you: Tamara is alive and she's here."

"Tamara is dead and rotting in the earth. Feivl is one of your sweethearts."

"I swear by the bones of my parents that it isn't a sweetheart!"

There was a tense silence at the other end of the line.

"Tell me who she is," Masha insisted.

"A relative of mine. A broken woman who has lost her children. The 'Joint' brought her to America."

"Then why did you say Feivl Lemberger?" Masha asked.

"Because I know how suspicious you are. If you hear a woman mentioned, you immediately think that—"

"How old is she?"

"Older than I—a shattered remain. Do you really believe Reb Abraham Nissen Yaroslaver would put a notice in the paper for a sweetheart of mine? They're pious people. I told you to call them and find out for yourself."

"Well, maybe this time you're innocent. You'll never know what I've been through these last few days."

"Little idiot, I love you! Where are you now?"

"Where am I? In a candy store on Tremont Avenue. I walked along on the street, smoking, and every few minutes a car stopped and some ruffian wanted to pick me up. The boys whistled as if I were a girl of eighteen. What they see in me, I'll never know. Where are we going on Monday?"

"We'll find some place."

"I'm afraid to leave my mother alone. What will happen if she has an attack? She can die and not a cock will crow."

"Ask one of the neighbors to take care of her."

"I avoid the neighbors. I can't suddenly drop in and ask them for favors. Besides, my mother is afraid of people. If someone knocks at the door, she thinks it's a Nazi. The enemies of Israel should enjoy life as much as I'm enjoying the prospect of this trip."

"If that's the case, we can stay here in the city."

"I miss the sight of green grass, a breath of fresh air. Even in the camps the air wasn't as polluted as it is here. I would take my mother along, but in her eyes I'm a harlot. God inflicts every form of misery on her and she trembles for fear lest she isn't doing enough for Him. The truth is that what He wanted, Hitler did."

"Then why do you light Sabbath candles? Why do you fast on Yom Kippur?"

"Not for Him. The true God hates us, but we have dreamed up an idol who loves us and has made us His chosen people. You said it yourself: 'The Gentile makes gods of stone and we of theories.' What time will you be here on Sunday?"

"Four o'clock."

"You're also a god and a murderer. Well, have a good Sabbath."

5

HERMAN and Masha took a bus to the Adirondacks. They got off at Lake George after a six-hour trip. There they found a room for seven dollars and decided to stay the night. They had started without any plan at all. Herman had found a map of New York State on a park bench and this was his guide. The window of their room overlooked a lake and hills. The breeze that came in carried the fragrance of pines. There was a distant sound of music. Masha had brought along a basketful of food that she and her mother had prepared—pancakes, pudding, a compote of apples, prunes, and raisins, and a home-baked cake.

Masha, smoking, stood looking out the window at the rowboats and motorboats on the lake and said playfully, "Where are the Nazis? What kind of a world is this without Nazis? A backward country, this America."

Before leaving, she had bought a bottle of cognac with some of her vacation pay. She had learned to drink in Russia. Herman took only one sip from the paper cup, but Masha kept refilling hers, becoming more and more cheerful, singing and whistling.

From early childhood, Masha had taken dancing lessons in Warsaw. Her calves were as muscular as a dancer's. Now she raised her arms and began to dance. In her slip and nylon stockings, a cigarette dangling from her lips, her hair loose, she reminded Herman of the girl performers in the circus that used to come to Tzivkev. She sang in Yiddish, Hebrew, Russian, Polish. She asked Herman to dance with her, urging him in a drunken voice, "Come, yeshiva boy, let's see what you can do."

They went to bed early, but their night was full of interruptions. Masha slept an hour and woke up. She wanted to do everything at once: to make love, smoke, drink, talk. The moon hung low over the water. Fish splashed about. The stars shook like tiny lanterns. Masha told Herman stories that aroused both anger and jealousy in him.

In the morning, they packed up and again boarded a bus. They spent the following night at Schroon Lake in a bungalow near the water. It was so cold that they had to put their clothing over their blankets to keep warm. After breakfast next morning, they rented a boat. Herman rowed while Masha stretched out to warm herself in the sun. Herman imagined he could read her thoughts through the skin of her forehead, through her closed eyelids.

He mused on how fantastic it was to be in America, in a free country, without fear of Nazis, the NKVD, border guards, informers. He hadn't even brought his "first papers" with him. In the United States no one was asked for documents. But he could never quite forget that, on a street between Mermaid and Neptune Avenues, Yadwiga waited for him. On East Broadway, in Reb Abraham Nissen Yaroslaver's house, was Tamara, who had come back and was waiting for any crumb he might throw her way. He would never be totally free of the claims these women had on him. Even Rabbi Lampert had the right to complain about him. Herman had refused to accept the friendship the rabbi wanted to impose on him.

Surrounded by the light-blue sky, the yellow-green water, he nevertheless felt less guilty. The birds had announced the new day as if it were the morning after creation. Warm breezes carried the scent of the woods and the smell of food being prepared in the hotels. Herman imagined that he heard the screech of a chicken or a duck. Somewhere on this lovely summer morning, fowl were being slaughtered; Treblinka was everywhere.

Masha's food supply had given out, but she refused to eat in a restaurant. She went to a market and bought bread, tomatoes, cheese, and apples. She came back laden with enough groceries to feed an entire family. Along with her playful frivolity, she had the instincts of a mother. She didn't squander money as loose women do. In the bungalow, Masha found a little naphtha stove and she made coffee. The smell of naphtha and smoke reminded Herman of his student years in Warsaw.

Flies, bees, and butterflies flew in through the open window. The flies and bees settled on some spilled sugar. A butterfly hovered over a slice of bread. It didn't eat, but seemed to savor the odor. To Herman these were not parasites to be driven away; he saw in each of these creatures the manifestations of the eternal will to live, experience, comprehend. As the fly's antennae stretched out toward the food, it rubbed its hind legs together. The wings of the butterfly reminded Herman of a prayer shawl. The bee hummed and buzzed and flew out again. A small ant crawled about. It had survived the cold night and was creeping across the table—but where to? It paused at a crumb, then continued on, zigzagging back and forth. It had separated itself from the anthill and now had to make out on its own.

From Schroon Lake, Herman and Masha went to Lake Placid. There they found a room in a house on a hill. Everything in the house was old but spotless: the parlor, the stairs, the pictures and ornaments hanging on the walls, the towel with its embroidered emblem, imported from Germany, a leftover from pre-World War I days. On the wide bed lay thick pillows, like the ones in European inns. The window here looked out on the mountains. The sun had set, casting purple squares on the walls.

After a while Herman went downstairs to telephone. He had taught Yadwiga how to receive a collect phone call. Yadwiga asked him where he was and he mentioned the first name that came to mind. Generally Yadwiga didn't complain, but this time she talked excitedly: she was afraid at night, the neighbors laughed at her and pointed their fingers at her. Why did Herman need so much money? She was more than willing to go to work and help out so that he could stay at home like other men. Herman quieted her, apologized, and promised not to stay away too long. She sent him a kiss through the telephone and he made a kissing sound in return.

When he came upstairs, Masha wouldn't speak to him. She said, "Now I know the truth."

"What truth?"

"I heard you. You miss her, you can hardly wait till you're back with her again."

"She's all alone. Helpless."

"And what about me?"

They ate supper in silence. Masha didn't turn on the lights. She handed him a hard-boiled egg and he was suddenly reminded of the evening before Tisha Ba'av, the last meal before fasting, when one partakes of a hard-boiled egg sprinkled with ashes, a sign of mourning, a symbol that one's luck can roll like an egg and turn bad. Masha alternately chewed and smoked. He tried to talk to her, but she would not reply. Soon after the meal, she flung herself on the bed in her clothes, curling herself up so that it was difficult to know whether she was asleep or sulking.

Herman went outside. He walked down an unknown street, stopped to look into the windows of souvenir shops: Indian dolls, gold-laced sandals with wooden soles, amber beads, Chinese earrings, Mexican bracelets. He came to a lake which reflected a copper sky. Refugees from Germany strolled by—broad-backed men and portly women. They were talking about houses, shops, the stock market. "In what way are they my brothers and sisters?" Herman asked himself. "What does their Jewishness consist of? What is my Jewishness?" They all had the same wish: to assimilate as quickly as possible and get rid of their accents. Herman belonged neither to them nor to the American, Polish, or Russian Jews. Like the ant on the table that morning, he had torn himself away from the community.

Herman walked around the lake, past patches of woods, past a hotel built like a Swiss chalet. Fireflies glimmered, crickets chirped, a sleepless bird screeched among the treetops. The moon rose—the head of a skeleton. What was above? What was the moon? Who had created it? For what purpose? Perhaps an answer as simple as gravitation was waiting for someone to discover, as Newton was said to have done the instant he saw an apple falling from a tree. Perhaps the all-embracing truth could be contained in a single sentence. Or were the words that could define it still to be created?

It was late when he returned to the rooming house. He had walked miles. The room was dark. Masha was lying in the same position in which he had left her. He went up close to her and touched her face as if to make sure she was alive. "What do you want?" she said, startled.

He undressed and lay down beside her. He lay there until he fell asleep. When he opened his eyes, the moon was shining. Masha stood in the center of the room, drinking from the flask of cognac.

"Masha, this is not the way!"

"What is the way?"

She took her nightdress off and came to him. They kissed silently and made love. Afterward she sat up and lighted a cigarette. Suddenly she said, "Where was I five years ago at this time?" She searched her memory for a long while. Then she said, "Still among the dead."

6

HERMAN and Masha traveled on, stopping at a hotel not far from the Canadian border. They had only a few days of vacation left, and the hotel was inexpensive.

A row of bungalows belonging to the hotel fronted a lake. Women and men in bathing costumes were playing cards outdoors. On a tennis court a rabbi, wearing a skullcap and shorts, played tennis with his wife, who was wearing the wig of an Orthodox woman. In a hammock between two pine trees lay a young boy and girl, giggling incessantly. The boy had a high forehead, a head of disheveled hair, and a hairy, narrow chest. The girl wore a tight bathing suit and a Star of David around her neck.

The proprietress had told Herman that the kitchen was "strictly kosher" and that the guests were all "one happy family." She escorted him and Masha to a bungalow with unpainted walls and a bare-beamed ceiling. The guests ate together at long tables in the hotel dining room. At lunchtime scantily clad mothers stuffed food into their children's mouths, determined to bring up tall Americans, six-footers. The little ones cried, gagged, and spat up the vegetables that had been forced down. Herman imagined that their angry eyes were saying, "We refuse to suffer just to satisfy your vain ambitions." The tennis-playing rabbi poured forth witticisms. The waiters—college or yeshiva students—joked with the older women and flirted with the girls. They immediately started questioning Masha as to where she came from and showered her with insinuating compliments. Herman's throat tightened. He could swallow neither the chopped liver and onions, the kreplach, the fatty piece of beef, nor the stuffed derma. The women at the table complained, "What kind of a man is he? He doesn't eat."

Since his stay in Yadwiga's hayloft, in the DP camp in Germany and in the years of struggle in America, Herman had lost contact with this kind of modern Jewry. But here they were again. A Yiddish poet with a round face and curly hair was carrying on a discussion with the rabbi. The poet, who referred to himself as an atheist, talked about worldliness, culture, the Jewish territory in Bira Bidjan, anti-Semitism. The rabbi performed the ritual washing of the hands after the meal and mumbled the blessing as the poet continued to spout phrases. At moments the rabbi's eyes took on a glazed expression and he intoned a few words aloud. A fat woman argued that Yiddish was a jargon, a mishmash without grammar. A bearded Jew, wearing gold-rimmed spectacles and a velvet skullcap, stood up and delivered a speech about the newly established State of Israel and solicited contributions.

Masha was engaged in conversation with the other women. They called her Mrs. Broder, and wanted to know when she and Herman had been married, how many children they had, what Herman's business was. Herman lowered his head. Every contact with people evoked terror in him. There was always the possibility that someone might know him and Yadwiga from Brooklyn.

An elderly man from Galicia had latched on to the name Broder and began to cross-examine Herman about whether or not he had family in Lemberg, in Tarnow, in Brody, in Drohobitch. He himself had a relative of that name, a second or third cousin, a man ordained as a rabbi, who had become a lawyer and was now an important figure in the Orthodox Party in Tel Aviv. The more answers Herman gave, the more the other probed. He seemed determined to prove that he and Herman were related.

The women at the table all commented on Masha's beauty, her slender figure, her clothes. When they learned that Masha had made the dress she was wearing, they wanted to know if she would sew for others. They all had items of clothing that needed to be let out, taken in, lengthened, or shortened.

Although Herman had eaten little, he rose from the table with a heavy feeling in his stomach. He and Masha went for a walk. He had not realized how impatient he had become during his years of solitude, how removed from all human involvement. He had one desire: to get away as quickly as possible. He walked so rapidly that Masha fell behind.

"Why are you running? No one is chasing you."

They walked uphill. Herman kept looking back. Would one be able to hide from the Nazis here? Would there be anyone to hide him and Masha in a hayloft? He had only just finished lunch and was already worrying about how he would face these people at suppertime. He would not be able to sit among them, watch the children being forced to eat, making a mess of the food. He could not listen to all those empty words. In the city, Herman never stopped longing for nature, the out-of-doors, but actually he was not suited for this tranquillity. Masha was afraid of dogs. Every time she heard one barking, she grasped Herman's arm. She soon said she could walk no farther in her high-heeled shoes. The farmers they passed eyed the strolling couple with dislike.

When they returned to the hotel, Herman suddenly decided to take out one of the rowboats supplied for the use of the guests. Masha attempted to dissuade him. "You'll drown us both," she said. But in the end she seated herself in the boat and lighted a cigarette. Herman knew how to row, but neither he nor Masha could swim. The sky was clear and light blue and a wind was blowing. Waves rose and fell, slapping against the sides of the boat, rocking it like a cradle. At times, Herman heard a splash, as if some monster were lurking in the water, silently swimming after them, ready to capsize the boat at any moment. Masha watched him with a worried expression, instructing him, criticizing him. She had little faith in his physical prowess. Or perhaps it was her own luck she mistrusted.

"Look at that butterfly!"

Masha pointed with her finger. How on earth had it
flown so far from the shore? Would it be able to fly back?
It fluttered in mid-air. It zigzagged, flying in no particular
direction, and suddenly vanished. The waves, an alternat-
ing pattern of gold and shadow, turned the lake into a
giant fluid chessboard.

"Careful! There's a rock!"

Masha sat bolt upright, and the boat wobbled. Herman
quickly rowed backward. A rock was sticking out of the
water, jagged and pointed, covered with moss—a remnant
of the Ice Age and of the glacier that had once gouged out
this basin in the earth. It had withstood the rains, the
snows, the frost, the heat. It was afraid of no one. It did
not need redemption, it had already been redeemed.

Herman rowed the boat to the shore and he and Masha
got out. They went to their bungalow, got into bed, and
covered themselves with the woolen blanket. Masha's
closed eyes seemed to be smiling behind their lids. Then
her lips started to move. Herman stared at her. Did he
know her? Even her features seemed unfamiliar to him.
He had never really considered the structure of her nose,
chin, forehead. And what was going on in her mind?

Masha trembled and sat up. "I just saw my father."

She was silent awhile. Then she asked, "What day of
the month is it?"

Herman figured out the date.

"It's been seven weeks since I've had my visitor," Masha
said.

At first, Herman didn't understand what she was talking about. The women in his life each referred to their
menstrual period by a different name: the holy day, the
guest, the monthly. He became alert and calculated the
time along with her.

"Yes, it's late."

"It's never late with me. As abnormal as I may be in other ways, I'm one hundred percent normal in this one."

"See a doctor."

"They can't tell so soon. I'll wait another week. An abortion in America costs five hundred dollars." Masha changed her tone of voice. "And it's dangerous too. A woman who worked in the cafeteria had one. She got blood poisoning and that was the end of her. What an ugly way to die! And what would my mother do if anything happened to me? I'm sure you would let her starve."

"Don't get melodramatic. You're not dying yet."

"How far is living from dying? I've seen people die and I know."

7

THE rabbi had apparently prepared a new set of jokes for the evening meal; his store of anecdotes seemed inexhaustible. The women giggled. The student-waiters served the food noisily. Sleepy children didn't want to eat and their mothers slapped them on the hands. One woman, a recent arrival in America, sent back her serving and the waiter asked, "By Hitler you ate better?"

Afterward they all gathered in the casino, a remodeled barn. The Yiddish poet gave a speech, lauding Stalin, and recited proletarian poetry. An actress did impersonations of celebrities. She cried, laughed, screamed, and made faces. An actor who had played in a Yiddish vaudeville theater in New York told bawdy jokes about a betrayed husband, whose wife had hidden a Cossack under her bed, and about a rabbi who had come to preach to a loose

woman and had left her house with his fly open. The
women and young girls doubled over with laughter. "Why
is it all so painful to me?" Herman asked himself. The
vulgarity in this casino denied the sense of creation. It
shamed the agony of the holocaust. Some of the guests were
refugees from Nazi terror. Moths flew in through the open
door, attracted by the bright lights, deceived by a false
day. They fluttered about awhile and fell dead, having
beaten themselves against the wall, or singed themselves
on the lightbulbs.

Herman glanced around and saw that Masha was dancing with an enormous man in a plaid shirt and green
shorts that exposed his hairy thighs. He held Masha by
the waist; she barely reached his shoulder with her hand.
One of the waiters was blowing a trumpet and another
was banging a drum. A third blew on a home-made instru-
ment that looked like a pot with holes in it.

Since Herman had left New York with Masha, he had
had little chance to be alone. After some hesitation, he
walked out without letting Masha see him leave. The
night was moonless and chilly. Herman passed by a farm.
A calf stood in a pen. It gazed into the night with the be-
wilderment of a mute creature. Its large eyes seemed to
ask: Who am I? What am I here for? Cool breezes blew
from the mountains. Meteors streaked across the sky. The
casino grew smaller in the distance and lay down below like
a firefly. With all her negativism, Masha had retained the
normal instincts. She wanted a husband, children, a
household. She loved music, the theater, and laughed at
the actors' jokes. But in Herman there resided a sorrow
that could not be assuaged. He was not a victim of Hitler.
He had been a victim long before Hitler's day.

He came to the shell of a burned-out house and
stopped. Attracted by the pungent smell, the holes that

had been windows, the sooty entrance, the black chimney, he went inside. If demons did exist, they would be at home in this ruin. Since he could not stand humans, perhaps ghosts were his natural companions. Could he remain in this rubble for the rest of his life? He stood among the charred walls, inhaling the smell of the long-extinguished fire. Herman could hear the night breathing. He even imagined that it snored in its sleep. The silence rang in his ears. He stepped on coals and ashes. No, he could not be a part of all that acting, laughing, singing, dancing. Through a hole that had once been a window, he could see the dark sky—a heavenly papyrus filled with hieroglyphics. Herman's gaze fixed upon three stars whose formation resembled the Hebrew vowel "segul." He was looking at three suns, each probably with its planets, comets. How strange that a bit of muscle fitted into a skull should be capable of seeing such distant objects. How peculiar that a panful of brains should be constantly wondering and not able to arrive at any conclusion! They were all silent: God, the stars, the dead. The creatures who *did* speak revealed nothing . . .

He turned back toward the casino, which by now was dark. The building, so recently filled with noise, was quiet and abandoned, sunk in the self-absorption of all inanimate objects. Herman started to look for his bungalow, but he knew he would have difficulty finding it. He got lost wherever he went—in cities, in the country, on ships, in hotels. A single light was burning at the entrance of the house where the office was located, but there was no one there.

The thought ran through Herman's mind: perhaps Masha had gone to bed with that dancer in the green shorts. It was unlikely, but anything was possible among modern people stripped of all faith. What did civilization consist of if not murder and fornication? Masha must have recognized his footsteps. A door opened and he heard her voice.

8

MASHA took a sleeping pill and fell asleep, but Herman remained awake. First he waged his usual war with the Nazis, bombed them with atomic bombs, blasted their armies with mysterious missiles, lifted their fleet out of the ocean and placed it on land near Hitler's villa in Berchtesgaden. Try as he might, he could not stop his thoughts. His mind worked like a machine out of control. He was again drinking that potion which enabled him to fathom time, space, "the thing in itself." His pondering always brought him to the same conclusion: God (or whatever He may be) was certainly wise, but there was no sign of His mercy. If a God of mercy did exist in the heavenly hierarchy, then he was only a helpless godlet, a kind of heavenly Jew among the heavenly Nazis. As long as one does not have the courage to leave this world, one can only hide and try to get by, with the help of alcohol, opium, a hayloft in Lipsk, or a small room at Shifrah Puah's.

He fell asleep and dreamed of an eclipse of the sun and funeral processions. They followed one after another, long catafalques, pulled by black horses, ridden by giants. They were both the dead and the mourners. "How can this be?" he asked himself in his dream. "Can a condemned tribe lead itself to its own burial?" They carried torches and sang a dirge of unearthly melancholy. Their robes dragged along the ground, the spikes of their helmets reached into the clouds.

Herman started and the rusty springs of the bed jangled. He awoke frightened and perspiring. His stomach was distended and his bladder full. The pillow under his head was wet and twisted like a piece of wrung-out washing. How long had he slept? One hour? Six? The bungalow was pitch black and wintery cold. Masha was sitting up in bed, her pale face like a spot of light in the dark. "Herman, I'm afraid of an operation!" she cried out hoarsely, her voice not unlike Shifrah Puah's. It was a few moments before Herman realized what she was talking about.

"Well, all right."

"Perhaps Leon will divorce me. I'll speak frankly to him. If he won't divorce me, the child will bear his name."

"I can't divorce Yadwiga."

Masha fell into a rage. "You can't!" she shouted. "When the king of England wanted to marry the woman he loved, he gave up his throne, and you can't get rid of a stupid peasant! There's no law that can force you to live with her. The worst that can happen is that you'll have to pay alimony. I'll pay the alimony. I'll work overtime and pay!"

"You know that a divorce would kill Yadwiga."

"I know nothing of the sort. Tell me, were you married to the bitch by a rabbi?"

"By a rabbi? No."

"How then?"

"A civil marriage."

"That's not worth a thing according to Jewish law. Marry me in a Jewish ceremony. I don't need their Gentile papers."

"No rabbi will perform a marriage without a license. This is America, not Poland."

"I'll find a rabbi who will."

"It would still be bigamy—worse, polygamy."

"No one will ever know. Only my mother and I. We'll move out of the house and you can use whatever name you like. If your peasant is so dear to you that you can't live without her, then go spend one day a week with her. I'll make my peace with that."

"Sooner or later, they'll arrest me and deport me."

"As long as there is no marriage certificate, no one can prove that we're man and wife. You can burn the ketuba right after the wedding ceremony."

"You have to register a child."

"We'll work something out. It's enough that I'm prepared to share you with such an idiot. Let me finish." Masha changed her tone. "I've been sitting here and thinking a full hour. If you won't agree, you can leave this minute and not come back. I'll find a doctor who will perform the operation, but don't you ever show your face to me again. I'll give you one minute to answer. If it's no, get dressed and get out. I don't want you here another second."

"You're asking me to break the law. I'll be afraid of every policeman in the street."

"You're afraid anyhow. Answer me!"

"Yes."

Masha was silent for a long time.

"Are you just saying that?" she said finally. "Or will I have to start all over again tomorrow?"

"No, it's settled."

"It takes an ultimatum to get you to decide anything. First thing tomorrow morning I'll telephone Leon and tell him he must give me a divorce. If he won't, I'll destroy him."

"What will you do? Shoot him?"

"I'm capable of doing that too, but I have other ways of getting at him. Legally he's as unkosher as pork. If I wanted to report him, he could be deported tomorrow."

"According to Jewish law, our baby will be a bastard anyhow. It was conceived before the divorce."

"Jewish law and all the other laws mean as much to me as last year's frost. I'm only doing it for my mother, only for her."

Masha got out of bed and moved about in the dark. A rooster crowed; other roosters answered him. A bluish light shone in through the window. The summer night was over. The birds started chirping and whistling all at the same time. Herman could no longer stay in bed. He got up, put on his trousers and shoes, opened the door.

The outdoors was occupied with its early-morning tasks. The rising sun had executed a childish painting on the night sky—spots, smears, a mess of colors. Dew had settled on the grass and a milky-white mist hung over the lake. Three young birds perched on the branch of a tree near the bungalow, kept their soft beaks wide open while the mother bird fed them little bits of stems and worms from her beak. She flew back and forth, with the single-minded diligence of those who know their duties. The sun rose behind the lake. Flames ignited the water. A pine cone fell, ready to fructify the earth, to bring forth a new pine.

Masha went out barefoot in her long nightgown, a cigarette between her lips.

"I've wanted your child since the day we met."

· PART TWO ·

· CHAPTER FIVE ·

1

HERMAN was again getting ready for one of his trips. He had invented a new lie about going on the road to sell the Encyclopedia Britannica, and had told Yadwiga that he would have to spend a whole week in the Middle West. Since Yadwiga hardly knew the difference between one book and another, the lie was superfluous. But Herman had got into the habit of making up stories. Besides, lies wore thin and had to be repaired constantly, and recently Yadwiga had been grumbling about him. He was away the first day of Rosh Hashanah and half of the second. She had prepared carp's head, apple and honey, and had baked the special New Year challah exactly as her neighbor had taught her to, but apparently Herman sold books even on Rosh Hashanah.

The women in the house were now trying to convince Yadwiga—speaking half in Yiddish, half in Polish—that her husband must have a mistress somewhere. One old woman had advised her to consult a lawyer, get a divorce from Herman, and demand alimony. Another had taken her to the synagogue to hear the blowing of the ram's horn. She stood among the wives and at the horn's first wailing sound had burst into tears. It had reminded her of Lipsk, of the war, of her father's death.

Now after only a few days with her, Herman was leaving again, to join not Masha but Tamara, who had rented a bungalow in the Catskill Mountains. He had had to lie to Masha too. He had told her that he was going with Rabbi Lampert to Atlantic City to attend a two-day rabbinical conference.

It was a lame excuse. Even Reformed rabbis did not hold conferences during the Days of Awe. But Masha, who had succeeded in getting Leon Tortshiner to give her a divorce and expected to marry Herman when the ninety-day waiting period was over, had stopped making jealous scenes. The divorce and her pregnancy seemed to have changed her outlook. She behaved toward Herman as a wife. And she showed more devotion than ever to her mother. Masha had found a rabbi, a refugee, who had agreed to perform the wedding ceremony without a license.

When Herman told her that he would be back from Atlantic City before Yom Kippur, she didn't question him. He also told her that the rabbi would pay him a fee of fifty dollars—and they needed the money.

The entire adventure was fraught with danger. He had promised to phone Masha and he knew that the long-distance operator might mention where the call was coming from. Masha might decide to phone Rabbi Lampert's office and discover that the rabbi was in New York. But since Masha had not called Reb Abraham Nissen Yaroslaver to check on him, she probably would not call Rabbi Lampert. One additional danger did not make that much difference. He had two wives and was about to marry a third. Even though he feared the consequences of his actions and the scandal that would follow, some part of him enjoyed the thrill of being faced with ever-threatening catastrophe. He both planned his actions and improvised. The "Unconscious," as von Hartmann called it, never made a mistake. Herman's words seemed to issue from his mouth of their own accord and only later would he realize what stratagems and subterfuges he had managed to invent. Behind this mad hodgepodge of emotions, a calculating gambler throve on daily risk.

Herman could easily free himself from Tamara. She had said several times that if he needed a divorce, she would give him one. But this divorce would not be of much help to him. There was probably little difference in the eyes of the law between a bigamist and a polygamist. Furthermore, a divorce would cost money and Herman would have to produce his papers. But there was something more: Herman saw in Tamara's return a symbol of his mystical beliefs. Whenever he was with her, he re-experienced the miracle of resurrection. Sometimes, as she spoke to him, he had the feeling he was at a séance at which her spirit had materialized. He had even played with the thought that Tamara wasn't really among the living, but that her phantom had returned to him.

Herman had been interested in occultism even before the war. Here in New York, when he could spare the time, he would go to the public library on Forty-second Street and look up books on mind-reading, clairvoyance, dybbuks, poltergeists—anything pertaining to parapsychology. Since formal religion was as good as bankrupt and philosophy had lost all meaning, occultism was a valid subject for those who still sought the truth. But souls existed on various levels. Tamara behaved—at least on the surface—like a living person. The refugee organization gave her a monthly allowance, and her uncle, Reb Abraham Nissen Yaroslaver, helped her as well. She had rented a bungalow at a Jewish hotel in Mountaindale. She didn't want to stay in the main building and eat in the dining room. The proprietor, a Jew from Poland, had agreed to have two meals a day brought to her bungalow. Her two weeks were almost over and Herman had not yet kept his promise to spend a few days with her. He had received a letter from her at his Brooklyn address chiding him for not keeping his word. She said at the end, "Make believe I'm still dead and come to visit my grave."

Before he left, Herman accounted for all eventualities. He gave money to Yadwiga; he paid the rent in the Bronx; he bought a gift for Tamara. He also put into his suitcase one of Rabbi Lampert's manuscripts to work on.

Herman arrived at the terminal too early and sat on a bench, his suitcase at his feet, waiting for the Mountaindale bus to be announced. It would not take him directly to where Tamara was stopping and he would have to change at some point along the route.

He had bought a Yiddish newspaper, but read only the headlines. The sum total of the news was always the same: Germany was being rebuilt; the Nazis' crimes were being forgiven by both the Allies and the Soviets. Each time Herman read such news, it awakened in him fantasies of vengeance in which he discovered methods for destroying whole armies, for ruining industries. He managed to bring to trial all those who had been involved in the annihilation of the Jews. He was ashamed of these reveries, which filled his mind at the slightest provocation, but they persisted with childish stubbornness.

He heard them call out Mountaindale and hurried to the exit where the buses were waiting. He lifted his suitcase up onto the rack and for the moment felt lighthearted. He was barely aware of the other passengers who had boarded the bus. They were speaking Yiddish and carrying packages wrapped in Yiddish newspapers. The bus started, and after a while a breeze smelling of grass, trees, and gasoline blew in through the partially opened window.

The ride to Mountaindale, which should have taken five hours, took almost a whole day. The bus halted at some terminal where they had to wait for another bus. It was still summery weather outside, but the days were already growing shorter. After sunset, a quarter moon came out and soon disappeared behind clouds. The sky became dark and starry. The driver of the second bus had to shut off the inside lights, because they disturbed his vision on the narrow, winding road. They drove through woods and suddenly a brightly lighted hotel materialized. On the veranda, men and women were playing cards. It had the insubstantiality of a mirage as they drove quickly by.

Gradually the other passengers got off at various stops and vanished into the night. Herman remained alone on the bus. He sat with his face pressed against the window-pane and tried to memorize each tree, shrub, stone along the way, as if America were destined for the same destruction as Poland, and he must etch every detail on his memory. Would not the entire planet disintegrate sooner or later? Herman had read that the whole universe was expanding, and was actually in the process of exploding. A nocturnal melancholy descended from the heavens. The stars gleamed like memorial candles in some cosmic synagogue.

The lights in the bus went on as it pulled up in front of the Hotel Palace, where Herman was to get off. It was exactly like the one they had already passed: the same veranda, the same chairs, tables, men, women, the same absorption in cards. "Had the bus been traveling in a circle?" he wondered. His legs felt stiff from having sat for so long, but he bounded up the wide steps of the hotel with vigor.

Suddenly Tamara appeared, wearing a white blouse, dark skirt, and white shoes. She looked tanned and younger. She had combed her hair differently. She ran toward him, took his suitcase, and introduced him to some women at a card table. One woman, who was wearing a bathing suit, with a jacket over her shoulders, threw a quick glance at her cards before saying in a hoarse voice, "How can a man leave such a pretty wife alone for such a long time? The men buzz around her like flies around honey."

"Why did it take so long?" Tamara asked, and her words, her Polish-Yiddish accent, the familiar intonations, shattered all his occult fantasies. This was no specter from the other world. She had put on some weight.

"Are you hungry?" she asked. "They've kept supper for you." She took him by the arm and led him into the dining room, where a single light was burning. The tables were already set for breakfast. Someone was still puttering about in the kitchen and the sound of running water could be heard. Tamara went into the kitchen and returned with a young man who carried Herman's supper on a tray: a half melon, soup with noodles, chicken with carrots, compote and a slice of honey cake. Tamara joked with the man and he answered her familiarly. Herman noticed that he had a blue number tattooed on his arm.

The waiter left and Tamara became silent. The youthfulness and even the suntan Herman had noticed upon his arrival seemed to fade. Shadows and the hints of pouches appeared under her eyes.

"Did you see that boy?" she said. "He was at the very doors of the ovens. In another minute, he would have been a heap of ashes."

2

TAMARA lay in her bed and Herman rested on the roll-away cot that had been brought into the bungalow for him, but neither of them could sleep. Herman had dozed off for a moment, but awakened with a start. The cot creaked under him.

"You aren't sleeping?" Tamara said.

"Oh, I'll fall asleep."

"I have some sleeping pills. If you like, I'll give you one. I take them, but I stay wide awake. And if I do fall asleep, it really isn't a sleep at all, but a sinking into emptiness. I'll get you a pill."

"No, Tamara, I'll get along without one."

"Why should you toss and turn all night?"

"If I were lying with you, I would sleep."

Tamara didn't speak for a time.

"What's the sense of it? You have a wife. I'm a corpse, Herman, and one doesn't sleep with a corpse."

"And what am I?"

"I thought you were faithful to Yadwiga, at least."

"I told you the whole story."

"Yes, you did tell me. It used to be that when someone told me something, I knew exactly what he was talking about. Now I hear the words clearly, but they don't seem to get through to me. They roll off me like water on oil-cloth. If you aren't comfortable in your bed, come into mine."

"Yes."

Herman got out of the cot in the dark. He crawled

under the covers and felt the warmth of Tamara's body and something he had forgotten over the years of separation, something both maternal and utterly strange. Tamara lay on her back, motionless. Herman lay on his side with his face toward her. He didn't touch her, but he noticed the fullness of her breasts. He lay still, as embarrassed as a bridegroom on his wedding night. The years separated them as effectively as a partition. The blanket was tightly tucked under the mattress, and Herman wanted to ask Tamara to loosen it, but he hesitated.

Tamara said, "How long has it been since we've lain together? It seems like a hundred years to me."

"It's less than ten."

"Really? To me it's been an eternity. Only God can cram so much into such a short time."

"I thought you didn't believe in God."

"After what happened to the children, I stopped believing. Where was I on Yom Kippur in 1940? I was in Russia. In Minsk. I sewed burlap sacks in a factory and somehow earned my ration of bread. I lived in the suburbs with Gentiles. When Yom Kippur came, I decided I was going to eat. What was the sense of fasting there? Also, it wasn't wise to show the neighbors you were religious. But when evening came and I realized that somewhere Jews were reciting *Kol Nidre,* the food wouldn't go down."

"You said that little David and Yocheved come to you."

Herman regretted his words immediately. Tamara didn't move, but the bed itself started to groan as if it had been shocked by his words. Tamara waited for the scraping sounds to stop before she said, "You won't believe me. I'd better not say anything."

"I believe you. Those who doubt everything are also capable of believing everything."

"Even if I wanted, I couldn't tell you. There's only one

way to explain it—that I'm crazy. But even insanity has to
have an origin."

"When do they come? In your dreams?"

"I don't know. I told you, I don't sleep but sink into an
abyss. I fall and fall and never reach bottom. Then I hang
suspended. That's only one example. I experience so
many things I can neither remember nor tell anyone
about. I get through the days all right, but my nights are
filled with terror. Perhaps I should go to a psychiatrist,
but how can he help me? All he can do is give these
things a Latin name. When I do go to a doctor, it's for
only one thing: a prescription for sleeping pills. The
children—yes, they come. Sometimes they visit till morning."

"What do they say?"

"Oh, they talk all night, but when I wake up, I don't
remember any of it. Even if I do remember a few words, I
soon forget them. But a feeling remains: that they exist
somewhere and want to be in contact with me. Sometimes
I go with them or I fly, I'm not sure which. I also hear
music, but it's a kind of music without sound. We come to
a border and I can't cross. They tear themselves away
from me and float over to the other side. I can't remember
what it is—a hill, some barrier. Sometimes I imagine I see
stairs and someone is coming to meet them—a saint or a
spirit. Whatever I say, Herman, it won't be accurate because there are no words to describe it. Naturally, if I'm
mad, then it's all part of my madness."

"You aren't mad, Tamara."

"Well, that's nice to hear. Does anyone really know
what madness is? Since you're here, why don't you move a
bit closer? It's all right. For years I've lived with the conviction that you were no longer among the living, and one
has different accounts to settle with the dead. When I

found out you were alive, it was too late to change my at-
titude."

"The children never talk about me?"

"I think they do, but I'm not sure."

For a moment the silence was total. Even the crickets
grew still. Then Herman heard the gushing sound of
water like a running brook, or was it a drainpipe? A stomach rumbled, but he wasn't sure whether it was his or Tamara's. He felt an itch and had the urge to scratch, but re-
strained himself. He wasn't exactly thinking. Nevertheless,
some thought process was going on in his brain. Suddenly
he said, "Tamara, I want to ask you something." Even as
he spoke, he didn't know what he was going to ask.

"What?"

"Why did you remain alone?"

Tamara didn't answer. He thought she might have
dozed off, but then she spoke, wide awake and clearly.
"I've already told you that I don't consider love a sport."

"What does that mean?"

"I can't have to do with a man I'm not in love with. It's
as simple as that."

"Does that mean you still love me?"

"I didn't say that."

"During all these years you've never had one single
man?" Herman asked with a tremor in his voice, ashamed
of his own words and the agitation they evoked in him.

"Supposing there had been someone? Would you jump
out of bed and walk back to New York?"

"No, Tamara. I wouldn't even consider it wrong. You
may be perfectly honest with me."

"And later you'll call me names."

"No. As long as you didn't know I was alive, how could
I demand anything? The most devout widows remarry."

"Yes, you're right."

"Then what is your answer?"

"Why are you shaking? You haven't changed one bit."

"Answer me!"

"Yes, I did have someone."

Tamara spoke almost angrily. She turned on her side, with her face toward him, thereby moving somewhat closer to him. In the dark he saw the glint of her eyes. As she turned, Tamara touched Herman's knee.

"When?"

"In Russia. Everything happened there."

"Who was it?"

"A man, not a woman."

There was suppressed laughter in Tamara's reply, mixed with resentment. Herman's throat tightened. "One? Several?"

Tamara sighed impatiently. "You don't have to know every detail."

"If you've told me this much, you might as well tell me everything."

"Well—several."

"How many?"

"Really, Herman, this isn't necessary."

"Tell me how many!"

It was quiet. Tamara seemed to be counting to herself. Herman became filled with grief and lust, amazed by the caprices of the body. One part of him mourned for something irrevocably lost: this betrayal, no matter how trivial compared to the world's iniquity, was a blot forever. Another part of him yearned to plunge himself into this treachery, to wallow in its degradation. He heard Tamara say, "Three."

"Three men?"

"I didn't know you were alive. You had been cruel to me. You made me suffer all those years. I knew that if you

were alive, you would do the same. In fact, you married
your mother's servant."

"You know why."

"There were 'whys' in my case, too."

"Well, you're a whore!"

Tamara made a sound like a laugh. "Didn't I tell you."
And she stretched out her arms to him.

3

HERMAN had fallen into a deep sleep, out of which someone was waking him. He opened his eyes in the dark and
didn't know where he was. Yadwiga? Masha? "Have I
gone off with another woman?" he wondered. But his con-
fusion lasted only a few seconds. Of course it was Tamara.
"What is it?" he asked.

"I want you to know the truth." Tamara spoke with the
trembling voice of a woman barely holding back her tears.

"What truth?"

"The truth is that I had no one—not three men, not
one, not even half a man. No one so much as touched me
with his little finger. That is God's truth."

Tamara was sitting up, and in the dark he sensed her
intensity, her determination not to let him go to sleep
again until he heard her out.

"You're lying," he said.

"I'm not lying. I told you the truth the very first time
when you asked me. But you seemed disappointed. What's
wrong with you—are you perverse?"

"I'm not perverse."

"I'm sorry, Herman, I'm as pure as the day you married

me. I say I'm sorry because, if I had known that you would feel so cheated, I might have tried to accommodate you. There was certainly no lack of men who wanted me."

"Since you talk out of both sides of your mouth so easily, I'll never be able to believe you again."

"Well, then, don't believe me. I told you the truth when we met in my uncle's house. Perhaps you'd like me to describe some imaginary lovers just to satisfy you. Unfortunately, my imagination isn't good enough. Herman, you know how sacred the memory of our children is to me. I would sooner cut out my tongue than desecrate their memories. I swear by Yocheved and David that no other man has touched me. Don't think it was such an easy thing to accomplish. We slept on floors, in barns. Women gave themselves to men they hardly knew. But when someone tried to get close to me, I pushed him away. I always saw the faces of our children before me. I swear by God, by our children, by the blessed souls of my parents, that no man so much as kissed me all those years! If you don't believe me now, then I beg you to leave me alone. God himself couldn't force a stronger vow from me."

"I believe you."

"I told you—it could have happened, but something didn't allow it. What it was I don't know. Though reason told me that there wasn't a trace left of your bones, I felt that you existed somewhere. How can one understand it?"

"It isn't necessary to understand it."

"Herman, there is something else I want to say to you."

"What?"

"I beg you, don't interrupt me. Before I came here, the American doctor at the consulate examined me and told me that I was in perfect health. I had survived everything —the hunger, the epidemics. I worked hard in Russia. I sawed logs, dug ditches, dragged wheelbarrows filled with rocks. At night, instead of sleeping, I often had to tend the sick who lay near me on planks. I never knew that I possessed so much strength. I'll soon get a job here, and no matter how hard it may be, it will be easier than what I had to do there. I don't want to go on accepting money from the 'Joint,' and I want to return the few dollars my uncle insisted on giving me. I'm telling you this so that you will know that I won't, God forbid, have to come to you for help. When you told me that you made your living by writing books for some rabbi who published them under his own name, I understood your situation. That's no way to live, Herman. You're destroying yourself!"

"I'm not destroying myself, Tamara. I've been a ruin for a long time."

"What will become of me? I shouldn't say this, but I can't ever be with anyone else. I know it as surely as I know that it's night now."

Herman didn't answer. He closed his eyes as if to get another moment of sleep.

"Herman, I have nothing to live for any more. I've wasted almost two weeks, eating, strolling, bathing, talking with all kinds of people. And all the while I've been saying to myself: 'Why am I doing this?' I try to read, but the books have no appeal for me. The women keep making suggestions about what I should do with myself, but I change the subject with jokes and meaningless banter. Herman, there's no other way out for me—I must die."

Herman sat up. "What do you want to do? Hang yourself?"

"If a piece of rope would make an end of it, then God bless the ropemaker. Over there I still had some hope. Actually, I had planned to settle in Israel, but when I found out you were alive, everything changed. Now I'm entirely without hope, and one dies of that more quickly than of cancer. I've observed it many times. I saw the opposite too. A woman in Jambul was lying on her deathbed. Then she received a letter from abroad and a package of food. She sat up and instantly became well. The doctor wrote a report about it and sent it to Moscow."

"And she's still alive?"

"She died of dysentery a year later."

"Tamara, I too am without hope. My only prospects are imprisonment and deportation."

"Why should you be imprisoned? You haven't robbed anyone."

"I have two wives and soon I'll have a third."

"Who is the third one?" Tamara asked.

"Masha, the woman I told you about."

"You said she already had a husband."

"He divorced her. She's pregnant."

Herman didn't know why he was revealing this to Tamara. But apparently he needed to confide in her, perhaps to shock her with his entanglements.

"Well, congratulations. You're going to be a father again."

"I'm going crazy, that's the bitter truth."

"Yes, you can't be in your right mind. Tell me, what sense does it make?"

"She's afraid of an abortion. When it comes to such things, a person can't be forced. She doesn't want the child to be illegitimate. Her mother is pious."

"Well, I must promise myself never to be surprised again. I'll give you a divorce. We can go to the rabbi tomorrow. You shouldn't have come to me under these circumstances, but talking consistency to you is like discussing colors with a blind man. Were you always like this? Or did the war do it? I don't really remember what kind of

human being you used to be. I told you, there are periods
of my life about which I've forgotten almost everything.
And you? Are you just frivolous, or is it that you enjoy
suffering?"

"I'm caught in a vise and can't free myself."

"You'll soon be free of me. You can also get rid of Yadwiga. Give her her fare and send her home to Poland. She
sits there alone in the apartment. A peasant has to work,
have children, go out into the fields in the morning, not
stay cooped up like an animal in a cage. She can go out of
her mind that way, and if, God forbid, you are arrested,
what will become of her?"

"Tamara, she saved my life."

"Is that why you want to destroy her?"

Herman didn't reply. It had begun to grow light. He
could make out Tamara's face. It was taking shape out of
the darkness—a patch here, a patch there, like a portrait
in the process of being painted. Her eyes stared at him
wide open. On the wall opposite the window, the sunlight
suddenly cast a spot that resembled a scarlet mouse. Herman became aware of how cold it was in the room. "Lie
down. You'll catch your death," he said to Tamara.

"The devil isn't taking me away so soon."

Nevertheless, she lay down again and Herman covered
them both with the blanket. He embraced Tamara and she
didn't resist him. They lay together without speaking,
overcome by both the complexities and the contradictory
demands of the body.

The fiery mouse on the wall grew paler, lost its tail, and
soon vanished altogether. For a while, night returned.

4

HERMAN spent the day and night before Yom Kippur eve at Masha's house. Shifrah Puah had bought two sacrificial hens, one for herself and one for Masha; she had wanted to buy a rooster for Herman but he had forbidden it. For some time now he had been thinking of becoming a vegetarian. At every opportunity, he pointed out that what the Nazis had done to the Jews, man was doing to animals. How could a fowl be used to redeem the sins of a human being? Why should a compassionate God accept such a sacrifice? This time Masha agreed with Herman. Shifrah Puah swore that if Masha didn't go through with the ceremony, she would leave the house. After reluctantly agreeing and twirling the hen above her head, uttering the prescribed prayers, Masha refused to take the fowl to the ritual slaughterer.

The two hens, one white, one brown, lay on the floor, their feet bound, their golden eyes looking sideways. Shifrah Puah had to take the hens to the slaughterer herself. As soon as her mother left the house, Masha burst into tears. Her whole face became contorted and wet. She fell into Herman's arms and cried out, "I can't take any more of this! I can't! I can't!"

Herman gave her a handkerchief to blow her nose. Masha went into the bathroom and he could hear her muffled crying. Afterward, she came into the room with a flask of whiskey in her hand. She had already drunk part of it. She was half laughing, half crying, with the mischievousness of a spoiled child. It occurred to Herman that as her pregnancy progressed she was becoming inappropriately babyish. She was full of little-girl mannerisms, giggly, even playfully naïve. He remembered Schopenhauer's statement that the female never really becomes fully mature. The bearer of children remains a child herself.

"In this kind of a world, there is only one thing left—whiskey. Here, have a drink!" Masha said, putting the flask to his lips.

"No, it's not for me."

Masha didn't come to him that night. She fell asleep right after supper, having taken a sleeping pill. Fully clothed, she lay on her bed in a drunken stupor. Herman turned off the light in his room. The hens, about which Shifrah Puah and Masha had quarreled, were already soaked, rinsed, and in the icebox. A not quite three-quarter moon shone in through the window. It cast its glow on the evening sky. Herman fell asleep and dreamed of things that had nothing to do with his mood. Somehow he was sliding down a hill of ice, using a contraption that was a combination of skates, a sled, and skis.

The next morning after breakfast, Herman said goodbye to Shifrah Puah and Masha and went to Brooklyn. On the way, he telephoned Tamara. Sheva Haddas had bought a seat for her in the women's section of their synagogue so that she might attend the midnight prayers. Tamara, after wishing Herman well like a pious wife, added, "No matter what happens, there is no one closer to me than you."

Yadwiga hadn't performed the ritual hen-twirling ceremony, but she had, on the day before Yom Kippur, prepared challah, honey, fish, kreplach, and chicken. Her kitchen smelled exactly the same as Shifrah Puah's. Yadwiga fasted on Yom Kippur. She paid for a ticket at the synagogue with ten dollars that she had managed to save out of her household money. She now poured out her resentment at Herman, accused him of running around with other women. He tried to defend himself, but couldn't conceal his annoyance. Finally he even pushed and kicked her, knowing that in her village in Poland, for wives to be beaten by their husbands was an affirmation of love. Yadwiga began to wail: she had saved his life and he was repaying her by a beating on the eve of the holiest day of the year.

The day was over and night fell. Herman and Yadwiga ate the last meal before fasting. Yadwiga drank eleven gulps of water as her neighbors advised her to—a prevention against thirst during the fast.

Herman fasted but did not go to the synagogue. He couldn't bring himself to be like one of those assimilated Jews who only prayed on the High Holy Days. He sometimes prayed to God when he was not fighting with Him, but to stand in a House of God with a holiday prayer book in his hands and praise Him according to the prescribed custom—this he couldn't do. The neighbors knew that Herman the Jew stayed at home while his Gentile wife went to pray. He could visualize them spitting at the mention of his name. In their own way, they had excommunicated him.

Yadwiga had dressed in a new frock that she had bought cheaply at a close-out sale. She had wrapped her hair in a kerchief, put a necklace of false pearls around her neck. The wedding ring Herman had bought for her, even though he had not stood beneath the wedding canopy with her, shone on her finger. She took a holiday prayer book with her to the synagogue. It was printed in Hebrew and English on facing pages: Yadwiga couldn't read either language.

Before leaving, she kissed Herman and said maternally, "Ask God for a happy year."

Then she burst into tears like a good Jewish woman.

The neighbors were waiting for Yadwiga downstairs, eager to include her in their circle, to teach her the Judaism that remained from their mothers and grandmothers and which the years in America had diluted and distorted.

Herman paced back and forth. Generally, when he found himself alone in Brooklyn, he would immediately phone Masha, but on Yom Kippur Masha didn't talk on the phone, nor did she smoke. Nevertheless, he did try to call her, because he noticed that there were not yet three stars in the sky. But there was no reply.

Alone in the apartment, Herman felt as if he were with all three women: Masha, Tamara, Yadwiga. Like a mind reader, he could read their thoughts. He knew, or at least he thought he knew, how the mind of each one of them functioned. Their grudges against God blended with their grudges against him. His women prayed for his health, but they also asked the omnipotent God that He reform Herman's ways. On this day, when God received so much homage, Herman was in no mood to bare his soul to Him. He went to the window. The street was empty. The leaves were beginning to turn and fell with each gust of wind. The Boardwalk was deserted. On Mermaid Avenue, all the shops were boarded up. It was Yom Kippur and quiet in Coney Island—so quiet that from his apartment he could hear the roar of the waves. Perhaps it was always Yom Kippur for the sea and it also prayed to God, but its God was like the sea itself—flowing eternally, infinitely wise, boundlessly indifferent, awesome in its unlimited power, bound by unchangeable laws.

Standing there, Herman tried to send telepathic messages to Yadwiga, Masha, and Tamara. He comforted them all, wished them a good year, promised them love and devotion.

Herman went into the bedroom and stretched out on the bed in his clothes. He didn't want to admit it, but of all his fears, the greatest was his fear of again becoming a father. He was afraid of a son and more afraid of a daughter, who would be an even stronger affirmation of the positivism he had rejected, the bondage that had no wish to be free, the blindness that wouldn't admit it was blind.

Herman fell asleep and Yadwiga awakened him. She told him that at the synagogue the cantor had sung *Kol Nidre* and that the rabbi had delivered a sermon soliciting funds for the yeshivas of the Holy Land and for other Jewish causes. Yadwiga had pledged five dollars. She told Herman in an embarrassed way that she didn't want him to touch her that night. It was forbidden. She bent over him and he saw in her eyes an expression that he used to see on the face of his mother during the high holidays. Yadwiga's lips trembled as if she were about to speak, but no sound came from them. Then she whispered, "I'm going to become Jewish. I want to have a Jewish child."

· CHAPTER SIX ·

1

HERMAN had spent the first two days of Succoth with Masha and had returned for Chol Hamoed, the intermediary days, to his apartment in Brooklyn.

He had eaten breakfast and was sitting at a table in the living room, working on a chapter of a book entitled *Jewish Life as Reflected in the Shulcan Aruch and the Responsa*. It had already been accepted by publishers in America and in England, and Rabbi Lampert was about to sign a contract with a French firm as well. Herman was to receive a percentage of the royalties. It was to be approximately fifteen hundred pages long, and had originally been planned for several volumes. But Rabbi Lampert had arranged that the work appear first as a series of monographs, each allegedly complete in itself, but prepared in such a way that they could later, with minor alterations, be bound into one large volume.

Herman wrote a few lines and paused. As soon as he sat down to work, his "nerves" began to sabotage him. He grew sleepy and could hardly keep his eyes open. He had to have a drink of water, he needed to urinate, he became conscious of a crumb between two loose teeth and tried to

get it out first with the tip of his tongue and then with a
thread drawn from the notebook binding.

Yadwiga had gone to the basement to do the laundry,
having taken a quarter from Herman to put in the washing machine. In the kitchen, Woytus was delivering an
avian lecture to Marianna, who was perched near him on
the stand. Her head was bowed guiltily, as if she were
being reprimanded for some inexcusable misdeed.

The telephone rang.

"What does she want now?" Herman wondered. He had
talked to Masha just a half hour before and she had told
him that she was going down to Tremont Avenue to shop
for the remaining days of the holiday—Shmini Atzeres
and Simchas Torah.

He lifted the receiver and said, "Yes, Mashele."

Herman heard a deep masculine voice, making the kind
of hesitant, throaty sound a man makes when he is about
to speak but is interrupted and loses his train of thought.
Herman started to say that the caller had the wrong number, when the voice asked for Herman Broder. Herman
couldn't decide whether or not to hang up. Was it a police detective? Had his bigamy been discovered? "Who is
it?" he said finally.

The person at the other end of the line coughed,
cleared his throat, and coughed again, like a speaker preparing for a speech. "I beg you to listen to me," he said,
speaking in Yiddish. "My name is Leon Tortshiner. I'm
Masha's former husband."

Herman's mouth became dry. It was the first direct contact he had ever had with Tortshiner. The man's voice
was deep and his Yiddish was different from Herman's
and Masha's. He spoke in an accent that was typical of a
small area of Poland, somewhere in the provinces between

Radom and Lublin. Each word ended in a slight vibrato, like the sound made by the bass notes of a piano.

"Yes, I know," Herman said. "How did you get my phone number?"

"What's the difference? I have it and that's what counts. If you must know, I saw it in Masha's address book. I have a good memory for numbers. I didn't know whose number it was, but eventually, as they say, I figured it out."

"I see."

"I hope I didn't wake you."

"No, no."

Tortshiner paused before he continued and Herman surmised from this pause that Tortshiner was a deliberate person, someone who thought ponderously and reacted slowly. "Can we get together?"

"For what reason?"

"It's a personal matter."

"He's not very clever," ran through Herman's mind. Masha had often said that Leon was a fool. "I'm sure you understand that this is extremely unpleasant for me," Herman heard himself stammer. "I can't see why it should be necessary. As long as you're divorced and—and—"

"My dear Mr. Broder, I wouldn't ring you up if it weren't necessary—for both of us."

He half chortled, half coughed, making a sound that was a combination of good-humored annoyance and the triumphant joviality of someone who has outsmarted his opponent. Herman felt the tips of his ears growing hot. "Perhaps we can talk about it over the phone?"

"There are things that have to be discussed face-to-face. Tell me where you live and I'll come over to your place, or we can meet in a cafeteria. You'll be my guest."

"At least give me an idea what it's about," Herman insisted.

It sounded as if Leon Tortshiner was smacking his lips together and struggling with words that were escaping his control.

The sounds finally became words. "What else can it be but about Masha?" Tortshiner was saying. "She is the link between us, so to speak. It's true Masha and I are divorced, but we were once man and wife, no one can deny that. I knew all about you even before she told me. Don't ask me how. I have, as they say, my sources of information."

"Where are you now?"

"I'm in Flatbush. I know you live somewhere in Coney Island, and if it's inconvenient for you to come to my place, then I'll come to yours. What is the saying? If Mohammed won't come to the mountain, then the mountain must come to Mohammed."

"There's a cafeteria on Surf Avenue," Herman said. "We can meet there." It was an effort for him to speak. He gave Tortshiner the exact location of the cafeteria and told him what subway would get him there. Tortshiner made him repeat the directions several times. He elaborated on everything and repeated phrases as if the very act of talking gave him pleasure. It was not actual dislike that he aroused in Herman so much as irritation at being forced into such an embarrassing situation. Herman was also suspicious. Who knows? It was not impossible that such a low character might be carrying a knife, or a revolver. Herman bathed and shaved hastily. He decided to wear his better suit; he didn't want to look shabby before this man. "One must please everyone," Herman thought ironically, "even the former husband of one's mistress."

He went to the basement and saw his underwear whirling wildly about through the window of the washing machine. The water foamed and splashed. Herman had the odd thought that these inanimate objects—the water, the soap, the bleach—were angry at man and the power he used to control them. Yadwiga was frightened at the sight of Herman. He had never before come down to the basement.

"I have to meet someone at a cafeteria on Surf Avenue," he told her. And though Yadwiga didn't question him, he described in detail where the cafeteria was located, thinking that if Leon Tortshiner were to attack him, Yadwiga would know where he was, or if necessary she would be able to appear as a witness in court. He even repeated Leon Tortshiner's name several times. Yadwiga gaped at him with the submission of the peasant who has long since given up trying to understand the city dweller and his ways. Still, her eyes betrayed a trace of distrust. Even on the days that belonged to her, he found reasons for getting away.

Herman looked at his wristwatch and timed himself so that he would not arrive at the cafeteria too early. He felt certain that a man like Leon Tortshiner would be at least half an hour late, and he decided to take a walk on the Boardwalk.

The day was sunny and mild, but the amusements had all been shut down. Nothing remained except boarded-up doors, faded and peeling posters. The performers had all left: the girl who was half snake, the strong man who ripped chains apart, the swimmer without hands and feet, the medium who called forth the spirits of the dead. The billboard announcing that the High Holy Days' services would be held in the auditorium of the Democratic Club was already ragged and weather-stained. Seagulls flew and shrieked above the ocean.

The waves surged toward the shore, hissing and foaming, receding again as they always had—barking packs of dogs, powerless to bite. In the distance, a ship with a gray sail rocked on the water. Like the ocean itself, it both moved and remained stationary—a shrouded corpse walking upon the water.

"Everything has already happened," Herman thought. "The creation, the flood, Sodom, the giving of the Torah, the Hitler holocaust." Like the lean cows of Pharaoh's dream, the present had swallowed eternity, leaving no trace.

2

HERMAN entered the cafeteria and saw Leon Tortshiner sitting at a table next to the wall. He recognized him from a photograph he had seen in Masha's album, though Tortshiner was now considerably older. He was a man of about fifty, large-boned, with a square-shaped head and thick dark hair that one could tell at a glance was dyed. His face was broad, with a prominent chin, high cheekbones, and a wide nose with large nostrils. He had thick eyebrows and his brown eyes were slanted like a Tartar's. There was a scar on his forehead that looked like an old knife wound. His somewhat coarse appearance was softened by the aura of Polish-Jewish affability. "He won't murder me," Herman thought. It seemed unbelievable that this boor had once been Masha's husband. The mere thought of it was ridiculous. But that was the way with facts. They punctured every bubble of conceit, shattered theories, destroyed convictions.

A cup of coffee was set in front of Tortshiner. A cigar with an inch of ash at its tip rested on an ashtray. At his left was a dish holding a partially eaten egg cake. Catching sight of Herman, Tortshiner made as if to rise, but fell back in his chair again.

"Herman Broder?" he asked. He stretched out a large, heavy hand.

"Sholom aleichem."

"Sit down, sit down," said Tortshiner. "I'll bring you some coffee."

"No, thanks."

"Tea?"

"No. Thanks."

"I'll get you some coffee!" Leon Tortshiner said decisively. "Since I invited you, you're my guest. I have to watch my weight, that's why I'm only eating an egg cake, but you can afford to eat a piece of cheesecake."

"Really, it's not necessary."

Tortshiner stood up. Herman watched him as he picked up a tray and took his place in the line at the counter. For his broad build, he was too short, with overly large hands and feet and with the shoulders of a strong man. This was how they grew in Poland: more in breadth than in height. He wore a brown striped suit, obviously chosen in an effort to look younger. He returned with a cup of coffee and a piece of cheesecake. He picked up the almost extinguished cigar quickly, puffed at it vigorously, and blew out a cloud of smoke.

"I pictured you altogether differently," he said. "Masha described you as a regular Don Juan." He obviously didn't intend the description to be derogatory.

Herman lowered his head. "Women's notions."

"I debated whether or not to call you for a long time. One doesn't do a thing like this easily, you know. I have

every reason to be your enemy, but I'll tell you right off
that I'm here for your sake. Whether you believe me or
not—that's, as they say, another matter."

"Yes, I understand."

"No, you don't understand. How can you understand?
You are, as Masha told me, something of a writer, but I'm
a scientist. Before one can understand, one must have the
facts, all the information. *A priori* we know nothing, only
that one and one make two."

"What *are* the facts?"

"The facts are that Masha bought the divorce from me
at a price that no honest woman should pay, even if her
life depended on it." Leon Tortshiner spoke in his deep
voice, without hurry, seemingly without anger. "I think
you should know this, because if a woman is capable of
paying such a price, one can never be altogether sure of
her integrity. She had lovers before she knew me and also
while she lived with me. That is the absolute truth.
That's the reason we separated. I'll be frank with you.
Normally, I would have no reason to take this interest in
you. But I struck up an acquaintance with a person who
knows you. He doesn't know our connection, if you want
to call it a connection, and he happened to tell me about
you. Why make a secret of it? His name is Rabbi Lampert. He told me that you suffered during the war, that
you spent years lying in a loft filled with hay, and all that.
I know you do some work for him. He calls it 'research,'
but you don't have to draw any diagrams for me. You're a
Talmudist, I specialized in bacteriology.

"As you know, Rabbi Lampert is working on a book to
prove that all knowledge stems from the Torah and he
wanted me to help him with the scientific part. I told him
plainly that modern knowledge is not to be found in the
Torah and there was no point looking for it there. Moses

knew nothing about electricity or vitamins. What's more, I don't want to waste my energy for a few dollars. I'd rather manage with less. The rabbi didn't actually mention your name, but when he spoke of a man who had hidden in a hayloft, I put two and two together, as they say. He praises you to the skies. But naturally he doesn't know what I know. He's a strange character. He immediately called me by my first name and that's not my style. Things must take their natural course. There has to be an evolution even in personal relationships. It's impossible to talk to him, because the telephone keeps ringing. I'll wager he has a thousand deals going on at the same time. Why does he need so much money? But I'll come to the point.

"I want you to know, Masha is a bum. Pure and simple. If you want to marry a bum, that's your privilege, but I thought I should warn you before she catches you in her net. Our meeting will, of course, remain a secret. That is the assumption on which I phoned you." Leon Tortshiner picked up his cigar and drew on it, but it had gone out.

While Tortshiner talked, Herman had been sitting with his head bent over the table. He was hot and wished he could open his collar. He felt a burning sensation behind his ears. A trickle of perspiration ran down his back, along his spine. When Tortshiner started to fuss with his cigar, Herman asked in a choked voice, "What price?"

Leon Tortshiner cupped his ear. "I can't hear. Speak a little louder."

"I said, 'What price?' "

"You know what price. You're not so naïve. You probably think I'm no better than she is and in a sense I can understand that. First of all, you're in love with her and Masha is a woman with whom one can fall in love. She drives men crazy. She almost drove me crazy. As primitive as she is, she has the perceptiveness of a Freud, Adler, and Jung put together, plus a little bit more. She's a brilliant actress too. When she wants to laugh, she laughs; and when she wants to cry, she cries. I told her straight out that if she stopped wasting her talents on foolishness, she could be a second Sarah Bernhardt. So, you see, it's no surprise to me that you're tangled up with her. I won't try to deny it—I still love her. Even a first-year student in psychology learns that one can love and hate at the same time. You're probably asking yourself, why should I tell you these secrets? What do I owe you? To understand, you'll have to hear me out with patience."

"I'm listening."

"Don't let the coffee get cold. Eat a piece of cheesecake. There. And don't be so upset. After all, the whole world is living through a revolution, a spiritual revolution. Hitler's gas chambers were bad enough, but when people lose all values, it's worse than torture. You undoubtedly come from a religious home. Where else did you learn Gemara? My parents weren't fanatics, but they were believing Jews. My father had one God and one wife, and my mother had one God and one husband.

"Masha probably told you that I studied at Warsaw University. I specialized in biology, worked with Professor Wolkowki, and helped him with an important discovery. Actually I made the discovery myself, though he received the credit. The truth is, they didn't reward him either. People think that thieves are to be found only on Krochmalna Street in Warsaw or the Bowery in New York. There are thieves among professors, artists, among the greatest in all fields. Ordinary thieves generally don't steal from one another, but plenty of scientists literally live by theft. Do you know that Einstein stole his theory from a mathematician who was helping him and no one really knows his name? Freud also stole, and so did Spinoza. This really has no connection with the subject, but I'm a victim of this sort of thievery.

"When the Nazis occupied Warsaw, I could have worked for them because I had letters from the greatest German scientists, and they would even have overlooked the fact that I was Jewish. But I didn't want to take advantage of such privileges and went through the whole Gehenna. Later I escaped to Russia, but our intellectuals there did an about-face and even started informing on one another. That's all the Bolsheviks needed. They sent them away to the camps. I myself had once been sympathetic to Communism, but actually, at the time when it would have paid me to be a Communist, I became fed up with the whole system and told them so openly. You can imagine how they treated me.

"In any case, I lived through the war, the camps, the hunger, the lice, and in 1945 I wound up in Lublin. There I met your Masha. She was the mistress, or the wife, of some Red Army deserter who had become a smuggler and a black marketeer in Poland. She apparently got enough to eat from the smuggler. I don't know exactly what happened between them. He accused her of being unfaithful and God knows what else. I don't have to tell you that she's an attractive woman—a few years ago she was a beauty. I had lost my whole family. When she heard I was a scientist, she became interested in me. The smuggler, I suppose, had another woman or half a dozen others. You must keep in mind that in all walks of life there is more chaff than wheat.

"Masha had found her mother and we all left for Germany. We had no papers and had to smuggle ourselves in. Every step of the way was fraught with peril. If you wanted to live, you had to break the law, because all laws

sentenced you to death. You were a victim yourself, so you
know how it was, though everyone has a different story to
tell. It's impossible to talk sensibly to refugees, because no
matter what you have to tell, someone will say that it happened just the other way around.

"But let's get back to Masha. We reached Germany and
they 'respectfully' interned us in a camp. Generally, couples lived together without the benefit of a marriage ceremony. Who needed such ceremonies at a time like that?
But Masha's mother insisted that we get married according to the laws of Moses and Israel. The smuggler probably gave her a divorce, or she hadn't been married to him
in the first place. I couldn't care less. I wanted to get back
to my scientific work as soon as I could, and I'm not religious. She wanted a wedding; I agreed to a wedding. Others in the camp started to do business immediately—
smuggling. The American Army brought all kinds of
goods to Germany and they handled it. Jews did business
everywhere, even in Auschwitz. If there is a hell, they'll
do business there too. I don't say this with malice. What
else could they do? The relief organizations provided
barely enough to exist on. After all those years of starvation, people wanted to eat well and to wear decent clothes
too.

"But what could I do if by nature I'm not a businessman? I stayed at home and lived on what the 'Joint' ra-
tioned out to me. The Germans didn't allow me near a
university or laboratory. There were a few other loafers
like me around and we read books or played chess. This
didn't please Masha. Living with her smuggler, she had
grown accustomed to luxury. When she met me, she had
been impressed because I was a scientist, but that didn't
satisfy her for long. She began to treat me like dirt; she
made terrible scenes. Her mother, I must tell you, is a

saint. She suffered every hell and remained pure. I loved
her mother dearly. How often does one find a holy person? Masha's father had also been a fine man, something
of a writer, a Hebraist. Who she takes after, I don't know.
She just couldn't resist gaiety wherever it was. The smugglers were always giving parties, dances. In Russia they
had gotten used to vodka and all its glories.

"When I met Masha in Lublin, it was my impression
that she was faithful to the smuggler. But soon it was obvious that she was having all kinds of affairs. The feeble
Jews had been killed off and those who were left had iron
constitutions, though, as it turns out, they were broken
people too. Their troubles are coming to the surface now.
In a hundred years, the ghettos will be idealized and the
impression created that they were inhabited only by
saints. There could be no greater lie. First of all, how
many saints are there in any generation? Second of all,
most of the really pious Jews perished. And among those
who managed to survive, the great drive was to live at any
cost. In some of the ghettos, they even ran cabarets. You
can imagine what cabarets! You had to step over dead
bodies to get in.

"My theory is that the human species is getting worse,
not better. I believe, so to speak, in an evolution in re-
verse. The last man on earth will be both a criminal and a
madman.

"I imagine that Masha told you the worst about me. As
a matter of fact, it was she who broke up the marriage.
While she was running around, I, like an idiot, sat home
with her mother. Her mother suffered from an eye dis-
ease, and I would read the Pentateuch and the American-
Yiddish newspapers out loud to her. But how long could I
lead such a life? I'm not old now, and in those days I was
in my prime. I was also beginning to meet people and

make contact with the scientific world. Women professors
used to visit from America—there are quite a number of
educated women here—and they became interested in me.
My mother-in-law, Shifrah Puah, told me openly that as
long as Masha left me alone all day and half the night, I
didn't owe her a thing. Shifrah Puah loves me to this day.
Once I met her in the street and she embraced me and
kissed me. She still calls me 'my son.'

"When my visa for America came through, all of a sud-
den Masha made up with me. I was granted the visa not
as a refugee but as a scientist. I got the visa, not she. She
was supposed to have gone to Palestine. Two famous
American universities were competing for me. Later I was
pushed out of one and then the other by intrigues. I
won't go into that now because it has no bearing on the
subject. I established theories and made discoveries that
the big companies didn't appreciate. The president of one
university told me frankly, 'We can't afford to have a second Wall Street crash.' What I had discovered was nothing more or less than new sources of energy. Atomic energy? Not exactly atomic. I would call them biological.
The atomic bomb would also have been ready years before it was if Rockefeller hadn't butted in.

"American billionaires hired thieves to rob the man
you see before you. They were after an apparatus I had
spent years building with my own hands. If this apparatus
had been put into operation—and it was only one step
from it—the American oil companies would have gone
bankrupt. But without me the machinery and chemicals
were of no value to the thieves. The companies tried to
buy me off. I've been having difficulties getting my citi-
zenship, and I'm sure they're behind it. You spit in Uncle
Sam's face ten times a day and he'll grin and bear it. But
try to touch his investments and he turns into a tiger.

"Where was I? Oh, yes, America. What would Masha have done in Palestine? She would have landed in a refugee camp, which would not have been much better than the camp in Germany. Her mother was sick and the climate there would have finished her. I'm not making myself out to be a saint. Soon after we got here, I became involved with another woman. She wanted me to divorce Masha. She was an American, the widow of a millionaire, and she was prepared to set me up in a laboratory so that I wouldn't have to be dependent on a university. But somehow I wasn't ready for a divorce. Everything must ripen, even a cancer. True, I no longer trusted Masha, and as a matter of fact, no sooner did we get here than she started all over again. But it seems that it is possible to love without trust. I once ran into an old schoolmate who told me openly that his wife was living with other men. When I asked him how he could stand it, he answered simply, 'One can overcome jealousy.' One can overcome anything but death.

"How about another cup of coffee? No? Yes, one can overcome anything. I don't know exactly how she met you and I don't care. What difference does it make? I don't blame you. You never swore any loyalty to me, and besides in this world we grab what we can. I grab from you, you grab from me. That there was someone before you, here in America, I know for sure, because I met him and he didn't make a secret of it. It was after she met you that she started asking me for a divorce, but since she ruined my life I didn't feel that I had any obligation to her. She could easily get a civil divorce, because we've been separated for some time. But no one could force me to give her a Jewish divorce, not even the greatest of rabbis. It's her fault that I'm still at loose ends. After the wreck of our marriage, I tried to pick up the threads of my career, but

I was so wound up I couldn't concentrate on serious work.
I began to hate her, though it isn't in my nature to hate. I
sit here with you as a friend and wish you only well. My
reasoning is simple: if it hadn't been you, it would have
been someone else. If I were as guilty as Masha tries to
make me appear, would her mother send me a New Year's
card on Rosh Hashanah with a personal note?

"Now I come to the point. A few weeks ago, Masha
called me up and asked me to meet her. 'What's happened?' I asked. She hemmed and hawed until finally I
told her to come to my place. She came, all dressed up, fit
to kill, as they say. I had heard about you, but she began
to tell me the whole story, as if it had only happened yesterday. All the details. She'd fallen in love with you; she
was pregnant. She wanted to have the baby. She wanted a
rabbi to perform the wedding ceremony because of her
mother. 'Since when have you become so concerned about
your mother?' I asked. I was in a bitter mood. She sat
down and crossed her legs like an actress posing for a photograph. I said to her, 'You behaved like a prostitute
when you were with me, now pay the price.' She hardly
protested. 'We're still man and wife,' she said. 'I guess it's
permitted.' To this day I don't know why I did it. Vanity,
perhaps. Then I met Rabbi Lampert and he told me
about you, your learning, the years of hiding in that attic,
and everything became clear, painfully clear. I realized
that she'd caught you in her net just as she had me. Why
she's attracted to intellectuals is a good question, though
undoubtedly she's been mixed up with roughnecks as
well.

"That, in short, is the story. I hesitated a long time before deciding to tell it to you. But I came to the conclusion that you had to be warned. I hope, at least, that the

child is yours. It looks as if she really loves you, but with such a creature one never can know."

"I won't marry her," Herman said. He spoke the words so quietly that Leon Tortshiner cupped his ear.

"What? Look, there's one thing I want to make sure. Don't tell her about our meeting. I really should have gotten in touch with you sooner, but as you see I am an impractical person. I do things and get myself into all kinds of trouble. If she knew that I told you what had happened, my life would be in danger."

"I won't tell her."

"You know you're not obliged to marry her. She's just the type to have a bastard. If there's someone to be pitied, it's you. Your wife—did she die?"

"Yes, she died."

"Your children too?"

"Yes."

"The rabbi told me that you live with a friend and that you don't have a telephone, but I remembered seeing your phone number in Masha's little book. She has a habit of outlining important phone numbers with circles and little drawings of flowers and animals. She drew a whole garden of trees and snakes around your number."

"How did you happen to be in Brooklyn today if you live in Manhattan?" Herman asked.

"I have friends here," Leon Tortshiner said, obviously lying.

"Well, I must go now," Herman said. "Thanks very much."

"What's your hurry? Don't go yet. I was only thinking of your own good. In Europe, people were accustomed to live secret lives. Maybe it made some sense there, but this is a free country and you don't have to hide from anyone.

Here you can be a Communist, an anarchist, whatever you want. There are certain religious sects who hold venomous snakes when they pray, because of some verse in the Book of Psalms. Others go around naked. Masha, too, carries around a whole pack of secrets. The trouble is that those who have secrets betray themselves. Man is his own betrayer. Masha told me things that she didn't have to tell me and that I never would have found out otherwise."

"What did she tell you?"

"Whatever she told me she'll tell you. It's just a matter of time. People like to show off about everything, even a hernia. I don't need to tell you that she doesn't sleep at night. She smokes and talks. I used to plead with her to let me sleep. But the demon in her won't let her rest. If she had lived in the Middle Ages, she would surely have been a witch and flown a broomstick Saturday night to keep a date with the devil. But the Bronx is one place where the devil would have died of boredom. Her mother is also a witch in her own way, but a good witch: half rebbetzin, half fortuneteller. Every female sits in her own net weaving like a spider. When a fly happens to come along, it's caught. If you don't run away, they'll suck the last drop of life out of you."

"I'll manage to run away. Goodbye."

"We can be friends. The rabbi is a savage, but he loves people. He has unlimited connections and he can be of use to you. He's angry at me because I won't read electronics and television into the first chapter of Genesis. But he'll find someone who will. Basically he's a Yankee, although I think he was born in Poland. His real name isn't Milton but Melech. He writes a check for everything. When he arrives in the next world and has to give an accounting, he'll take out his checkbook. But, as my grandmother Reitze used to say, 'Shrouds don't have pockets.' "

3
———————

THE telephone rang, but Herman didn't answer it. He
counted the rings and went back to the Gemara. He sat
at the table, which was covered with a holiday cloth, studying and intoning as he used to do in the study house in
Tzivkev.

Mishnah: "And these are the duties the wife performs
for the husband. She grinds, bakes, washes, cooks, nurses
her child, makes the bed, and spins wool. If she has
brought one servant with her, she doesn't grind, bake, or
wash. If she has brought two, she doesn't cook or nurse
the child; three, she doesn't make the bed or spin wool;
four, she sits in the salon. Rabbi Eliezer says: Even if she
brought him a houseful of servants, he should force her to
spin wool, because idleness leads to insanity."

Gemara: She grinds? But the water does that—the intention is that she prepares the grain to be ground. Or it
can mean a hand mill. This Mishnah doesn't concur with
Rabbi Chiyah, because Rabbi Chiyah said: A wife is
solely for beauty, for children. Rabbi Chiyah said further:
Whoever wishes his daughter to be fair should feed her
young chickens and make her drink milk during the time
before she becomes ripe—"

The telephone began to ring again and this time Herman didn't count the rings. He was through with Masha.
He had sworn to renounce all worldly ambitions, to give
up the licentiousness into which he had sunk when he
had strayed from God, the Torah, and Judaism. He had
stayed up the previous night trying to analyze the modern

Jew and his own way of life. He had once again arrived at
the same conclusion: if a Jew departed in so much as one
step from the Shulcan Aruch, he found himself spiritually
in the sphere of everything base—Fascism, Bolshevism,
murder, adultery, drunkenness. What could stop Masha
from being what she was? What could change Leon Tortshiner? Who and what could have controlled the Jewish
members of the GPU, the Capos, the thieves, speculators,
informers? What could save him, Herman, from sinking
even deeper into the mire in which he was caught? Not
philosophy, not Berkeley, Hume, Spinoza, not Leibnitz,
Hegel, Schopenhauer, Nietzsche, or Husserl. They all
preached some sort of morality but it did not have the
power to help withstand temptation. One could be a Spi-
nozaist and a Nazi; one could be versed in Hegel's phenom-
enology and be a Stalinist; one could believe in monads,
in the *Zeitgeist,* in blind will, in European culture, and
still commit atrocities.

At night he had taken stock of himself. He was deceiving Masha, Masha was deceiving him. Both had the same
goal: to get as much pleasure as possible out of life in the
few years left before darkness, the final end, an eternity
without reward, without punishment, without will, would
be upon them. Behind this *Weltanschauung* festered deception and the principle of "might is right." One could
escape from this only by turning to God. And to what
faith could he repair? Not to a faith which had, in the
name of God, organized inquisitions, crusades, bloody
wars. There was only one escape for him: to go back to
the Torah, the Gemara, the Jewish books. What about his
doubt? Even if one were to doubt the existence of oxygen,
one would still have to breathe. One could deny gravity,
but one would still have to walk on the ground. Since he
was suffocating without God and the Torah, he must

serve God and study the Torah. He rocked back and forth, intoning, "And she nurses her child. So I would say that the Mishnah does not agree with the School of Shamai. 'If she made an oath not to nurse her child,' the School of Shamai says, 'she removes the breast from its mouth,' and the School of Hillel says, 'The husband forces her and she must nurse it.' "

The telephone rang again. Yadwiga came in from the kitchen, holding an iron in one hand and a pan of water in the other.

"Why don't you answer the telephone?"

"I'll never answer the phone again on a holiday. And if you want to become Jewish, don't iron on Shmini Atzeres."

"You write on the Sabbath, not I."

"I won't write on the Sabbath any more. If we don't want to become like the Nazis, we must be Jews."

"Will you go to Kuffoth with me today?"

"Say Hakaffoth, not Kuffoth. Yes, I'll go with you. You'll have to go to the ritual bath too, if you want to become a Jewish woman."

"When will I become Jewish?"

"I'll talk to the rabbi. I'll teach you how to say the prayers."

"Will we have a child?"

"If God wills it, we'll have one."

Yadwiga's face turned red. She seemed overcome with joy.

"What shall I do with the iron?"

"Put it away till after the holidays."

Yadwiga stood there a while longer, then she returned to the kitchen. Herman grasped his chin. He hadn't shaved and his beard was beginning to grow. He had decided that he could no longer work for the rabbi, since

the work was a deception. He would have to find a position as a teacher or do something else. He would divorce
Tamara. What hundreds of generations of Jews before
him had done, he would do. Repent? Masha would never
repent. She was a modern woman through and through,
with all the modern woman's ambitions and delusions.

The wisest thing for him to do would be to leave New
York, settle in a distant state. If not, he would always be
tempted to go back to Masha. Even the thought of her
name excited him. In the repeated ringing of the phone,
he could hear her anguish, her wantonness, her attach-
ment to him. Reading Rashi's annotations to the Talmud,
he still couldn't keep her peppery words from intruding
—her teasing remarks, her contempt for those who desired her, running after her like hounds after a bitch.
Without question, she would have an explanation for her
behavior. She was capable of declaring a pig kosher and
propounding a plausible theory to prove it.

He sat over his Gemara, staring at the letters, at the
words. These writings were home. On these pages dwelt
his parents, his grandparents, all his ancestors. These
words could never be adequately translated, they could
only be interpreted. In context, even a phrase such as "a
woman is for her beauty's sake" had a deep religious sig-
nificance. It brought to mind the study house, the wom-
en's section of the synagogue, penetential prayers, lamen-
tations for martyrs, sacrifice of one's life in the Holy
Name. Not cosmetics and frivolity.

Could this be explained to an outsider? The Jew took
words from the marketplace, from the workshop, from the
bedroom, and sanctified them. In the Gemara the words
for thief and robber had another flavor, different associa-
tions from those they had in Polish or English. The sin-
ners in the Gemara stole and cheated solely so that Jews

would have a lesson to learn—so that Rashi could make a commentary, so that Tosafoth could write the great super-commentaries on Rashi; so that the learned teachers such as Reb Samuel Idlish, Reb Meir of Lublin, and Reb Shlomo Luria could seek even clearer answers and ferret out new subtleties and new insights. Even the idol-worshippers that are mentioned worshipped the gods so that a Talmudic tractate would set forth the perils of idolatry.

The phone rang again and Herman imagined that he heard Masha's voice through the ringing: "At least hear my side!" According to all the laws of justice, both sides were entitled to be heard. Although Herman knew that he was breaking his vows again, he could not prevent himself from getting up and lifting the receiver.

"Hello."

There was silence at the other end of the line. Apparently Masha could not speak.

"Who is it?" Herman asked.

No one answered.

"You whore!"

Herman heard the sound of a gasp. "Are you still alive?" Masha asked.

"Yes, I'm alive."

There was another long silence.

"What's happened to you?"

"What's happened is that I've found out you are a despicable creature!" Herman was shouting. He couldn't catch his breath.

"I believe you've gone out of your mind!" Masha replied.

"I curse the day I met you! Slut!"

"My God! What have I done?"

"Paid for your divorce with prostitution!" It seemed to Herman that it wasn't his voice shouting. This was the way his father used to scold a faithless Jew: Goy, fiend, apostate! It was the ancient Jewish outcry against those who broke the commandments. Masha began to cough. It sounded as if she were choking. "Who told you this? Leon?"

Herman had promised Leon Tortshiner not to mention his name. Just the same, he couldn't lie now. He didn't answer.

"He is a vicious devil and—"

"He may be vicious, but he spoke the truth."

"The truth is that he asked me, but I spat in his face. If I'm lying, may I not live to wake up in the morning and may I never have any rest in my grave. Bring us face to face. If he dares to repeat this ugly lie, I'll kill him and myself. Oh, Father in heaven!"

Masha was screaming, and her voice too was not like her own; it was like that of a Jewish woman of olden times who had been falsely accused of evil-doing. It seemed to Herman as if he were hearing a voice from generations past. "He isn't a Jew, he's a Nazi!"

Masha wailed so loudly that Herman had to hold the receiver away from his ear. He stood listening to her weeping. Instead of becoming less intense, it grew louder. Herman's anger was rekindled.

"You had a lover here in America!"

"If I had a lover in America, may I get cancer. May God hear my words and punish me. If Leon made it up, may the curse fall on him. Father in heaven, see what they're doing to me! If he's telling the truth, may the child in my womb die!"

"Stop it! You're swearing like a fishwife."

"I don't want to live any more!"

Masha was convulsed with sobs.

· *CHAPTER SEVEN* ·

1

ALL night the snow fell—dry and coarse as salt. On the street where Herman lived, one could barely make out the contours of the few cars buried beneath it. Herman imagined that this was the way the Pompeiian chariots had looked covered over with ash after the eruption of Vesuvius. The night sky turned violet as if, through some miracle or transformation in the heavens, the earth had entered an unknown constellation. Herman thought about his boyhood: Hanukkah, the rendering of chicken fat for the coming Passover, playing games with a dreidl, skating in the frozen gutters, reading the weekly portion of the Torah which begins with "And Jacob dwelt in the land of his fathers." The past existed! Herman spoke to himself. Granted that time is nothing more than a mode of thinking, as maintained by Spinoza, or a form of perception, as Kant thought, still the fact cannot be denied that in Tzivkev in wintertime the stove was heated with firewood; his father, blessed be his memory, studied the Gemara and its commentaries, while his mother cooked a barley stew of pearl kasha, beans, potatoes, and dried mushrooms. Herman could taste the flavor of the grits, hear his father mumbling as he read, his mother talking to Yadwiga in the kitchen, the tinkling of a bell on a sled carrying logs that a peasant was bringing in from the forest.

Herman, in his robe and slippers, was sitting in his apartment. Though it was winter, the window was opened slightly, letting in a sound like countless crickets chirping under the snow. It was too warm in the house. The janitor had provided heat all night long. The steam in the radiator whistled its one-note tune full of inarticulate longing. Herman imagined that the sound of the steam in the pipes was a lament: bad, bad, bad; grief, grief, grief; sick, sick, sick. There was no light on, but the room was filled with the snow-reflected glow that suffused the sky. It was a light, Herman imagined, similar to the Northern Lights he had read about in books. For a while he stared at the bookcase and at the volumes of the Gemara which again stood neglected and dusty. Yadwiga never dared to touch these sacred books.

Herman had been unable to sleep. He had been married to Masha by a rabbi, and she was, according to his calculations, in her sixth month, although it certainly wasn't apparent. Yadwiga had also missed her period.

Herman thought of the Yiddish saying that ten enemies can't harm a man as much as he can harm himself. Yet he knew he wasn't doing it all by himself; there was always his hidden opponent, his demon adversary. Instead of destroying him with dispatch, his enemy continued to invent new and baffling tortures for him.

Herman breathed the cold air that blew in from the ocean and the snowfall. He looked outside and had the desire to say a prayer, but to whom? How could he dare to speak to the higher powers now? And what should he pray for? After a while he returned to bed and lay down next to Yadwiga. It was their last night together. In the morning, he was leaving on one of his trips, which meant he would be going to stay with Masha.

Since their wedding, when he had placed the ring on Masha's index finger, she had busied herself improving the apartment and redecorating his room. At night she no longer had to come to him secretly because of her mother. She had promised not to quarrel with him about Yadwiga, but she broke her word. She cursed Yadwiga at every opportunity, even blurting out that she would like to kill her. Masha's hope that the marriage would still her mother's reproaches proved false. Shifrah Puah complained that Herman's idea of marriage was a mockery. She forbade him to call her "mother-in-law." Only the most necessary words passed between them. Shifrah Puah became even more engrossed in her prayers, in leafing through books, reading the Yiddish newspapers and the memoirs of Hitler victims. She spent a great deal of time in her darkened bedroom and it was difficult to know whether she was thinking or napping.

Yadwiga's pregnancy was a new catastrophe. The rabbi of the synagogue Yadwiga had attended on Yom Kippur had accepted her ten dollars, a woman had led her to the ritual bath, and now Yadwiga was a convert to Judaism. She observed the laws of purification and Kashruth. She asked Herman questions continually. Was it permitted to keep meat in the refrigerator when there was a bottle of milk in it? Was it all right to eat dairy food after fruit? Was she permitted to write to her mother, who, according to Jewish law, was no longer her mother? Her neighbors confused her with their conflicting suggestions, often based on shtetl superstitions. An elderly Jew, an immigrant peddler, tried to teach her the Yiddish alphabet. Yadwiga no longer tuned in to the Polish radio programs, but listened only to those in Yiddish. One always heard weeping and sighing on these stations; even the songs had a sobbing quality. She asked Herman to speak Yiddish to her, though she understood little. She reprimanded him more and more for not conducting himself like other Jews. He didn't go to synagogue, nor did he own a prayer shawl and phylacteries.

He would tell her to mind her own business, or say, "You won't have to lie on my bed of nails in Gehenna," or, "Do me a favor, and leave the Jews alone. We have enough trouble without you."

"May I wear the medallion Marianna gave me? It has a crucifix on it."

"You may, you may. Stop bothering me."

Yadwiga no longer kept her neighbors at a distance. They visited, shared secrets, and gossiped with her. These women, with little else to do, instructed Yadwiga in Judaism, showed her how to buy bargains, warned her about being exploited by her husband. An American housewife must have a vacuum cleaner, an electric mixer, an electric steam iron, and, if possible, a dishwasher. The apartment must be insured against fire and theft; Herman must take out a life-insurance policy; she must dress better and not go around in peasant's rags.

There was a controversy among the neighbors on what kind of Yiddish to teach Yadwiga. The women from Poland tried to teach her Polish Yiddish, and the Litvaks that of Lithuania. Continuously, they pointed out to Yadwiga that her husband spent too much time on the road and that, if she wasn't watchful, he might run off with another woman. In Yadwiga's mind, the insurance policy and the dishwasher were both necessary aspects of Jewish observances.

Herman fell asleep, woke up, dozed off, and woke

again. His dreams were as intricate as his waking life. He had discussed the possibility of an abortion with Yadwiga, but she wouldn't hear of it. Wasn't she entitled to have at least one child? Must she die and have no Kaddish? (She had learned the word from her neighbors.) Well, and what about him? Why should he remain like a withered tree? She would be a good wife to him; she was willing to go to work till the ninth month, to wash clothes for the neighbors, scrub floors, to help contribute toward the expenses. A neighbor, whose son had just opened a supermarket, offered Herman a job, so that he wouldn't have to travel around the country selling books.

Herman was supposed to have phoned Tamara at the furnished room into which she had moved, but days passed and he hadn't called. He was, as usual, behind in his work for the rabbi. Every day he was afraid of receiving a letter from the Department of Internal Revenue imposing heavy penalties on him for non-payment of taxes. Any investigation might expose all his involvements. He shouldn't continue living in this apartment now that Leon Tortshiner had his phone number. Tortshiner was capable of paying a visit unannounced. Herman considered it possible that Tortshiner was scheming to bring about his downfall.

Herman laid his hand on Yadwiga's hip. Her body gave off an animal warmth. His was cold by comparison. Yadwiga seemed to sense in her sleep that Herman desired her and responded mutteringly without waking up altogether. "There is no such thing as sleep," Herman thought. "It's all a sham and make-believe."

He again dozed off, and when he opened his eyes, it was broad daylight. The snow was dazzling in the sunshine. Yadwiga was in the kitchen—he could smell coffee. Woytus whistled and trilled. He was surely serenading Marianna, who rarely sang at all, but groomed herself all day plucking at the down under her wings.

For the hundredth time, Herman calculated his expenses. He owed rent here and in the Bronx, he had to pay the phone bills in the names of Yadwiga Pracz and Shifrah Puah Bloch. He hadn't paid the utilities for either apartment and the gas and electricity might be shut off. He had misplaced the bills. His papers and documents had a way of vanishing; perhaps he had even lost money. "Well, it's just too late to do anything," he thought.

After a while he went into the bathroom to shave. He looked at his lathered face in the mirror. The soap on his cheeks resembled a white beard. A pale nose and a pair of light-colored eyes, tired yet youthfully eager, could be seen peering out of the suds.

The phone rang. He went to it, lifted the receiver, and heard the voice of an older woman. She stammered and had trouble speaking. He was about to hang up when she said, "This is Shifrah Puah."

"Shifrah Puah? What has happened?"

"Masha—is sick—" And she began to sob.

"Suicide," ran through Herman's mind. "Tell me what has happened!"

"Come quickly—please!"

"What is it?"

"Please come!" Shifrah Puah repeated. And she hung up.

Herman had the impulse to call back to get more details, but he knew it was difficult for Shifrah Puah to speak over the phone and that her hearing was poor. He returned to the bathroom. The lather on his cheeks had dried up and was flaking off in bits. No matter what happened, he had to shave and shower. "As long as you're alive, you mustn't stink." He started to apply fresh lather to his face.

Yadwiga came into the bathroom. Usually she would open the door slowly and ask permission to come in, but this time she came without courtesy. "Who just phoned? Your mistress?"

"Leave me alone!"

"The coffee's getting cold."

"I can't have breakfast. I must go right away."

"Where to? To your mistress?"

"Yes, to my mistress."

"You made me pregnant and you go running to whores. You're not selling books. Liar!"

Herman was astonished. She had never spoken in such a venomous tone. Anger seized him. "Go back into the kitchen, or I'll throw you out of here!" he shouted.

"You have a mistress. You spend nights with her. You dog!"

Yadwiga shook her fist at him, and Herman pushed her out of the doorway. He heard her cursing at him in her peasant tongue: *"Szczerwa, cholera, lajdak, parch."* He hurried into the shower, but only cold water sprayed out. He dressed clumsily but as quickly as he could. Yadwiga had left the apartment, probably to tell the neighbors that he had beaten her. Herman took one gulp of coffee from the cup on the kitchen table and hurried out. He returned in a moment; he had forgotten his sweater and rubbers. Outside, the snow blinded him. Someone had dug a path between two walls of snow. He walked down to Mermaid Avenue, where the shopkeepers were clearing away the snow, shoveling it into heaps. He was engulfed by a cold wind from which no amount of clothing could protect him. He hadn't had enough sleep, he felt light from hunger.

He climbed up the stairs to the open station to wait for a train. Coney Island, with her Luna Park and Steeplechase, lay desolate in the winter snow and frost. The train rolled up to the platform and Herman stepped inside. Briefly, he could see the ocean from the window. The waves leaped and foamed with wintry fury. A man moved slowly along the beach, but it was impossible to imagine what he was doing there in the cold, unless he was trying to drown himself.

Herman took a seat over hot pipes. He felt a warm blast of air through the cane seating. The car was half empty. A drunk had stretched himself out on the floor. He wore summer clothes, and no hat. From time to time, he uttered a growl. Herman picked up a muddy newspaper from the floor and read an item about a maniac who had murdered his wife and six children. The train was slower than usual. Someone said that the tracks were covered with snow. It speeded up when it went underground, and finally pulled into Times Square, where Herman changed for a Bronx express. The trip took almost two hours, during which Herman read through the muddy newspaper: the columnists, the ads, even the horse-racing page and the obituaries.

2

WHEN he entered Masha's apartment, he saw Shifrah Puah, a stocky young man who was a doctor, and a dark-complexioned woman, probably a neighbor. Her head with its frizzly hair was too large for her small body.

"I thought you would never come," Shifrah Puah said.

"It's a long ride by subway."

Shifrah Puah was wearing a black kerchief on her head. Her face looked yellow and more wrinkled than usual.

"Where is she?" Herman asked. He didn't know whether he was asking about a living person or a dead one.

"She is asleep. Don't go in."

The doctor, round-faced, with moist eyes and curly hair, motioned toward Herman, and in a mocking tone asked, "The husband?"

"Yes," Shifrah Puah said.

"Mr. Broder, your wife wasn't pregnant. Who told you she was pregnant?"

"She did."

"She had a hemorrhage, but there was no baby. Did a doctor examine her?"

"I don't know. I'm not even sure she saw a doctor."

"Where do you people think you're living—on the moon? You're still in your little shtetl in Poland." The doctor spoke half in English, half in Yiddish. "In this country when a woman is pregnant, she is under the continuous care of a doctor. Her whole pregnancy was here!" the doctor said, pointing his index finger to his temple.

Shifrah Puah had already heard his diagnosis, but she clasped her hands together as if she were hearing it for the first time.

"I don't understand it, I don't understand. Her belly grew. The child kicked her."

"All nerves."

"Such nerves! Defend and protect us against such nerves. Father in heaven, she started to scream and go into labor. Oh, my wretched life!" Shifrah Puah wailed.

"Mrs. Bloch, I once heard of such a case," the neighbor said. "Everything happens to us refugees. We suffered so much under Hitler, we're half crazy. The woman I heard about got a huge stomach. Everybody said she was carrying twins. But in the hospital they found it was only gas."

"Gas?" Shifrah Puah asked, putting her hand to her ear as if she were deaf. "But I tell you, she didn't have her period all these months. Well, evil spirits are playing with us. We came out of Gehenna, but Gehenna followed us to America. Hitler has run after us."

"I'm leaving now," the doctor said. "She'll sleep till late tonight—maybe even tomorrow morning. When she wakes up, give her the medicine. You can give her some food too, but no cholent."

"Who eats cholent in the middle of the week?" Shifrah Puah asked. "We don't even have cholent on the Sabbath. The cholent that you have to cook in a gas oven has no taste."

"I was just kidding."

"You'll come again, Doctor?"

"I'll drop in tomorrow morning on the way to the hospital. You'll be a grandmother a year from now. She's completely normal inside."

"I won't live that long," Shifrah Puah said. "Only God in heaven knows what strength and life these few hours have cost me. I thought she was in her sixth month—her seventh month, at most. Suddenly she starts screaming that she has cramps and blood gushes out of her. That I'm still alive and standing on my feet is a miracle from above."

"Well, it was all up here." Again the doctor pointed to his forehead. He went out but paused at the doorway to beckon to the neighbor, who followed him. Shifrah Puah was silent, waiting suspiciously in case the woman might be listening at the door. Then she said, "I wanted so much to have a grandchild. At least someone to name after the murdered Jews. I'd hoped it would be a boy and he would be called Meyer. But with us nothing works because our luck is black. Oh, I shouldn't have saved myself from those Nazis! I should have stayed there with the dying Jews, and not run away to America. But we wanted to live. What use is my life to me? I envy the dead. All day I envy them. I can't even earn my death. I hoped my bones would be buried in the Holy Land, but it's fated that I should lie in an American cemetery."

Herman didn't answer. Shifrah Puah went over to the table and picked up the prayer book that was lying there. Then she put it down again. "Would you like something to eat?"

"No, thanks."

"Why did it take you so long? Well, I guess I'll say my prayers." She put on her eyeglasses, sat down on a chair, and began mumbling with her pale lips.

Herman opened the door to the bedroom carefully. Masha was sleeping in the bed in which Shifrah Puah usually slept. She looked pale and serene. He gazed at her for a long time. He was overcome with love for her as well as shame at himself. "What can I do? How can I repay her for all the pain I've caused her?" He closed the door and went to his room. Through the partially frosted-over window he could see the tree in the courtyard that not long ago had been covered with green leaves. It was laden with snow and icicles. Over the bits of scrap iron and metal grates that were strewn about, there lay a thick, bluish-white covering. The snow had made a graveyard of man's trash.

Herman lay down on the bed, and fell asleep. When he opened his eyes, it was evening and Shifrah Puah was standing over him, trying to wake him up.

"Herman, Herman. Masha's up. Go and see her."

It took a moment for him to realize where he was and to remember what had happened.

A single light was on in the bedroom. Masha lay in the same position as before, but her eyes were open. She looked at Herman and said nothing.

"How do you feel?" he asked.

"I have no feelings left."

3

IT was snowing again. Yadwiga was making a stew as it used to be cooked in Tzivkev—a mixture of groats, lima beans, dried mushrooms, and potatoes, sprinkled with paprika and parsley. A song from a Yiddish operetta, which Yadwiga took to be a religious chant, came from the radio. The parakeets reacted to the music in their own fashion. They screeched, whistled, tweeted, and flew around the room. Yadwiga had to put lids on the pots, so the birds wouldn't—God forbid—fall in.

In the midst of writing, Herman was overcome with fatigue. He put down the pen, leaned his head back against the armchair, and tried to take a little nap. In the Bronx, Masha had not yet returned to work, because she was still weak. She had fallen into a state of apathy. When he spoke to her, she replied briefly and to the point, but in such a way that they were left with nothing to talk about. Shifrah Puah prayed all day as if Masha were still dangerously ill. Herman knew that without Masha's earnings, they did not have enough money even for essentials, but he too was without funds. Masha had suggested the name of a loan association where he could borrow a hundred dollars at a high rate of interest, but how far would such a loan go? He might also need a co-signer.

Yadwiga came in from the kitchen. "Herman, the stew is finished."

"So am I, financially, physically, spiritually."

"Speak so that I can understand you."

"I thought you wanted me to speak Yiddish to you."

"Talk the way your mother did."

"I can't talk the way my mother did. She believed and I am not even an atheist."

"I don't know what you're babbling about. Come eat. I've made a Tzivkev barley stew."

Herman was about to get up, when the doorbell rang.

"One of your ladies has probably come to give you a lesson," Herman said.

Yadwiga went to open the door. Herman crossed out the last half page he had written, and muttered, "Well, Rabbi Lampert, the world will do with a somewhat shorter sermon." He suddenly heard a suppressed cry. Yadwiga ran back into the room, slamming the door shut. Her face was white and her eyes seemed to turn upward. She stood there trembling, with her hand holding the doorknob, as if someone were trying to force his way in. "A pogrom?" ran through Herman's mind. "Who is it?" he asked.

"Don't go! Don't go! Oh, God!" Spittle appeared on Yadwiga's lips as she tried to block his way. Her face became distorted. Herman glanced at the window. The fire escape was not off this room. He took a step toward Yadwiga and she grabbed him by the wrists. At that moment the door opened and Herman saw Tamara in a shabby fur coat, hat, and boots. He understood instantly.

"Stop shaking, idiot!" he screamed at Yadwiga. "She's alive!"

"Jesus, Maria!" Yadwiga's head jerked convulsively. She

pushed herself against Herman with all her strength, almost knocking him over.

"I didn't think she would recognize me," Tamara said.

"She's alive! She's alive! She isn't dead!" Herman shouted. He began wrestling with Yadwiga, trying both to calm her and to push her away. She clung to him, wailing. It was like the howling of an animal.

"She's alive! She's alive!" he shouted once again. "Calm down! Foolish peasant!"

"Oh, Holy Mother! My heart!" Yadwiga crossed herself. At once she realized that a Jewish woman doesn't make the sign of a cross and clasped her hands together. Her eyes bulged from their sockets, her mouth became twisted with cries she couldn't utter.

Tamara took a step backward. "It never occurred to me she would recognize me. My own mother wouldn't know me. Calm down, Yadzia," she said in Polish. "I'm not dead and I haven't come to haunt you."

"Oh, Little Father!"

And Yadwiga beat her head with both fists. Herman said to Tamara, "Why did you do this? She might have died of fright."

"I'm sorry, I'm sorry. I thought I was so changed. No resemblance. I wanted to see how and where you live."

"You could at least have telephoned."

"O God, O God! What will happen now?" Yadwiga cried. "And I'm pregnant." Yadwiga laid her hand on her belly.

Tamara looked surprised but also as if she were about to burst out laughing. Herman stared at her. "Are you crazy or drunk?" he asked.

As soon as he said the words, he became aware of the odor of alcohol. A week earlier Tamara had told him she was scheduled to go to the hospital to have the bullet removed from her hip. "Have you taken to hard liquor?" he said.

"When a person can't have the soft things of life, he takes to the hard ones. You're settled here quite comfortably." Tamara's tone changed. "When you lived with me, there was always a mess. Your papers and books were everywhere. Here it's spic and span."

"She keeps the place clean, and you ran around giving speeches to the Poalay Zion."

"Where's the crucifix?" Tamara asked in Polish. "Why isn't there a crucifix hanging here? Since there isn't a mezuzah, there must be a crucifix."

"There is a mezuzah," Yadwiga answered.

"There has to be a crucifix too," Tamara said. "Don't think I've come here to disturb your bliss. I learned how to drink in Russia, and when I have a glassful I become curious. I wanted to see for myself how you live. After all, we still have something in common. Both of you remember me when I was alive."

"Jesus! Maria!"

"I'm not dead, I'm not dead. I'm not alive and I'm not dead. The truth is that I have no claims on him," Tamara said, pointing to Herman. "He didn't know I was struggling to survive somewhere, and he probably always loved you, Yadzia. He surely slept with you before he did with me."

"No, no! I was an innocent girl. I came to him a virgin," Yadwiga said.

"What? Congratulations. Men love virgins. If men had their way, every woman would lie down a prostitute and get up a virgin. Well, I see that I'm an uninvited guest and I'll go now."

"Pani Tamara, sit down. You frightened me and that's the reason I screamed so. I'll bring coffee. God is my witness that if I had known that you were alive I would have kept away from him."

"I bear you no grudge, Yadzia. Our world is a greedy place. You didn't get much of a bargain in him, though," Tamara said, indicating Herman, "but anything is better than being alone. It's a nice apartment too. We never had such an apartment."

"I'll bring coffee. Would you, Pani Tamara, like something to eat?"

Tamara didn't answer. Yadwiga went to the kitchen, her house slippers clumsily slapping the floor. She left the door open. Herman noticed that Tamara's hair was mussed. There were yellowish pouches under her eyes.

"I didn't know you drank," he said.

"There's a lot you don't know. You think one can go through hell and come out unscathed. Well, one can't! In Russia, there was one cure for every illness—vodka. You drank your fill, lay down in the straw or on the bare earth, and stopped caring. Let God and Stalin do as they pleased. Yesterday I went to visit some people who own a liquor store—here in Brooklyn, but in another neighborhood. They gave me a whole shopping bag full of whiskey."

"I thought you were going to the hospital."

"I was supposed to go tomorrow, but I'm not sure I want to now. This bullet," Tamara said, placing her hand on her hip, "is my best souvenir. It reminds me that I once had a home, parents, children. If they take it away from me, I won't have anything left at all. It was a German bullet, but after lying in a Jewish body for so many years, it has become Jewish. It may decide to explode one day, but meanwhile it lies there quietly and we get along fine. Come, touch it, if you like. You're a partner in this too. The same revolver may have killed your children—"

"Tamara, I beg you—"

Tamara made a spiteful face and stuck her tongue out at him.

"Tamara, I beg you!" she mimicked him. "Don't be afraid. She won't divorce you. If she does, you can always go to the other one. What's her name again? And if she throws you out too, then you can come to me. Here's Yadzia with the coffee!"

Yadwiga came in, carrying a tray with two cups of coffee, cream, sugar, and a plate of home-made cookies. She had put on an apron and looked just like the servant she had once been. This was how she had served Herman and Tamara before the war, when they had come from Warsaw to visit. Yadwiga's face, which a while ago had been pale, was now red and moist. Beads of perspiration stood out on her forehead. Tamara looked at her with both astonishment and laughter.

"Set it down. Bring a cup for yourself," Herman said.

"I'll drink mine in the kitchen."

And again Yadwiga's slippers slapped back to the kitchen. This time she shut the door behind her.

4

"I SEEM to have blundered in like a bull into a china shop," Tamara said. "When things go wrong, it's hard to do anything right. It's true I did have a drink, but I'm far from drunk. Please call her in. I must explain to her."

"I'll explain it to her myself."

"No, call her in. She probably thinks I've come to take her husband away."

Herman went into the kitchen, closing the door behind him. Yadwiga was standing at the window with her back to the room. His footsteps startled her and she turned around quickly. Her hair was mussed up, her eyes were filled with tears, her face was red and puffy. She seemed to have aged. Before Herman could say anything, she raised her fists to her head and began to wail, "Where will I go now?"

"Yadzia, everything will be just as it was."

A cry like the hissing of a goose tore from Yadwiga's throat. "Why did you tell me she was dead? You weren't selling books, you were staying with her!"

"Yadzia, I swear by God that it isn't so. She only recently came to America. I had no idea she was alive."

"What shall I do now? She's your wife."

"You're my wife."

"She came first. I'll go away. I'll go back to Poland. If only I weren't carrying your child." Yadwiga began rocking from side to side, in the keening gesture of peasants mourning their dead: "Ay-ay-ay."

Tamara opened the door. "Yadzia, don't cry like that. I haven't come to take your husband away. I just wanted to see how you were living."

Yadwiga lurched forward as if to fall at Tamara's feet.

"Pani Tamara, you are his wife and that's how it will remain. If God granted you life, it's a gift. I'll step aside. It's your house. I'll go home. My mother won't turn me away."

"No, Yadzia, you don't need to do that. You're carrying his child and I'm already, as they say, a barren tree. God took my children Himself."

"Oh, Pani Tamara!" Yadwiga dissolved into tears, slapping her cheeks with both palms. She rocked back and forth, bending over as if she were looking for a place to fall down. Herman glanced at the door, afraid that the neighbors might hear her.

"Yadzia, you must calm yourself," Tamara said firmly. "I'm alive but I am as good as dead. They say dead people sometimes come back to pay a visit and in a way I'm that kind of visitor. I came to see how things are, but don't worry, I won't come again."

Yadwiga took her hands away from her face, which had turned the color of raw flesh.

"No, Pani Tamara, you stay here! I'm a simple peasant, uneducated, but I have a heart. It's your husband and your home. You suffered long enough."

"Be still! I don't want him. If you want to go back to Poland, go back, but not because of me. I wouldn't live with him even if you were to go away."

Yadwiga quieted down. She peered sideways at Tamara, doubtful and suspicious. "Where will you go? Here there's a home and a household for you. I'll cook and clean. I'll be a servant again. That's the way God wants it."

"No, Yadwiga. You have a good heart, but I can't accept such a sacrifice. A slit throat cannot be sewn together again."

Tamara, preparing to go, adjusted her hat and tidied some loose strands of hair. Herman took a step toward her. "Don't go. Since Yadwiga knows, we can all be friends. I'll have a few less lies to tell."

At that moment, they heard the doorbell. It was a long, loud ring. The two parakeets, who had been perched on the roof of the cage listening to the conversation, were startled and began to fly about. Yadwiga ran from the kitchen into the living room. "Who is it?" Herman called.

He heard muffled talk, but couldn't make out whether the voice was a man's voice or a woman's. He opened the door. Standing in the hall were a small couple. The woman had a sallow, wrinkled face, yellowish eyes, and carrot-colored hair. The lines in her forehead and cheeks looked as if they had been sculpted in clay. Nevertheless, she didn't seem old, not more than in her forties. She wore a house dress and slippers. She had brought some knitting along and was working the needles as she waited at the door. Next to her stood a tiny man wearing a felt hat with a feather in it, a checked jacket that was too light for a cold winter day, a pink shirt, striped trousers, tan shoes, and a tie that was a mixture of yellow, red, and green. He appeared outlandishly comical, as if he had just flown in from a hot climate and hadn't had time to change his clothes. His head was long and narrow and he had a hooked nose, sunken cheeks, and a pointed chin. His dark eyes had a humorous expression, as if the visit he was making was nothing more than a joke.

The woman spoke in a Polish-accented Yiddish. "You don't know me, Mr. Broder, but I know you. We live downstairs. Is your wife at home?"

"She's in the living room."

"A dear soul. I was with her when she was converted. It was I who took her to the ritual bath and told her what to do. Women who were born Jewish should love Jewishness the way she does. Is she busy?"

"Yes, a little."

"This is my friend, Mr. Pesheles. He doesn't live here. He has a house in Sea Gate. He has, may no evil eye befall him, houses in New York and Philadelphia too. He came to visit us, and we told him about you, that you sell books and write, and he would like to talk to you about some business."

"Not business! Not business at all!" Mr. Pesheles interrupted. "My business isn't books but real estate and I don't do that any more either. After all, how much business does a person need? Even Rockefeller can't eat more than three meals a day. It's just that I love to read, whether it's a newspaper, a magazine, a book, whatever I can lay my hands on. If you have a few minutes, I'd like to have a chat with you."

Herman hesitated. "I'm terribly sorry, but I'm really very busy."

"It won't take long—ten or fifteen minutes," the woman urged. "Mr. Pesheles only comes to see me once every six months and sometimes not that often. He's a rich man, may no evil eye befall him, and if you're ever looking for an apartment, he may be able to do you a favor."

"What kind of favor? I don't do any favors. I myself have to pay rent. This is America. But if you need an apartment, I can recommend you and it won't do you any harm."

"Well, come in. Forgive me for receiving you in the kitchen. My wife is indisposed."

"What's the difference where? He didn't come here to be honored. He gets, may no evil eye befall him, plenty of honors. They just made him president of the biggest home for the aged in New York. All over America they know who Nathan Pesheles is. And he just built two Yeshivas in Jerusalem—not one yeshiva, but two yeshivas—where hundreds of boys will be able to study Torah, at his expense—"

"Please, Mrs. Schreier, I don't need any publicity. If I need a publicity agent, I'll hire one. He doesn't have to know about all that. It's not for praise that I do it." Mr. Pesheles spoke quickly. He spat out his words like dried peas. His mouth was sunken, with almost no lower lip. He smiled knowingly and had the ease of a rich man visiting the poor. The two of them had continued standing at the door, but now they moved into the kitchen. Before Herman had a chance to introduce Tamara, she said, "I'd better go now."

"Don't run away. No need to go because of me," Mr. Pesheles said. "You're a pretty woman, but I'm not a bear and I don't swallow people."

"Sit down, sit down," Herman said. "Don't go, Tamara," he added. "I see there aren't enough chairs, but we'll soon go into the other room. One second!"

He went into the living room. Yadwiga was no longer crying. She stood there, staring at the door apprehensively with a peasant's fear of strangers. "Who is it?"

"Mrs. Schreier. She brought a man with her."

"What does she want? I can't see anyone now. Oh, I'm going out of my mind!"

Herman returned to the kitchen with a chair. Mrs. Schreier was already seated next to the kitchen table. Woytus was perched on Tamara's shoulder, pulling at an earring. Herman heard Mr. Pesheles saying to Tamara, "Only a few weeks? But you're not like a greenhorn at all. In my time you could spot an immigrant from a mile away. You look like an American. Absolutely."

5

"Yadwiga doesn't feel well. I don't think she'll join us," Herman said. "I'm sorry, it's not very comfortable here."

"Comfortable!" Mrs. Schreier interrupted. "Hitler taught us how to get along without comfort."

"You come from there too?" Herman asked.

"Yes, from there."

"From the concentration camps?"

"From Russia."

"Where were you in Russia?" Tamara asked.

"In Jambul."

"In the camp?"

"In the camp too. I lived on Nabroznaya Street."

"God in heaven, I also lived on the Nabroznaya," Tamara cried, "with a rebbetzin from Dzikow and her son."

"Well, it's a small world, a small world," Mr. Pesheles said, clapping his hands together. He had pointed fingers and freshly manicured fingernails. "Russia is a vast country, but no sooner do two refugees meet than they are either related or were in the same camp together. You know what? Let's all go down to your place," he said, addressing Mrs. Schreier. "I'll send out for bagels, lox, and maybe even some cognac. Since both of you are from Jambul, you'll have a lot to talk about. Come down, Mr. er-er-Broder. I remember people, but I forget names. Once I forgot my own wife's name—"

"That's something all men forget," Mrs. Schreier said with a wink.

"Unfortunately, it's not possible," Herman said.

"Why not? Bring your wife and come on down. Nowadays a Gentile converting to Judaism is no small matter. I heard she hid you for years in a loft. What kind of books do you sell? I'm interested in old books. I once bought a book with Lincoln's signature in it. I like to go to auctions. I was told you do some writing too. What do you write?"

Herman was about to answer, but the telephone rang. Tamara looked up and Woytus began flying around again. The phone was located near the kitchen, in a small foyer that led to the bedroom. Herman became angry at Masha. Why was she calling? She knew he was coming.

Perhaps he shouldn't answer it? He picked up the receiver and said, "Hello."

It occurred to him that it might be Leon Tortshiner. Herman had expected a call from him ever since their meeting in the cafeteria. Herman heard a man's voice, but it wasn't Leon Tortshiner's. It was a deep bass voice asking in English, "Is this Mr. Herman Broder?"

"Yes."

"This is Rabbi Lampert." It was quiet. In the kitchen, they had stopped talking.

"Yes, Rabbi."

"So you do have a telephone, and not in the Bronx, but in Brooklyn. Esplanade 2 is somewhere in Coney Island."

"My friend moved," Herman mumbled, knowing the lie would only lead to new complications.

The rabbi cleared his throat. "He moved and had a phone installed? Sure, sure. I really am a damn fool, but not such a damn fool as you think." The rabbi's voice rose a pitch. "Your whole comedy is altogether superfluous. I know everything, absolutely everything. You got married and you didn't even tell me so I could congratulate you. Who knows? I might even have given you a nice wedding present. But if this is the way you want it, it's your privilege. I'm calling you because in your cabala article you made several serious errors which do neither of us any credit."

"What errors?"

"I can't tell you now. Rabbi Moscowitz called me up— something about the Angel Sandalphon or Metatron. The article is in type. When he caught the mistakes, they were going to press. They'll have to take out the pages and rearrange the whole magazine. That's what you've done to me."

"I'm very sorry, but in that case I resign, and you don't have to pay me for the work I've done."

"How will that help me? I depend on you. Why didn't you check? That's why I hired you, to do research so I wouldn't look like a simpleton in the eyes of the world. You know I'm busy and—"

"I don't know what errors I made, but if there are errors, I shouldn't be doing this work."

"Where will I get someone else now? You kept secrets from me. Why? If you love a woman, that's no sin. I treated you like a friend and opened my heart to you, but you made up some story about a landsman from the old country, a Hitler victim. Why can't I know that you have a wife? At least I have the right to wish you mazel tov."

"Certainly. Thank you very much."

"Why are you speaking so quietly? Do you have a sore throat or something?"

"No, no."

"I told you all along that I can't work with a man who won't give me his address and phone number. I must see you right away, so tell me where you live. If we make the corrections, they'll hold the presses till tomorrow."

"I don't live here, but in the Bronx."

Herman was practically whispering into the phone.

"Again in the Bronx? Where in the Bronx? Honestly, I can't figure you out."

"I'll explain everything to you. I'm just here temporarily."

"Temporarily? What's the matter with you? Or do you have two wives?"

"Maybe."

"Well, when will you be there in the Bronx?"

"Tonight."

"Give me the address. Once and for all! Let there be an end to this muddle!"

Reluctantly, Herman gave him Masha's address. He covered his mouth with his hand so he wouldn't be heard in the kitchen.

"What time will you be there?"

Herman told him the time.

"Is this definite, or are you bluffing again?"

"No, I'll be there."

"Well, I'll come over. You don't have to be so nervous. I won't steal your wife."

Herman returned to the kitchen and saw Yadwiga. She had come out of the living room. Her face and eyes were still red and she stood with her fists on her hips, looking over to where he had been standing. She had apparently been listening to his conversation. Herman heard Mrs. Schreier asking Tamara, "How did they send you to Russia, with the echelons?"

"No, we were smuggled across the border," Tamara answered.

"We rode in cattle cars," Mrs. Schreier said. "Three weeks we rode, packed in like herring in a barrel. If we needed to eliminate—you should excuse me—we had to do it through a small window. Picture it, men and women together. How we survived, I'll never be able to understand. And some didn't survive. They died standing up. They simply threw the dead bodies out of the train. We came to a forest in a terrible frost and first we had to chop down the trees with which to build the barracks. We dug ditches in the frozen earth and that's where we slept—"

"I know it only too well," Tamara said.

"Do you have relatives here?" Mr. Pesheles asked Tamara.

"An uncle and aunt. They live on East Broadway."

"East Broadway? And what is he to you?" Mr. Pesheles asked, indicating Herman.

"Oh, we're friends."

"Well, come down to Mrs. Schreier's and we'll all become friends. With all this talk about starvation, I'm feeling hungry. We'll eat, drink, and have a talk. Come on, Mr. er-er-Broder. On such a cold day, it's good to pour out one's heart."

"I'm afraid I must leave now," Herman said.

"I have to go too," Tamara added.

Yadwiga seemed suddenly to wake up.

"Where is Pani Tamara going? Please stay here. I'll make supper."

"No, Yadzia, another time."

"Well, it looks as if you're not going to accept my invitation," Mr. Pesheles said. "Come, Mrs. Schreier, we didn't succeed this time. If you have any old volumes, we can do a little business another time. I am, as I've mentioned, a bit of a collector. Other than that—"

"We'll talk later," Mrs. Schreier said to Yadwiga. "Maybe Mr. Pesheles won't be such an infrequent guest in the future. What that man did for me, only God knows. Others were content to moan about the fate of the Jews, but he sent visas. I wrote him a letter, a total stranger— only because his father had been my father's partner, they both handled produce—and four weeks later an affidavit arrived. We went to the consulate and they already knew about Mr. Pesheles. They all knew."

"Well, enough. Don't praise me, don't praise me. What's an affidavit? A piece of paper."

"With such pieces of paper, they could have rescued thousands of people."

Pesheles stood up. "What's your name?" he asked Tamara. She looked questioningly at him, at Herman, at Yadwiga.

"Tamara."

"Miss? Missus?"

"Whatever you like."

"Tamara what? Surely you have a last name."

"Tamara Broder."

"Also Broder? Are you brother and sister?"

"Cousins," Herman answered for Tamara.

"Well, it's a small world. Extraordinary times. Once I read a story in the paper about a refugee who was eating supper with his new wife. Suddenly the door opened and in walked his former wife, who he thought had died in the ghetto. That's the kind of mess Hitler and Stalin and the rest of their gangs cooked up."

Mrs. Schreier's face broke into a smile. Her yellow eyes sparkled with flattering laughter. The creases of her face grew even deeper, becoming like the tattoo lines sometimes seen on the faces of primitive tribes.

"What's the point of the story, Mr. Pesheles?"

"Oh, nothing really. In life, anything can happen. Especially nowadays, when everything is turned upside down."

Mr. Pesheles lowered the lid of his right eye and puckered his lips as if about to whistle. He put his hand in his breast pocket and handed Tamara two calling cards.

"Whoever you are, let's not be strangers."

6

No sooner did the guests leave than Yadwiga burst into tears. In a moment, her face was once again contorted.

"Where are you going now? Why are you leaving me? Pani Tamara! He doesn't sell books. It's a lie. He has a mistress and he goes to her. Everyone knows it. The neighbors laugh at me. And I saved his life! I took the last bite of food out of my mouth and brought it to him in the hayloft. I carried out his excrement."

"Please, Yadwiga, stop!" Herman said.

"Herman, I must go! I just want to tell you one thing, Yadzia. He didn't know that I was alive. I came here from Russia only a short time ago."

"She telephones every day, his sweetheart. He thinks I don't understand, but I understand. He spends days with her and comes home exhausted and penniless. The old landlady comes every day to ask for the rent and threatens to throw us out in the middle of winter. If I weren't pregnant, I could work in a factory. Here you have to reserve a hospital and a doctor. Here nobody gives birth at home—I won't let you go, Pani Tamara." Yadwiga ran to the door and spread her arms out, barring it.

"Yadzia, I have to go," Tamara said.

"If he wants to go back to you, I'll give the baby away. Here you can give children away. They even pay—"

"Stop talking nonsense, Yadzia. I won't go back to him and you don't need to give your baby away. I'll find you a doctor and a hospital."

"Oh, Pani Tamara!"

"Yadzia, let me out!" Herman said. He had put on his coat.

"You're not going!"

"Yadzia, a rabbi's waiting for me. I work for him. If I don't meet him now, we'll remain without a crust of bread."

"It's a lie! A whore's waiting for you, not a rabbi."

"Well, I see what's going on here," Tamara said, half to

herself and half to Yadwiga and Herman. "I really have to leave now. If I change my mind and decide to go to the hospital, I must wash some things and get ready. Let me out, Yadzia."

"You've decided to go, after all? Which hospital are you going to? What's the name of it?" Herman asked.

"What difference does it make? If I live, I'll come out, and if I don't, they'll bury me somehow. You don't have to visit me. If they find out you're my husband, they'll make you pay. I told them I have no relatives and that's the way it must remain."

Tamara went over to Yadwiga and kissed her. For a moment Yadwiga laid her head on Tamara's shoulder. She cried loudly and kissed Tamara on the forehead, cheeks, both hands. She almost sank to her knees, mumbling in her peasant dialect, but it was impossible to make out what she was saying.

As soon as Tamara left, Yadwiga placed herself in front of the door again. "You won't leave today!"

"We'll soon see."

Herman waited till he could no longer hear Tamara's footsteps. Then he grabbed Yadwiga by the wrists and wrestled with her in silence. He pushed her and she fell to the floor with a thud. He unlocked the door and ran out. He hurried down the uneven stairs two at a time and heard a sound that was both a cry and a groan. He remembered something he had once learned: when you break one of the Ten Commandments, you break them all. "I'll end up a murderer," he said to himself.

He hadn't noticed that dusk had fallen. The stairway was already dark. Doors opened, but he didn't turn around. He went outside. Tamara stood in the snowdrifts, waiting for him.

"Where are your rubbers? You can't go like that!" she shouted.

"I must."

"Are you trying to commit suicide? Go get your rubbers, unless you want to catch pneumonia."

"What I'll catch is no concern of yours. Go to the devil —the lot of you!"

"Well, it's the same Herman. Wait here, I'll go up and bring your rubbers down to you."

"No, you're not going!"

"So we'll have one idiot less in the world."

Tamara picked her way through the snowdrifts. They looked blue and crystalline. The street lights had gone on, but it was still twilight. The sky was overcast with yellowish, rust-red clouds, stormy and threatening. A cold wind blew in from the bay. Suddenly an upper-story window opened and one rubber fell down, then another. Yadwiga was throwing Herman his rubbers. He looked up at the window, but she closed it immediately and drew the curtains. Tamara turned back toward him and laughed. She winked and shook her fist at him. He managed to put on the rubbers, but his shoes were filled with snow. Tamara waited until he caught up with her.

"The worst dog gets the best bone. Why is it?"

She took him by the arm and together they made their way through the snow, carefully and slowly like an elderly couple. Chunks of snow and ice fell from the roofs. Mermaid Avenue was covered with high drifts. A dead pigeon lay in the snow, its red feet protruding. "Well, holy creature, you've already lived your life," Herman addressed it in his thoughts. "You're lucky." He was gripped with sorrow. "Why did you create her, if this was to be her end? How long will you be silent, Almighty sadist?"

Herman and Tamara walked to the station, where they boarded a train. Tamara was going only as far as Fourteenth Street, and Herman to Times Square. All the seats were occupied except for a small corner bench, and Herman and Tamara squeezed into it.

"So you've decided to go through with the operation," Herman said.

"What have I got to lose? Nothing more than my wretched life."

Herman bowed his head. As they approached Union Square, Tamara took leave of him. He stood up and they kissed.

"Think of me once in a while," she said.

"Forgive me!"

Tamara hurried out of the train. Herman sat down again in the dimly lighted corner. It seemed to him that he heard his father's voice saying, "Well, I ask you, what have you accomplished? You've made yourself and everyone else wretched. We're ashamed of you here in heaven."

Herman got off at Times Square and crossed over to the IRT subway. He walked to Shifrah Puah's street from the station. The rabbi's Cadillac practically filled the snow-covered street. All the lights in the house had been turned on and the car seemed to glow in the dark. Herman was ashamed to enter this brightly lighted house with his pale face, frozen, red nose, and shabby clothes. In the dark entryway, he shook off the snow and rubbed his cheeks to give them color. He fixed his tie and wiped the moisture from his forehead with a handkerchief. It occurred to Herman that the rabbi might not have found any mistakes in the article at all. His call might simply have been an excuse to interfere in Herman's affairs.

The first thing Herman noticed when he entered the door was a huge bouquet of roses in a vase on the dresser.

On the cloth-covered table, between the cookies and oranges, stood a magnum of champagne. The rabbi and Masha were clicking their glasses together; they obviously hadn't heard Herman come in. Masha was already tipsy. She spoke in a loud voice and laughed. She had put on a party dress. The rabbi's voice thundered. Shifrah Puah was in the kitchen, frying pancakes. Herman heard the sound of sizzling oil and smelled the browning potatoes. The rabbi was wearing a light-colored suit and seemed strangely tall and broad in this crowded apartment with its low ceilings.

The rabbi got up and reached Herman in one long stride. Clapping his hands, he called out loudly, "Mazel tov, bridegroom!"

Masha set down her glass. "He's here at last!" And she pointed at him and shook with laughter. Then she too got up and went to Herman. "Don't stand at the door. It's your home. I'm your wife. Everything here is yours!"

She threw herself into his arms and kissed him.

· CHAPTER EIGHT ·

1

THE snow was falling for the second day There was
no heat in Shifrah Puah's apartment. The janitor,
who lived in the basement, lay in his room in a drunken
stupor. The furnace had broken down and there was no
one to repair it.

Shifrah Puah wandered about the house in heavy boots,
huddled in a ragged fur coat which she had brought from
Germany, her head wrapped in a woolen shawl. Her face
was sallow with cold and vexation. She put on her eyeglasses and paced up and down as she read her prayer
book. She alternately prayed and cursed the swindling land-
lords who allowed poor tenants to freeze in winter. Her
lips had turned blue. She read a verse aloud and said, "As
if we didn't have enough trouble before coming here.
Now we can add America to the list. It's not so much better than the concentration camps. All we need is a Nazi to
come in and beat us up."

Masha, who had skipped work that day because she was
getting ready to go to a party at Rabbi Lampert's, scolded
her mother. "Mama, you should be ashamed of yourself!
In Stutthoff, if you had had what you have now, you
would have gone out of your mind with joy."

"How much strength does a person have? There we at least had hope to sustain us. There isn't a part of my body that isn't frozen. Maybe you can buy a fire pot. My blood is congealing."

"Where can you get a fire pot in America? We'll move out of here. Just wait till spring comes."

"I won't last till spring."

"Old witch, you'll outlive us all!" Masha's voice was shrill with impatience.

The party to which the rabbi had invited Masha and Herman had driven her into a frenzy. At first she had refused to go, arguing that Leon Tortshiner was probably behind the invitation and had some trick in mind. Masha suspected that the rabbi's visit to her house, his getting her drunk on champagne, were all part of a plot on Leon Tortshiner's part to separate her from Herman. Masha kept belittling the rabbi, calling him a spineless creature, a braggart, a hypocrite. And when she finished with him, she reviled Leon Tortshiner as a maniac, impostor, provocateur.

Since her false pregnancy, Masha had not been able to sleep at night, even with the help of pills. When she finally fell asleep, nightmares awakened her. Her father appeared to her in his shrouds, shouting verses from the Bible in her ear. She saw fantastic beasts with coiled horns and pointed snouts. They had pouches, teats, and were covered with sores. They barked, roared, and drooled over her. She was menstruating painfully every two weeks and passing blood clots. Shifrah Puah urged her to go to the doctor, but Masha said she didn't believe in doctors and swore that they poisoned their patients.

But suddenly Masha had changed her mind and decided to go to the party. Why should she be afraid of Leon Tortshiner? She had got both a civil and a rabbinical divorce from him. If he greeted her, she would turn her back on him; if he tried any tricks, she would simply spit in his face.

Herman observed once again how Masha went from one extreme to the other. She began to get ready for the party with growing enthusiasm. She flung open closets, dresser drawers, dragged out dresses, blouses, shoes, most of which she had brought from Germany. She decided to remodel a dress. She sewed, ripped out the basting, smoked cigarette after cigarette, pulled out heaps of stockings, lingerie. She chattered all the while, telling stories of how men had pursued her—before the war, during the war, after the war, in the camps, the offices of the "Joint" —and insisted that Shifrah Puah verify her words. For a moment she abandoned her sewing to dig up old letters and photographs as proof.

Herman understood that what she craved was to be a success at the party, to outshine all the other women with her elegance, her good looks. He had known from the beginning that, despite Masha's initial opposition, she would eventually decide to go. With Masha, everything had to be made into drama.

The radiator began to hiss unexpectedly—the furnace had been repaired. The apartment became steamy and Shifrah Puah complained that the drunken janitor was surely trying to set the house on fire. They would have to leave the apartment and run out into the frost. It smelled of smoke and coal fumes. Masha filled the tub with hot water. She did everything at once: prepared her bath, sang songs in Hebrew, Yiddish, Polish, Russian, and German. With amazing speed, she had turned an old dress into a new one, found a pair of matching high-heel shoes and a stole that someone had given her as a gift in Germany.

By evening it had stopped snowing, but the air was icy

cold. The streets in the east Bronx might have been the winter streets of Moscow or Koybishev.

Shifrah Puah, who deprecated the idea of the party, mumbled about Jews not having the right to celebrate after the holocaust, but she inspected Masha's appearance and suggested improvements. In her preoccupation, Masha had forgotten to eat, and her mother prepared some rice and milk for her and Herman. The rabbi's wife had phoned Masha and told her how to get to West End Avenue in the Seventies, where they lived. Shifrah Puah insisted that Masha wear a sweater, or a pair of warm underpants, but Masha wouldn't hear of it. Every few minutes, she took a swig from a bottle of cognac.

Night was already falling when Herman and Masha left. A freezing wind gripped his shoulders and ripped his hat from his head; he caught it in mid-air. Masha's party dress fluttered and filled up like a balloon. The deep snow gripped one of her boots as she tried to walk, and her stockinged foot got wet. Her carefully set hair, only partially protected by her hat, became white with snow, as if she had aged in a second. She held on to her hat with one hand and with the other held down the hem of her dress. She shouted something to Herman, but the wind carried her voice away.

The walk to the El, which normally took a few minutes, now became a major undertaking. When they finally got there, a train had just pulled out. The cashier, who sat in a booth heated by an iron stove, told them that trains were stalling on the snow-covered tracks and there was no telling when the next one would come. Masha shivered and hopped up and down to warm her feet. Her face was sickly pale.

Fifteen minutes passed and no train arrived. A large

group of waiting passengers had collected: men wearing rubber boots, galoshes, and carrying lunch boxes; women clad in heavy jackets, with kerchiefs on their heads. Each face in its own way seemed to express dullness, greed, anxiety. The low foreheads, the troubled gazes, the broad noses with large nostrils, the square chins, the full breasts and wide hips refuted all visions of Utopia. The caldron of evolution was still simmering. One scream could instigate a riot here. The right bit of propaganda could rouse this group into a pogrom-making rabble.

A whistle blew and the train rushed in. The cars were half empty. Their windows were white with frost. It was cold in the car, and the floor was covered with slush, soiled newspapers, chewing gum. "Can there be anything uglier than this train?" Herman wondered. "Everything here is as dismal as if it were made to order for the purpose." A drunkard began making a speech, prattling about Hitler and the Jews. Masha took a little mirror out of her bag and strained to see her reflection in the fogged-up glass. She moistened her fingertips and tried to smooth her hair, which the wind would only disarrange again when they got out.

As long as the train ran aboveground, Herman looked out through a bit of window he had wiped clear of mist. Newspapers fluttered in the wind. A grocer was throwing salt on the sidewalks near his store. An automobile was trying to get out of a ditch, but its wheels spun helplessly in one spot. Herman was suddenly reminded of his resolution to become a good Jew, to return to the Shulchan Aruch, the Gemara. How many times had he made such resolutions! How many times had he tried to spit in the face of worldliness, and each time been tricked away. Yet here he was on his way to a party. Half of his people had been tortured and murdered, and the other half were giving parties. He was overcome with pity for Masha. She looked underweight, wan, sick.

It was late when Herman and Masha stepped out of the train into the street. A wild wind was blowing from the frozen Hudson River. Masha clung to Herman. He had to lean into the wind with all his weight in order not to be blown back. Snow covered his eyelids. Masha, gasping, shouted something to him. His hat tried to tear itself off his head. His coattails and trousers whipped about his legs. It was a miracle that they were able to make out the number on the rabbi's house. He and Masha ran breathlessly into the lobby. Here it was warm and tranquil. Gold-framed pictures hung on the walls; carpets covered the floors; chandeliers diffused soft light; sofas and easy chairs awaited guests.

Masha went up to a mirror to try to repair some of the damage inflicted on her dress and appearance. "If I can survive this, I'll never die," she said.

2

SHE twisted a last lock into place and walked toward the elevator. Herman straightened his tie. His collar felt loose around his neck. A full-length mirror reflected all the defects of his figure and attire. His back was stooped and he looked haggard. He had lost weight: his overcoat and his suit seemed too big for him. The elevator man hesitated an instant before opening the elevator door. When he stopped at the rabbi's floor, he watched suspiciously as Herman rang the bell.

No one came. Herman could hear noise, the sound of talking, and the rabbi's loud voice within the apartment. After a while, a black maid in white apron and white cap opened the door. Behind her was the rabbi's wife, the rebbetzin. She was a tall, statuesque woman, even taller than her husband. She had wavy, blond hair, a turned-up nose, and wore a long, gold-colored dress. She was bedecked with jewelry. Everything about this woman appeared bony, pointed, long, Gentile. She looked down on Herman and Masha and her eyes lighted.

Suddenly the rabbi appeared.

"Here they are!" he bellowed. And he stretched out both hands, one to Herman and one to Masha, at the same time kissing Masha.

"She's really a beauty!" he shouted. "He's nabbed the prettiest woman in America. Eileen, look at her!"

"Give me your coats. It's cold, isn't it? I was afraid you might not be able to make it. My husband has told me so much about you. I'm really happy that—"

The rabbi put his arms around Masha and Herman and led them into the living room. He pushed his way through the crowd, introducing them as they went along. Through the haze, Herman saw clean-shaven men with tiny skullcaps perched on top of their thick hair, as well as men without skullcaps, and men with goatees or with full beards. There was as much variety in the women's hair coloring as there was in the shades of their dresses. He heard English, Hebrew, German, even French. There was a smell of perfume, liquor, chopped liver.

A butler approached the new guests and asked what they wanted to drink. The rabbi led Masha to the bar, leaving Herman behind. He put his hand around Masha's waist, leading her as if they were dancing. Herman wished he could sit down somewhere, but he didn't see an empty chair. A maid offered him a tray of assorted fish, cold cuts, eggs, crackers. He tried to spear a half egg with a toothpick, but it slipped away. People were speaking so loudly that he was deafened by the noise. A woman shrieked with laughter.

Herman had never been to an American party. He had anticipated that the guests would be seated and that dinner would be served. But there was neither room to sit down nor was a meal served. Someone spoke to him in English, but in all the din he couldn't make out the words. Where on earth was Masha? She seemed to have been swallowed up in the throng. He stopped in front of a painting and stood looking at it for no particular reason.

He walked into a room with several armchairs and couches. The walls were lined with books from floor to ceiling. Some men and women were sitting around, holding drinks in their hands. A vacant chair stood in a corner and Herman sank into it. The group was discussing a professor who had received a five-thousand-dollar grant to write a book. They were ridiculing him and his writing. Herman heard the names of universities, foundations, scholarships, grants, publications on Judaica, socialism, history, psychology. "What kind of women are these? How is it they are so well informed?" Herman thought. He was self-conscious about his shabby clothing, apprehensive that they might try to draw him into their conversation. "I don't belong here. I should have remained a Talmudist." He angled his chair still farther away from the group.

For the sake of something to do, he took a copy of Plato's *Dialogues* from the bookcase. He opened it at random to "Phaedo" and read these words: "It may seem unlikely that those who are sincerely concerned with philosophy actually are merely studying how to die and how to be dead." He leafed back a few pages to the "Apologia" and his eye fell on the words, "Because I believe it is against nature that a better man should be hurt by a lesser one." Was this really so? Was it against nature that the Nazis should have murdered millions of Jews?

A servant came to the door and announced something which Herman didn't understand. Everyone got up and left the room. Herman remained alone. He imagined that the Nazis were in New York, but someone—perhaps even the rabbi—had boarded him up in this library. His food was served through an opening in the wall.

A person who looked familiar appeared in the doorway. He was a small man wearing a dinner jacket; his laughing eyes expressed recognition and irony. "Whom do I see?" he said in Yiddish. "Well it's really, as they say, a small world."

Herman stood up.

"You don't recognize me?"

"I'm so confused here, that—"

"Pesheles! Nathan Pesheles! I came to your apartment a few weeks ago—"

"Yes, of course."

"Why are you sitting here by yourself? Did you come here to read books? I didn't know that you know Rabbi Lampert. But who doesn't know him? Why don't you get something to eat? They're serving food in the other room cafeteria-style. You take it yourself from a buffet. Where is your wife?"

"She's here somewhere. I've lost her."

As soon as Herman uttered these words, he realized that Pesheles was talking not about Masha but about Yadwiga. The catastrophe Herman had dreaded was upon him. Pesheles took him by the arm.

"Come, let's find her together. My wife couldn't come tonight. She has the grippe. There are women who get sick whenever they have to go somewhere."

Pesheles led Herman into the living room. The crowd was standing with plates in hand, eating and chatting. Some sat on windowsills, on the radiator, wherever they could find a spot. Pesheles drew Herman toward the dining room. A large group of people were clustered around a long table covered with food. Herman caught sight of Masha. She was with a short man, who held her by the arm. He was obviously saying something very amusing to her, because Masha laughed out loud and clapped her hands together. When she saw Herman, she squirmed out of the man's grip and made her way to his side. Her companion followed. Masha's face was flushed and her eyes shone with high spirits.

"Here is my long-lost husband!" she called out. She threw her arms around Herman's neck and kissed him as if he had just returned from a journey. Her breath reeked of alcohol.

"This is my husband; this is Yasha Kotik," Masha said, indicating the man to whom she had been talking. He was wearing a European tuxedo with worn lapels; a broad satin stripe adorned each side of his trousers. His black hair was parted and glossy with pomade and he had a crooked nose and cleft chin. His youthful figure contrasted oddly with his wrinkled forehead and lined mouth, which revealed a set of false teeth when he smiled. There was something mocking and shrewd in his gaze, in his smile, in his mannerisms. He stood with his arm bent, as if waiting to escort Masha off again. He puckered his lips, creating more creases in his face.

"So this is your husband?" he asked, clownishly lifting one eyebrow.

"Herman, Yasha Kotik is the actor I told you about. We were together in the camp. I didn't know he was in New York."

"Someone told me that she went to Palestine," Yasha Kotik said to Herman. "I thought she was somewhere near the Wailing Wall, or at Rachel's Tomb. I look around—she's standing and drinking whiskey in Rabbi Lampert's living room. That's America for you, crazy Columbus, ha!"

Simulating a gun with his thumb and index finger, he made a shooting gesture. Everything about him moved with acrobatic agility. His face was in constant motion, grimacing and mimicking simultaneously. He raised one eye in mock surprise while the other one drooped as if crying. He inflated his nostrils. Herman had heard a great deal about him from Masha. It was said he told jokes while digging his own grave and the Nazis had been so amused by him that they let him go. Similarly, his buffoonery also stood him in good stead with the Bolsheviks. He had been able to overcome countless perils with his gallows humor and comic antics. Masha had boasted to Herman that Yasha had been in love with her but she had discouraged him.

"That means you are the husband and she's the wife?" Kotik said to Herman. "How did you catch her? I've been searching for her through half the world, and you marry her just like that. Who gave you the right? It's, you should pardon me, rank imperialism—"

"You're still a buffoon," Masha said. "It seems to me I heard you were in Argentina."

"I was in Argentina. Where haven't I been? Blessed be the airplane. You sit down, knock off a glass of schnapps, and before you start snoring and dreaming about Cleopatra, you're in South America. Here it's Shevuot and peo-

ple are swimming in Coney Island and there it's Shevuot
and you shudder in an apartment without heat. How deli-
cious can a Shevuot dairy meal taste when it's freezing
outside? Hanukkah you melt from the heat, and everyone goes to cool off at Mar-del-Plata. But just duck into
the casino and lose your few pesos, and it's hot again.
What did you see in him that made you marry him?"
Yasha Kotik said to Masha, underscoring his question
with an exaggerated raising of his shoulders. "What, for
example, does he have that I don't? I want to know."

"He's a serious person and you're a pain in the neck,"
Masha replied.

"Do you know what you have here?" Yasha Kotik said,
addressing Herman and pointing to Masha. "She's not just
a woman. She's a firebrand, whether from heaven or hell I
still can't decide. Her wit kept us all alive. She could have
convinced Stalin himself if he had paid a visit to the
camp. Whatever happened to Mosheh Feifer?" Yasha
asked, turning to Masha. "I thought you went away with
him—"

"With him? What are you jabbering about? Are you
drunk, or do you just want to make trouble between my
husband and me? I don't know a thing about Mosheh Feifer, nor do I want to. The way you talk, someone might
think he and I were lovers. He had a wife and everyone
knew it. If they're both alive, they're surely together."

"Well, I didn't say a thing. You don't have to be jealous, Mr.—what's your name? Broder? Let it be Broder.
During the war, none of us was human. The Nazis made
soap out of us, kosher soap. And to the Bolsheviks we
were manure for the revolution. What can you expect
from manure? If it were up to me, I would just wipe those
years from the calendar."

"He's as drunk as Lot," Masha muttered.

3

PESHELES had been standing one step behind the group throughout their conversation. He had raised his eyebrows in astonishment, waiting with the patience of a card player who knows he has an ace in the hole. A smile was frozen on his lipless mouth. Herman in his consternation had forgotten about him and he now turned to him. "Masha, this is Mr. Pesheles."

"Pesheles? Seems to me I once met a Pesheles. In Russia or Poland—I don't remember where now," Masha said.

"I come from a small family. We probably had a grandmother named Peshe or Peshele. I met Mr. Broder in Coney Island, in Brooklyn—I didn't know—"

Pesheles blurted out the last words with a cackle. Masha looked questioningly at Herman. Yasha Kotik roguishly scratched his head with the nail of his pinky.

"Coney Island? I played there once, or tried to—what's it called? Oh, yes, Brighton. A whole theater full of old women. Where do they get so many old women in America? They're not only deaf, they've forgotten Yiddish. How can you be a comedian to an audience that doesn't hear you and couldn't understand if they did? The manager, or whatever he called himself, kept bending my ear about success. Go be a success in an old-age home! As you see me, I've been in Yiddish show business for forty years. I started when I was eleven. When they didn't let me perform in Warsaw, I went to Lodz, Vilna, Ishishok. I performed in the ghetto too. Even a hungry audience is better than a deaf audience. When I got to New York, the actors' union made me audition. They asked me to play Cuny Leml while the union experts played cards as they watched. I didn't make it—diction, schmiction. In short, I met a man who ran a Rumanian restaurant in a cellar. He called it Night-Spot Cabaret. Jewish ex-truck drivers go there with their shiksehs. Every one of the men is over seventy. They all have wives and grandchildren who are already professors. The women wear expensive mink coats and Yasha Kotik has to amuse them. My specialty is that I speak a bad English and throw in Yiddish words. And that's what I get for saying no to the gas chambers, for refusing to lie down and die for Comrade Stalin in Kazakhstan. Just my luck, I've developed arthritis here in America and my heart is beginning to act up. What do you do, Mr. Pesheles? Are you a businessman?"

"What's the difference? I don't take anything away from you."

"Take!"

"Mr. Pesheles deals in real estate," Herman said.

"Maybe you have a house for me?" Yasha Kotik asked. "I'll give you a written guarantee that I won't eat the bricks."

"What are we standing here for?" Masha interrupted. "Let's get something to eat. Honestly, Yashele, you haven't changed one bit. Still the same square peg in a round hole."

"You've become extremely pretty."

"How long have you two been married?" Pesheles asked Masha.

Masha frowned. "Long enough to start thinking about a divorce."

"Where do you live? Also in Coney Island?"

"What's all this talk about Coney Island? What happened in Coney Island?" Masha asked suspiciously.

"Well, here it is!" Herman said to himself. It surprised him that his anticipation of the catastrophe had been much worse than the actuality. He was still on his feet. He hadn't fainted away. Yasha Kotik closed one eye and wiggled his nose. Pesheles took a step closer.

"I'm not making it up, Mrs.—what shall I call you? I was in Mr. Broder's home in Coney Island. What street is it on? Between Mermaid and Neptune? I thought the woman who was converted was his wife. It turns out he has a pretty little wife here. I tell you, these greenhorns know how to live. With us Americans, when you get married, you stay that way, whether you like it or not. Or you get divorced and pay alimony, and if you don't pay, you go to prison. What happened to that other pretty little woman—Tamara? Tamara Broder? I even wrote her name down in my notebook."

"Who is this Tamara? Your dead wife was called Tamara, wasn't she?" Masha asked.

"My dead wife is in America," Herman replied. As he spoke, his knees trembled and he felt sick to his stomach. Was he going to faint after all, he asked himself.

Masha's face became angry. "Has your wife risen from the dead?"

"So it seems."

"Is it the one you went to see at her uncle's on East Broadway?"

"Yes."

"You told me she was old and ugly."

"That's what all men tell all wives," Yasha Kotik said, laughing. He stuck out the tip of his tongue and rolled one eye. Pesheles stroked his chin.

"I'm not sure now who's mixed up—I or everyone else." He turned to Herman. "I visited Mrs. Schreier in Coney Island and she told me about a woman upstairs

who had converted to Judaism and that you were her husband. She described you as an author, a rabbi or whatever
you are, and said you sold books. I have a weakness for lit-
erary matters, whether Yiddish, Hebrew, or Turkish. She
praised you to the skies, saying this and that, and since I
have a library and collect odds and ends, I thought I
might be able to buy something from you. Now who is
Tamara?"

"I don't know, Mr. Pesheles, what you want or why
you're interfering in other people's business," Herman
said. "If you think there's something wrong, why not call
the police."

Fiery rings appeared before his eyes as he spoke. They
oscillated slowly in his line of vision. It was a phenome-
non he remembered experiencing ever since childhood. It
seemed the little rings lurked behind his eyes, ready to appear at times of stress. One ring swung off to the side, but
floated back. Can one faint and remain standing, Herman
wondered.

"What police? What are you talking about? I'm not, as
they say, God's cossack. As far as I'm concerned, you can
have a whole harem. You don't live in my world. I
thought I might be able to help you. After all, you're a
refugee, and a Polish Gentile who becomes Jewish is nothing to sneeze at. They told me you travel around selling
encyclopedias. It happened that a few days after I saw you
I had occasion to visit a woman in the hospital who had
undergone an operation for female troubles. She is the
daughter of an old friend. I come in and see your Tamara; they were sharing a room. She had a bullet removed
from her hip. New York is such a vast city, a whole world,
but it is also a little village. She told me she was your wife
—perhaps she was talking in a state of delirium."

Herman opened his mouth to answer, but just then the

rabbi joined them. His face glowed with the liquor he had drunk.

"I've been looking all over for them and here they are!" he shouted. "You all know each other? My friend Nathan Pesheles knows everyone and everyone knows him. Masha, you're the most beautiful woman at the party! I never knew there were such lovely women left in Europe. And here's Yasha Kotik too!"

"I knew Masha before you did," Yasha Kotik said.

"Well, my friend Herman hid her from me."

"He's hiding more than one," Pesheles added insinuatingly.

"You think so? You must know him well. With me he plays the role of an innocent lamb. I began to think he was a eunuch and—"

"I wish I were such a eunuch," Pesheles interrupted.

"You can't hide from Mr. Pesheles." The rabbi laughed. "He has his spies everywhere. What do you know? Let me in on it."

"I don't reveal other people's secrets."

"Come eat. Come into the dining room. We'll stand on line with all the others."

"Excuse me, Rabbi, I'll be right back," Herman said abruptly.

"Where are you running to?"

"I'll be right back."

Herman walked away quickly and Masha hurried after him. They had to push their way through the crowd.

"Don't follow me. I'll be right back," Herman insisted.

"Who is this Pesheles? Who is Tamara?" Masha grabbed Herman's sleeve.

"I beg you, let go of me!"

"Give me a straight answer!"

"I have to vomit."

He tore himself away from Masha and ran to find a bathroom. He bumped into people and they pushed him back. A woman yelled at him because he had stepped on her corns. He went out into the hallway and saw a number of doors through the smoke-filled air, but he couldn't tell which one led to a bathroom. His head began to spin. The floor rocked beneath him like a ship. A door opened and someone came out of a bathroom. As Herman hurried in, he became entangled with another man coming out, who scolded him.

He ran to the toilet bowl and vomit poured from his mouth. There was a ringing in his ears, a hammering in his temples. Spasmodically, his stomach brought up acids, bitter tastes, and stenches he had forgotten existed. Each time he thought his stomach was emptied and he started to wipe his mouth with paper, he was gripped by another spasm. He groaned and retched, bending lower and lower. He vomited one last time and stood up, feeling drained. Someone banged on the door and tried to push it open. He had soiled the floor tiles, splattered the walls, and he had to clean up. He looked in the mirror which reflected his pale face. He removed a hand towel from the rack and wiped off his jacket lapels. He tried to open the window to let the smell out, but he didn't have the strength to raise it. He made one last effort and the window opened. Hardened snow and icicles hung from the frame. Herman breathed in deeply and the fresh air revived him. Again he heard the door being pounded on, the knob rattling. He opened it and saw Masha.

"Are you trying to break the door?"

"Shall I call a doctor?"

"No doctor. We have to get out of here."

"You're all dirty."

Masha took a handkerchief from her purse. As she

wiped him off, she asked, "How many wives do you have? Three?"

"Ten."

"May God shame you as you've shamed me."

"I'm going home," Herman said.

"Go ahead, but to your peasant, not to me," Masha answered. "Everything is over between us."

"Over is over."

Masha returned to the living room and Herman went in search of his coat, hat, and rubbers, but he didn't know where to look. The rabbi's wife, who had taken them from him, had disappeared. The maid was nowhere to be seen. He wandered among the crowd in the foyer. He asked a man where the coats were, but the man just shrugged his shoulders. Herman went into the library and dropped into an armchair. Someone had left half a glass of whiskey and part of a sandwich on an end table. Herman ate the bread and the smelly cheese and drank the remains of the whiskey; the room spun round him like a carousel. A network of spots and lines swung before his eyes, the blazing colors he sometimes saw when he pressed his eyelids with his fingertips. Everything seemed to shimmer, quiver, change form. People stuck their heads in the door, but Herman didn't really see them. Their faces swam around indistinctly. Someone spoke to him, but Herman's ears felt as if they were full of water. He was being rocked on a stormy sea. How strange that there was any order at all in this chaos. The forms he saw were all geometrical, though distorted. The colors changed rapidly. He recognized Masha when she came in. She came up to him with a drink in her hand and said, "You're still here?"

He heard her words as if from a distance, astonished at the change in his sense of hearing and at his feeling of in-

difference to himself. Masha pulled up a chair and sat
down, almost touching his knee with hers.

"Who is this Tamara?"

"My wife is alive. She's in America."

"We're through, but I think you owe it to me to be
honest with me for the last time."

"It's the truth."

"Who is Pesheles?"

"I don't know."

"Rabbi Lampert has offered me a job—supervisor in a
convalescent home. The pay is seventy-five dollars a
week."

"What will you do with your mother?"

"There will be a place for her there too."

Herman fully understood what all this meant, but it no
longer mattered. He seemed to be experiencing the "dis-
integration of the limbs," the Hasidic description for the
achievement of a state of selflessness. "If only I could always be this way!" he thought.

Masha waited. Then she said, "You wanted all this to
happen. You planned it this way. I'll lock myself up with
the old and sick people. Since there is no nunnery for
Jewish women, that will be my nunnery—until my
mother dies. After that, I'll make an end to the whole
comedy. Can I get you something? It's not your fault you
were born a charlatan."

Masha left. Herman leaned his head against the back of
the chair. His one desire was to be able to lie down somewhere. He heard talking, laughter, footsteps, the clatter of
dishes and glassware. Then gradually the fuzziness in his
brain diminished; the room stopped spinning; the chair
stood on firm ground again. His mind reintegrated itself.
All that remained was the weakness in his knees and the

bitter aftertaste in his mouth. He even felt a slight pang of hunger.

Herman thought of Pesheles and Yasha Kotik. It was clear that if he survived this ordeal he would never be able to work for Rabbi Lampert again. In all the turmoil there existed a plan engineered by the Powers who controlled human affairs. The rabbi was clearly trying to take Masha away from him. He would never pay seventy-five dollars a week to a woman without training or experience for such a job. Nor would he take care of her mother in addition, at the cost of another seventy-five dollars a week, if not more.

Herman suddenly remembered what Yasha Kotik had said about Mosheh Feifer. The party had destroyed once and for all the few illusions about Masha to which he had clung. He waited a long time, but Masha hadn't returned. "Who knows? She may have gone to call the police," he fantasized. He pictured how they would arrive, arrest him, send him to Ellis Island, and then deport him to Poland.

Mr. Pesheles stood before him. He looked at Herman, his head cocked to one side, and said mockingly, "Oh, so here you are! They're looking for you."

"Who?"

"The rabbi, the rebbetzin. Your Masha is a pretty woman. Piquant. Where do you find them? No offense, but to me you look like a nothing."

Herman didn't answer.

"How do you do it? I too would like to know how."

"Mr. Pesheles, you don't need to envy me."

"Why not? In Brooklyn, a Gentile woman has herself converted for your sake. You have here a woman as pretty as a picture. And Tamara is nothing to sneeze at either. I didn't mean any harm, but I told Rabbi Lampert about the Gentile woman who was converted because of you, and now he's totally confused. He told me that you're writing a book for him. Who is this Yasha Kotik? I don't know him at all."

"I don't know him either."

"He seems to be quite friendly with your wife. It's a crazy world, isn't it? The more you live, the more you see. Still and all, you must be a little bit more careful here in America. For years nothing happens and then the fat is in the fire. There was once a racketeer who associated with the top people: governors, senators—you name it. Suddenly someone started to make trouble and now he's cooling his heels in prison and they'll soon send him back to Italy where he came from. I'm not making any comparisons, God forbid, but for Uncle Sam the law is the law. My advice to you is, at least don't keep them in the same state. Tamara is a woman who's suffered. I tried to arrange a match for her and she told me that she was married to you. Naturally it's a secret and I won't tell anyone."

"I didn't know she was alive."

"But she told me that from Europe she sent an announcement to the 'Joint' or Hias to be printed in the newspapers here. You probably don't read the papers?"

"Perhaps you know where I can find my coat?" Herman said. "I want to leave, but I can't find it."

"Is that so? All these women you could find, and your coat you can't find? I'll bet you're quite an actor yourself. Don't worry, no one will steal your coat. I imagine that the wraps are in the bedroom. Nobody in New York has enough closets to hang all the coats at a party. But what's the rush? You certainly won't leave without your wife. I hear our rabbi has just offered her a good job. Do you smoke?"

"Occasionally."

"Here, have a cigarette. It relaxes the nerves." Mr. Pesheles produced a gold cigarette case and a lighter also made of gold. The cigarettes were imported ones, shorter than American cigarettes, with gilded tips. "Then again, why worry about the future?" he said. "No one knows what tomorrow will bring. Whoever doesn't take what he can today has nothing. What happened to all the fortunes in Europe? A heap of ashes." Mr. Pesheles inhaled and blew smoke rings. In a minute, his face became aged, melancholy. He looked as if he were reflecting upon some inner sorrow for which there could be no comfort.

"I'd better see what's doing out there," he said, pointing toward the door.

4

HERMAN, left alone, sat with his head bowed. He had noticed a copy of the Bible on the shelf near his chair and he leaned over and took it out. He leafed through the pages and found Psalms: "Be gracious unto me, O Lord, for I am in distress. Mine eye wasteth away with vexation, yea, my soul and my body. For my life is spent in sorrow, and my years in sighing. My strength faileth because of mine iniquity and my bones are wasted away. Because of mine adversaries, I am become a reproach, yea, unto my neighbors exceedingly, and a dread to mine acquaintances."

Herman read the words. How was it that these sentences fitted all circumstances, all ages, all moods, while secular literature, no matter how well written, in time lost its pertinence.

Masha staggered in, obviously drunk. She was carrying a plate and a glass of whiskey. Her face was pale, but her eyes shone with derision. Unsteadily, she set the plate on the arm of Herman's chair.

"What are you doing?" she asked. "Reading the Bible? You lousy hypocrite!"

"Masha, sit down."

"How do you know I want to sit down? Maybe what I really want to do is lie down. On second thought, I think I'll sit right in your lap."

"No, Masha, not here."

"Why not? I know he's a rabbi, but his apartment isn't a temple. During the war, even the temple didn't stop anyone. They drove Jewish women into the temple and—"

"Nazis did that."

"And who were the Nazis? Also men. They wanted the same thing you, Yasha Kotik, even the rabbi, want. Maybe you would have done exactly the same. They slept with plenty of Nazi women in Germany. They bought them for a pack of American cigarettes, for a bar of chocolate. You should have seen how the daughters of the master race went to bed with the ghetto boys, and how they hugged and kissed them. Some even married them. So why make so much of the word Nazi? We're all Nazis. The whole human race! You're not only a Nazi but a coward afraid of his own shadow."

Masha tried to laugh, but she soon became serious again. "I've had too much to drink. There was a bottle of whiskey and I kept pouring it out. Go ahead and eat if you don't want to drop dead from hunger." Masha fell into a chair. She took a pack of cigarettes out of her bag, but she couldn't find any matches. "Why are you looking at me like that? I won't sleep with the rabbi."

"What went on between you and Yasha Kotik?"

"My lice slept with his lice. Who is Tamara? Tell me once and for all."

"My wife is alive, as I've tried to tell you."

"Is that the truth or are you still leading me on?"

"It's the truth."

"But they shot her."

"She's alive."

"The children too?"

"No, not the children."

"Well. There is a hell that is even too much for Masha. Does your shikseh know about her?"

"She paid us a visit."

"It's all the same to me. I believed that when I came to America I'd get out of all the filth, but I seem to have landed in the thickest muck of all. This may be the last time I talk to you and I want to tell you that you're the worst fraud I've known in my life. And believe me, I've known plenty of rats. Where is your resurrected wife? I'd like to meet her, at least take a look at her."

"She lives in a furnished room."

"Give me her address and phone number."

"What for? All right, I'll give it to you, but I don't have my address book with me."

"If you hear that I'm dead, don't come to my funeral."

5

WHEN Herman got outside and realized how fiercely cold it was, something in him began to laugh—the laughter that sometimes accompanies total misery. A biting wind blew from the Hudson, whistling and whining. The cold penetrated Herman's body in a few seconds. It was one o'clock in the morning. He hadn't the strength to undertake the long trip to Coney Island. He clung to the door, afraid to move. If only he had enough money for a hotel. But he had less than three dollars in his pocket, and there was not a room to be had for three dollars anywhere except perhaps on the Bowery. Should he go back and borrow some money from the rabbi? There were guests upstairs with cars who would undoubtedly take Masha home. "No, I'd rather die!" he muttered. He started walking toward Broadway. The wind was calmer there. Even the frost wasn't as piercing and it was more brightly lighted than West End Avenue. The snow had stopped, but once in a while a single flake fluttered down either from the sky or from a roof. Herman noticed a cafeteria. He hurried across the street and a taxicab almost ran him down. The driver shouted at him. Herman shook his head and waved his hand in a sign of apology.

He stumbled into the cafeteria, breathless and stiff with cold. Here in the light and warmth, breakfast was already being served. There was a clattering of dishes. People were reading morning newspapers, eating French toast with syrup, oatmeal with cream, wheat cereal with milk, waffles with sausages. The mere smell of food made Herman feel faint. He found a table next to the wall and hung up his hat and coat. He realized that he hadn't picked up a check and went back to the cashier to explain.

"Yes, I saw you come in," the cashier said. "You looked frozen through and through."

Herman ordered oatmeal, eggs, a roll, and coffee at the food counter. The whole meal came to fifty-five cents. As he carried the tray back to his table, his legs trembled and he could hardly bear up under its weight. But as soon as he started to eat, his vitality returned. The aroma of coffee was intoxicating. He now had only one wish—that the cafeteria remain open all night.

A Puerto Rican came to the table to clear away the dishes. Herman asked when the cafeteria closed, and the man said, "Two o'clock."

In less than an hour, he would be out in the snowy cold again. He had to make some plan, come to some decision. There was a phone booth opposite him. Maybe Tamara was still awake. She was now the only one who wasn't at war with him.

He went into the phone booth, inserted a coin, and dialed Tamara's number. A woman answered the phone and went to call her. In less than a minute, he heard her voice.

"I hope I didn't wake you. It's me, Herman."

"Yes, Herman."

"Were you asleep?"

"No, I was reading the newspaper."

"Tamara, I'm in a cafeteria on Broadway. They close at two o'clock. I have nowhere to go."

Tamara hesitated a moment. "Where are your wives?"

"They're both not speaking to me."

"What are you doing on Broadway at this hour?"

"I was at a party at the rabbi's."

"I see. Would you like to come here? It's bitter cold. I've pulled the sleeves of a sweater over my legs. There's a wind whistling through the house as if there wasn't a pane in the windows. Why are your wives fighting with you? On second thought, why don't you come right over? I was thinking of calling you tomorrow. There's something I have to talk to you about. The only problem is that they lock the outside door. You can ring the bell for two hours and the janitor won't come to open it. When will you be here? I'll go down and open it myself."

"Tamara, I'm ashamed to be bothering you like this. It's just that I've no place to sleep and don't have the money to pay for a hotel."

"Now, when she's pregnant, she's started a campaign against you?"

"She's being egged on from all sides. I don't want to blame you, but why did you have to tell Pesheles about us?"

Tamara sighed. "He came to the hospital and descended on me with a thousand questions. I still can't figure out how he got there. He sat down next to my bed and cross-examined me like a prosecutor. He tried to make a match for me too. It was soon after the operation. What kind of people are these?"

"I've got myself into such a mess that everything is hopeless," Herman said. "I'd better go back to Coney Island."

"At this hour? It will take you all night. No, Herman, come to my place. I can't sleep. I'm up all night anyhow."

Tamara was about to say something else, but the operator interrupted to ask for another coin, which Herman didn't have. He told Tamara he would be over as soon as he could, and hung up. He left the cafeteria and walked to the subway station on Seventy-ninth Street. An empty Broadway stretched out before him. The street lights, burning brightly, somehow created a wintry, holiday mood, mysterious and fairy-like. Herman descended the stairs to the station and stood waiting for a local train. The only other person on the platform was black. He wasn't wearing a coat despite the icy weather. Herman waited for fifteen minutes and still no train appeared, nor did any other person. The lights glared. Snow as fine as flour began to sift down through a grate in the ceiling.

Now he regretted having phoned Tamara. It might have been wiser for him to go to Coney Island. At least he might have got a few hours of warm sleep—that is, if Yadwiga would have left him in peace. He realized that in order to hear the doorbell Tamara would have to get dressed and wait downstairs in the cold entryway.

The tracks started to vibrate and a train roared in. There were only a few men sitting in the car—a drunk who mumbled and made faces; a man with a broom and a box of signal lights used by track workers; a laborer carrying a metal lunch box and a wooden last. Muddy puddles surrounded the men's shoes, their noses were red and shiny from the cold, their fingernails were ragged and dirty. A restlessness peculiar to people who turn the night into day hung in the air. Herman imagined that the walls, the lights, the windowpanes, the advertisements were tired of the cold, the noise, the harsh light. The train kept whistling and howling its warning siren, as if the motorman had lost control or had gone through a red signal light and realized his mistake. On Times Square Herman made the long walk to the shuttle that went to Grand Central Station.

Again Herman had to wait a long time for a local train to Eighteenth Street. The other people waiting seemed to be in situations similar to his: men separated from their families, drifters whom society could neither assimilate nor reject, whose faces expressed failure, regret, guilt. Not one of these men was properly shaved or dressed. Herman observed them, but they ignored him and each other. He got off at Eighteenth Street and walked the block to Tamara's house. The office buildings stood unlighted, abandoned. It was difficult to believe that, just a few hours ago, swarms of people were doing business there. Above the rooftops, the sky glowed somberly, starless. Herman walked up the few slippery steps to the glass door of Tamara's house. He saw Tamara in the dim light of a single electric bulb. She was waiting for him in an overcoat, the bottom of her nightgown showing below the hem, her face gray with sleeplessness, her hair uncombed. She opened the door silently and they shuffled up the stairs, because the elevator wasn't in operation.

"How long have you been waiting?" Herman asked.

"What's the difference? I'm used to waiting."

It seemed incredible to him that this was his wife, the same Tamara whom he had met for the first time almost twenty-five years ago at a lecture where the subject under discussion had been "Can Palestine Solve the Jewish Question?" On the third floor, Tamara paused and said, "Oh, my legs!"

His calves, too, felt strained.

Tamara caught her breath, and now asked, "Does she have a hospital yet?"

"Yadwiga? The neighbors have taken over completely."

"But it's your child, after all."

He wanted to say, "So what?" but he kept silent.

6

HERMAN had slept an hour and had awakened. He hadn't undressed, but lay in bed wearing his jacket, trousers, shirt, and socks. Tamara had again pulled the sleeves of a sweater over her feet. She had thrown her mangy fur coat and Herman's overcoat on top of the blanket.

She was saying: "Thank God, my time of suffering isn't

over. I'm still right in the midst of it. This, more or less, is the way we had to struggle in Jambul. You won't believe me, Herman, but I find some comfort in it. I don't want to forget what we went through. When it's warm in the room, I imagine that I've betrayed all the Jews in Europe. My uncle feels that Jews should observe an eternal shiva. The entire people should squat on low stools and read from the Book of Job."

"Without faith, one can't even mourn."

"That in itself is reason enough to mourn."

"You said on the phone that you had been planning to call me. What about?"

Tamara was thoughtful. "Oh, I don't know how to begin. Herman, it isn't in me to lie continually the way you do. My aunt and uncle confronted me about us. Since I had already confessed the truth to a nobody like Pesheles, how could I keep the facts from the only relatives I have left in the world? I didn't mean to complain about you, Herman. It's my shame too, but I felt I had to tell them. I thought they would die of shock when I told them that you're married to a Gentile. But my uncle just sighed and said, 'If you perform an operation on someone, there are afterpains.' Who knows that better than I? The suffering only started the morning after the operation. Naturally, he wants us to get a divorce. He has in mind not one but ten matches for me—learned men, fine Jews, all refugees who have lost their wives in Europe. What am I to say? I have as much desire to get married as you have to dance on the roof. But my uncle and aunt both insisted that either you divorce Yadwiga and come back to me or I divorce you. From their point of view, they're right. My mother, blessed be her memory, once told me a story about dead people who don't know they've died. They eat, drink, even get married. So, since we once lived together, had children together, and now are roaming about the World of Delusion, why do we need a divorce?"

"Tamara, they can put a corpse in prison too."

"No one is going to imprison you. And why are you so afraid of prison? You might be better off than you are now."

"I don't want them to deport me. I don't want to be buried in Poland."

"Who will inform on you? Your mistress?"

"Maybe Pesheles."

"Why should he inform on you? And what proof does he have? You didn't marry anyone in America."

"I gave Masha a Jewish marriage contract."

"What will she do with it? My advice is, go back to Yadwiga and make peace with her."

"Is this what you wanted to tell me? I can't work for the rabbi any more. It's out of the question now. I owe rent. I hardly have enough to get through tomorrow."

"Herman, I want to say something, but don't be angry with me."

"What is it?"

"Herman, people like you are incapable of making decisions for themselves. It's true, I'm not very good at it either, but sometimes it's easier to deal with others' problems than with one's own. Here in America, some people have what is called a manager. Let me be your manager. Put yourself entirely in my hands. Pretend that you're in a concentration camp and must do whatever you're told to do. I'll tell you what to do and you do it. I'll find you a job too. In your state, you're in no position to help yourself."

"Why should you do this? And how?"

"That's not your concern. I'll do something. Beginning tomorrow, I'll take care of all your needs and you must be ready to do whatever I ask. If I tell you to go out and dig ditches, you must go and dig ditches."

"What will happen if they put me in jail?"

"Then I'll send you packages in jail."

"Really, Tamara, this is just a way of giving me your few dollars."

"No, Herman. You won't be taking anything away from me. Starting tomorrow, I'm taking over all your affairs. I know I'm a greenhorn, but I'm used to living in strange places. I can see that things have become too much for you and you're about to fall under the burden."

Herman was silent. Then he said, "Are you an angel?"

"Maybe. Who knows what angels are?"

"I told myself it was madness to phone you so late at night, but something made me do it. Yes, I'll put myself in your hands. I have no strength left—"

"Get undressed. You're ruining your suit."

Herman got out of bed and took off his jacket, trousers, and tie, keeping on only his underwear and socks. In the dark, he laid his clothes over the chair. While undressing, he heard steam hissing in the radiator.

He got into bed again and Tamara moved closer to him, laying her hand on his ribs. Herman dozed. Every once in a while he opened an eye. Slowly the darkness lifted. He could hear noises, footsteps, the opening and closing of doors in the hallway. The roomers must be working people who got up early to go to work. Even to live in these miserable rooms, one had to earn money. After some time, Herman fell asleep. When he woke up, Tamara was already dressed. She told him she had taken a bath in the hall bathroom. She looked at him appraisingly, and her face took on a decisive expression.

"Do you remember our agreement? Go wash up. Here's a towel."

He put his coat around his shoulders and went out in
the hallway. All morning, people had been waiting to get
into the bathroom, but now the door stood open. Herman
found a piece of soap which someone had left behind, and
washed himself at the sink. The water was lukewarm.
"Where does her goodness come from?" Herman wondered. He remembered Tamara as stubborn and jealous.
But now, despite the fact that he had exchanged her for
others, she alone was prepared to help him. What did it
mean?

He returned to the room and dressed. Tamara told him
to walk down to the floor below and ring for the elevator
there. She didn't want people in the house to know that a
man had spent the night with her. She told him to wait
for her outside. Outdoors the morning light blinded him
for an instant. Nineteenth Street was jammed with trucks
unloading packages, boxes, crates. On Fourth Avenue
huge machines were shoveling the snow. The sidewalks
were swarming with passers-by. Pigeons that had survived
the night were scavenging in the snow; sparrows hopped
after them. Tamara took Herman to a cafeteria on
Twenty-third Street. The smells were the same as they
had been the previous night on Broadway, but here they
were combined with a disinfectant used to wash the floors.
Tamara didn't even ask what he wanted to order. She
seated him at a table and brought him orange juice, a roll,
an omelet, and coffee. She watched him eat for a moment,
then went to get breakfast for herself. Herman held his
cup of coffee in both hands, not drinking, but warming
himself with it. His head bent lower and lower. Women
had ruined him, but they had also showed him compas-
sion. "I'll manage to live without Masha too," he consoled
himself. "Tamara is right—we're not really alive any
more."

· *CHAPTER NINE* ·

1

WINTER was over. Yadwiga was walking about with a pointed belly. Tamara had reserved a bed for her in a clinic and talked to her every day on the phone in Polish. The neighbors hovered over her. Woytus sang and warbled from early morning till evening. Marianna had laid a little egg. Though Yadwiga had been cautioned not to do too much physical work, she never stopped cleaning and scrubbing. The floors gleamed. She bought paint and with the help of a neighbor who had been a painter in Europe redecorated the walls. In New Jersey, Masha and Shifrah Puah celebrated the Passover seder with the aged and infirm at the rabbi's convalescent home. Tamara helped Yadwiga prepare for the holiday.

The neighbors were told that Tamara was Herman's cousin. They had something new to wag their tongues about, but if a man chooses to be an outcast and has found a woman who will tolerate his ways, there was little to be done about it. The older tenants were eager to chat with Tamara, to question her about the concentration camps, about Russia and the Bolsheviks. Most of these people were anti-Communists, but among them was a for-

mer peddler, who insisted everything the newspapers reported about Russia was untrue. He accused Tamara of
lying. The slave-labor camps, the starvation, the black
market, the purges—all were figments of her imagination. Whenever he listened to Tamara's accounts, he
would comment, "I still say, blessed be Stalin!"

"Why don't you go to him then?"

"They will come here." He complained because his
wife, who kept a strictly kosher kitchen, forced him to say
the blessing over the wine each Friday evening and insisted that he go to synagogue. Before Passover, the whole
building smelled of matzo and borscht, which the women
prepared themselves, of sweet wine, horse-radish, and
other foods that had immigrated from the old country and
now blended their odors with the smell of the bay and the
ocean.

Herman could barely believe it himself, but Tamara
had found him a job. Reb Abraham Nissen Yaroslaver
and his wife Sheva Haddas had decided to go on a long
visit to Israel. Reb Abraham Nissen even hinted that he
might settle there permanently. He had saved several
thousand dollars and was receiving Social Security pay-
ments. He wanted to be buried in Jerusalem on the
Mount of Olives, not among the shaved Jews in a New
York cemetery. He had been wanting to sell his bookstore
for some time, but to sell it for the low prices he had been
offered would have shown a lack of respect for the books
he had so carefully accumulated. Besides, there was always
the possibility that he might not want to remain in Israel.
Tamara had talked her uncle into leaving the store in her
hands. Herman would help her run it. Whatever else Herman might be, he was honest in money matters. Tamara
would live in her uncle's apartment and pay the rent.

Reb Abraham Nissen sent for Herman and showed him

the stock—all old books. Reb Abraham Nissen had never been able to organize them. Books lay about in dusty heaps on the floor, many of them with torn bindings and peeling covers. Somewhere he had an inventory, but it was not to be found. He never bargained with a customer: whatever was offered, he accepted. What did he and Sheva Haddas need? The old building on East Broadway where they lived was rent-controlled.

Though he knew about Herman's behavior and kept urging Tamara to divorce him, the old man nevertheless managed to find excuses for him. Why should these young people be expected to have faith when he himself was plagued by doubts? How could those who had lived through the destruction believe in the Almighty and in His mercy? Deep in his heart, Reb Abraham Nissen had no sympathy for those Orthodox Jews who tried to pretend that the holocaust in Europe had never taken place.

Reb Abraham Nissen expressed these thoughts to Herman during their long talk before he left for Israel. He wanted to settle in the Holy Land to save himself the arduous journey through the underground caverns which the dead must traverse before reaching the Holy Land, there to be resurrected when the Messiah came. The old man made no written contract with Herman. They agreed verbally that Herman was to take out of the business whatever he needed to live on.

Since Masha had accepted the job at the convalescent home, Herman no longer felt that he was in control of things, nor did he want to be. He had become a fatalist in practice as well as in theory. He was willing to let the Powers lead him, whether they were called Chance or Providence or Tamara. His only problem was this matter of hallucinations: in the subway he would see Masha in a train on the opposite track. The telephone in the store would ring and he would hear Masha's voice. It would be several seconds before he realized that it was not she. The most frequent calls came from young Americans asking whether they could sell or give away books left to them by fathers who had died. How they knew about Reb Abraham Nissen's bookstore Herman had no idea, since the old man had never advertised anywhere.

It was all one great riddle to Herman: Reb Abraham Nissen's trust in him, Tamara's readiness to help him, her devotion to Yadwiga. Since that night in the Catskill Mountains, Tamara would have nothing to do with him physically. Their relationship was entirely platonic.

A latent business sense had awakened in Tamara. With Herman's help, she catalogued the books, set prices, and sent the torn books out to a bindery to be repaired. Before Passover, Tamara had stocked up on Haggadahs, seder trays, matzo covers, skullcaps of all styles and colors, even candles and matzo plates. She acquired a supply of prayer shawls, phylacteries, prayer books printed in both English and Hebrew, as well as texts boys used in studying for their bar mitzvahs.

The lie about selling books that Herman had so often repeated to Yadwiga had become a reality. One morning he took Yadwiga downtown with him to see the store. Tamara later took her home, because Yadwiga was still afraid to travel alone by subway, especially now that she was in the last months of pregnancy.

How strange it was to be sitting at the seder table with Tamara and Yadwiga and to be reciting the Haggadah with the two of them. They had insisted that he wear a skullcap and go through the entire ceremony—the blessing over the wine, the symbolic partaking of parsley, chopped apples with nuts and cinnamon, the eggs and salt water. Tamara asked the Four Questions. For him, and probably for Tamara too, it was all a game, an expression of nostalgia. But then, what wasn't a game? Nowhere could he find anything that was "real," not even in the so-called "exact sciences."

In Herman's private philosophy, survival itself was based on guile. From microbe to man, life prevailed generation to generation by sneaking past the jealous powers of destruction. Just like the Tzivkever smugglers in World War I, who stuffed their boots and blouses with tobacco, secreted all manner of contraband about their bodies, and stole across borders, breaking laws and bribing officials—so did every bit of protoplasm, or conglomerate of protoplasm furtively traffic its way from epoch to epoch. It had been so when the first bacteria appeared in the slime at the ocean's edge and would be so when the sun became a cinder and the last living creature on earth froze to death, or perished in whichever way the final biological drama dictated. Animals had accepted the precariousness of existence and the necessity for flight and stealth; only man sought certainty and instead succeeded in accomplishing his own downfall. The Jew had always managed to smuggle his way in through crime and madness. He had stolen into Canaan and into Egypt. Abraham had pretended that Sarah was his sister. The whole two thousand years of exile, beginning with Alexandria, Babylon, and Rome and ending in the ghettos of Warsaw, Lodz, and Vilna had been one great act of smuggling. The Bible, the Talmud, and the Commentaries instruct the Jew in one strategy: flee from evil, hide from danger, avoid showdowns, give the angry powers of the universe as wide a berth as possible. The Jew never looked askance at the deserter who crept into a cellar or attic while armies clashed in the streets outside.

Herman, the modern Jew, had extended this principle

one step: he no longer even had his faith in the Torah to depend on. He was deceiving not only Abimelech but Sarah and Hagar as well. Herman had not sealed a covenant with God and had no use for Him. He didn't want to have his seed multiply like the sands by the sea. His whole life was a game of stealth—the sermons he had written for Rabbi Lampert, the books he sold to rabbis and yeshiva boys, his acceptance of Yadwiga's conversion to Judaism, and Tamara's favors.

Herman read the Haggadah and yawned. He raised his wineglass and poured off ten drops to indicate the ten plagues visited on Pharaoh. Tamara praised Yadwiga's dumplings. A fish from the Hudson River or some lake had paid with its life so that Herman, Tamara, and Yadwiga should be reminded of the miracles of the exodus from Egypt. A chicken had donated its neck to the commemoration of the Passover sacrifice.

In Germany and even in America, neo-Nazi parties were being organized. In the name of Lenin and Stalin, Communists had tortured elderly teachers, and annihilated whole villages in China and Korea in the name of "cultural" revolution. In the Munich taverns, murderers who had played with the skulls of children sipped beer from tall steins and sang hymns in church. In Moscow they had liquidated all the Jewish writers. Yet Jewish Communists in New York, Paris, and Buenos Aires praised the murderers and reviled yesterday's leaders. Truth? Not in this jungle, this saucer of earth perched over hot lava. God? Whose God? The Jews'? Pharaoh's?

Both Herman and Yadwiga begged Tamara to stay overnight, but she insisted on going home, promising to return in the morning to help prepare the second seder. She and Yadwiga washed the dishes. Tamara wished Yadwiga and Herman a happy holiday and left for home.

Herman went into the bedroom and lay down on the bed. He didn't want to think about Masha, but his thoughts kept returning to her. What was she doing? Did she ever think of him?

The telephone rang and Herman ran to pick up the receiver, hoping that it was Masha and afraid that she would change her mind. He almost tripped and shouted a breathless hello into the phone.

There was no answer.

"Hello! Hello! Hello!"

It was an old trick of Masha's to call and not say a word. Perhaps she just wanted to hear his voice.

"Don't be an idiot, say something!" he said.

There was still no answer.

"You left, not I," he found himself saying.

No one replied. He waited a moment and said, "You can't make me more miserable than I am."

2

WEEKS went by. Herman had fallen asleep and had dreamed about Masha. The telephone rang, he threw off his blankets and bolted out of bed. Yadwiga continued snoring. He ran into the hall, bruising his knee in the dark. He lifted the receiver and called hello, but there was no answer.

"If you don't answer, I'm going to hang up," he said.

"Wait!" It was Masha's voice. It sounded choked, and she was swallowing her words. After a time, her speech became clearer. "I'm in Coney Island," she said.

"What are you doing in Coney Island? Where are you?"

"At the Manhattan Beach Hotel. I've been trying to reach you all evening. Where have you been? I decided to try once more, but then I fell asleep."

"What are you doing at the Manhattan Beach Hotel? Are you alone?"

"I'm alone. I've come back to you."

"Where's your mother?"

"In the home in New Jersey."

"I don't understand."

"I've arranged for her to stay there. The rabbi will get her a stipend or something. I told him everything—that I couldn't live without you and that my mother was the only obstacle. He tried to talk me out of it, but logic doesn't help."

"You know Yadwiga's about to give birth."

"He'll take care of her too. He's a great man, though he's mad. He has more heart in his fingernail than you have in your whole being. How I wish I could love him! But I can't. When he so much as touches me, I shudder with disgust. He'll be talking to you himself. He wants you to finish the work you started for him. He loves me and would divorce his wife if I agreed to marry him, but he understands my feelings. I never believed he could have so much heart."

Herman waited a moment before speaking.

"You could have told me all this from New Jersey," he said with a tremor in his voice.

"If you don't want me, I won't force myself on you. I swear that if you turn me away this time, I'll never look at your face again. Everything has come to a climax. I want to know once and for all: yes or no?"

"You gave up your job?"

"I've given up everything. I've packed a suitcase and I've come back to you."

"What will happen to your apartment? Have you given that up too?"

"We'll liquidate everything. I don't want to stay in New York. Rabbi Lampert gave me a wonderful reference and I can get a job anywhere. The people at the home were crazy about me. I literally brought people back to life. The rabbi has a convalescent home in Florida, and if I want to work for him there, I can start right away at a hundred a week. If you don't like Florida, he also has a home in California. You can work for him too. He's as good as an angel from heaven."

"I can't leave her now. She may go into labor any day."

"And after she gives birth, you'll have other reasons. I've made up my mind. Tomorrow I'm flying to California and you'll never hear from me again. I swear by the bones of my father."

"Wait a minute!"

"For what? For new excuses? I'll give you one hour to pack and get here. Rabbi Lampert will take care of your peasant's hospital bills and everything else. He's the president of some lying-in hospital—I've forgotten the name of it. I didn't hide anything from him. He was shocked, but he understands. He may be vulgar but he's a saint just the same. Or have you found a new lover?"

"I don't have a new lover, but I do have a bookstore."

"What? You have a store?"

Herman told her the story briefly

"You've gone back to your Tamara?"

"Absolutely not. But she's also an angel."

"Introduce her to the rabbi. Two angels may bring forth a new God. We're both devils, and we only hurt each other."

"I can't start packing my things now in the middle of the night."

"Don't pack anything. What do you have anyway? The rabbi gave me a loan, or an advance, depending on what I do. Leave everything, like that slave in the Bible."

"What slave? This will kill her."

"She's a strong peasant. She'll find somebody and be happy. She can give the child up for adoption. The rabbi is connected with such an agency too. He has a hand in everything. If you like, we'll have a child. But the time for talking is over. If Abraham could sacrifice Isaac, you can sacrifice Esau. Maybe later we can take her child to live with us. What's your answer?"

"What exactly do you want me to do?"

"Get dressed and come here. Such things are done every day."

"I'm afraid of God."

"If you're afraid, stay with her. Good night forever!"

"Wait, Masha, wait!"

"Yes or no?"

"Yes."

"I'll give you my room number."

Herman hung up. He listened attentively. Yadwiga was still snoring. He remained beside the phone. He hadn't realized how intensely he had longed for Masha. He stood there in the darkness with the mute submissiveness of one who has surrendered his will. It was a while before he could act. He remembered that he had a flashlight somewhere in a drawer. He found it and focused it on the telephone, so that he could make a call. He had to talk to Tamara. He dialed Reb Abraham Nissen Yaroslaver's number. It rang for minutes until at last he heard Tamara's sleepy voice.

"Tamara, forgive me," he said. "This is Herman."

"Yes, Herman, what's the matter?"

"I'm leaving Yadwiga. I'm going away with Masha."

Tamara did not speak for a time. "Do you know what you're doing?" she asked finally.

"I know and I'm doing it."

"A woman who demands such sacrifices doesn't deserve them. I didn't think you'd lost your grip on yourself so completely."

"These are the facts."

"What about the store?"

"It's all in your hands. The rabbi for whom I used to work wants to do something for Yadwiga. I'll give you his address and phone number. Get in touch with him."

"Wait, I'll get a pencil and paper."

It was quiet as he held the receiver and waited. Yadwiga's snoring had stopped.

"I wonder what time it is," Herman thought. Usually he had a keen sense of time. He could often guess the time exactly to the minute. But now he seemed to have lost the knack. He begged the very God against whom he was sinning to keep Yadwiga from wakening. Tamara returned to the phone. "What's the number?"

Herman gave her Rabbi Lampert's name and phone number.

"Couldn't you at least wait till she has the baby?"

"I can't wait."

"Herman, you have the keys to the store. Can you open up in the morning? I'll be there at ten o'clock."

"I'll be there."

"Well, you've made your bed, and you'll have to sleep in it," Tamara said, and hung up.

He stood in the dark, listening to his inner self. Then he went to look at the clock in the kitchen. He was surprised to find it was only fifteen minutes past two. He hadn't slept more than an hour, though it seemed as if he had slept through the night. He looked for a suitcase in which to pack shirts and underwear. He carefully opened a drawer and removed a few shirts, some underwear and pajamas. He sensed that Yadwiga was awake and only pretending to be asleep. Who knows? Could it be that she wanted to get rid of him? Maybe she was tired of it all? She might also be waiting to make a scene at the last moment. As he crammed his clothes into the suitcase, he remembered the rabbi's manuscript. Where was it? He heard Yadwiga getting up.

"What's the matter?" she called.

"I must go somewhere."

"Where? Oh, never mind." Yadwiga lay down again. He heard the bed creak.

He dressed in the dark, perspiring although he felt cold. Loose change fell out of his trouser pockets. He kept bumping into furniture.

The telephone rang and he hurried to answer it. It was Masha again. "Are you coming or aren't you?"

"Yes. You've given me no choice."

3

HERMAN was afraid that at any moment Yadwiga might change her mind and try to prevent him from leaving by force, but she lay quietly. She had been awake throughout his preparations. Why wasn't she saying anything? For the first time since he had known her, she was behaving unpredictably. It was as if she had become part of a plot against him and knew something that was unknown to him. Or had she really achieved the ultimate stage of resignation? It was a riddle that made him uneasy. She might still spring at him with a knife at the last moment. Before he left, he went into the bedroom and said, "Yadwiga, I'm going now."

She didn't reply.

He wanted to close the door without a sound, but it shut with a bang. He descended the stairs quietly so as not to waken the neighbors. He crossed Mermaid Avenue and walked down Surf Avenue. How quiet and dark Coney Island was in the early morning! The amusement concessions were closed and the lights were out. The avenue stretched out before him as empty as a country road. He could hear the rush of the waves from beyond the Boardwalk. It smelled of fish and other sea things. Herman could make out a few stars in the sky. He saw a taxi and hailed it. All he had was ten dollars. He opened a window of the taxi to clear out the cigarette smoke. A breeze was blowing, but his forehead remained damp. He took a deep breath of air. Despite its nighttime coolness, it already held the promise of a warm day to come. The thought flashed through his mind that this must be the way a murderer felt when he was about to kill someone. "She's my enemy! My enemy!" he muttered, meaning Masha. He had the uncanny feeling that he had already experienced this event at some other time. But when? Could he have dreamed it? He had a strong sensation of thirst, or was it yearning for Masha?

The taxi stopped at the Manhattan Beach Hotel. Herman was concerned that the driver might not have change for ten dollars, but the man silently counted out the money for him. It was quiet in the lobby. The clerk was dozing behind the counter in front of the key boxes. Herman was sure that the elevator man would ask him where he was going at that hour, but the man took him up to the floor he asked for, without a word. Herman soon found the room. He knocked at the door and Masha opened it immediately. She was wearing a negligee and slippers. The only illumination came from the street lights. They fell into each other's arms and clutched each other wordlessly, locked together in grim silence. The sun rose and Herman hardly noticed it. Masha tore herself away from him and went to lower the shades.

They had fallen asleep having hardly spoken. He slept deeply and awoke with renewed desire and a fear that was bound with a forgotten dream. All he could remember was disorder, screaming, and something derisive. Even this confused memory soon faded away. Masha opened her eyes. "What time is it?" she asked, and fell asleep again.

He woke her up to explain that he had to be at the bookstore at ten o'clock. They went into the bathroom to wash up. Masha began to speak. "The first thing we must do is go to my apartment. I still have some things there, and I have to close it up. My mother won't be coming back there."

"That can take days."

"No, a few hours. We can't stay here any longer."

Although he had just satisfied himself with her body, he couldn't imagine how he had been able to stand such a long separation from her. In those weeks she had become somewhat fuller; she looked more youthful.

"Did your peasant make a fuss?" she asked.

"No, she didn't say a word."

They dressed quickly and Masha checked out of the hotel. They walked to the subway station at Sheepshead Bay. The bay was sunlit and filled with boats, many of them just returned from early-dawn trips to the open sea. Fish that a few hours before had been swimming in the water now lay on the boat decks with glassy eyes, wounded mouths, bloodstained scales. The fishermen, well-to-do sportsmen, were weighing the fish and boasting about their catches. As often as Herman had witnessed the slaughter of animals and fish, he always had the same thought: in their behavior toward creatures, all men were Nazis. The smugness with which man could do with other species as he pleased exemplified the most extreme racist theories, the principle that might is right. Herman had repeatedly pledged himself to become a vegetarian, but Yadwiga wouldn't hear of it. They had starved enough in the village and later in the camp. They hadn't come to rich America to starve again. The neighbors had taught her that ritual slaughter and Kashruth were the roots of Judaism. It was meritorious for the hen to be taken to the ritual slaughterer, who recited a benediction before cutting its throat.

Herman and Masha stopped at a cafeteria to eat breakfast. He explained again that he couldn't go directly to the Bronx with her, because he had to meet Tamara and give her the keys to the store. Masha listened to him suspiciously. "She'll talk you out of it."

"Then come with me. I'll give her the keys and we can go home together."

"I have no energy left. The weeks in the home were one long hell. Every day my mother insisted that she wanted to go back to the Bronx, though she had a comfortable room, nurses, a doctor, and everything a sick person could wish for. They had a synagogue where men and women prayed. Each time the rabbi paid a visit, he brought her a gift. She couldn't have it better in heaven. But she never stopped accusing me of driving her into an old-age home. The other old people soon realized that there was no way of making her happy. There was a garden where everybody would sit to read the newspapers, or play cards—but she locked herself in her room. The old

people were sorry for me. What I told you about the
rabbi was the truth: he offered to leave his wife for me.
All I had to do was say the word."

Once in the subway, Masha became silent. She sat with
her eyes shut. Whenever Herman spoke to her, she would
start as if he had awakened her from sleep. Her face,
which that morning had looked so full and youthful, had
again become drawn. Herman noticed a white hair on her
head. Masha had finally brought their drama to a climax.
With her, things always came out twisted, wild, theatrical.
Herman kept looking at his watch. He was to have met
Tamara at the store at ten o'clock, but it was already
twenty minutes past and the train was still far from his
station. At last the train stopped at Canal Street and Herman rose quickly. He promised to phone Masha and come
to the Bronx as soon as he could. He ran up the stairs two
at a time. He rushed to the store, but Tamara wasn't
there. She must have gone home. He unlocked the door
and went in to call Tamara and to tell her that he had arrived. He dialed the number, but there was no answer.

Herman thought that Masha might have reached home
by this time and he phoned her. The phone rang many
times, but no one answered there either. He called again
and was about to hang up when he heard Masha's voice.
She was both shouting and crying, and at first he couldn't
make out what she was saying. Then he heard her wail,
"I've been robbed! They've taken all our things! They've
left nothing but the bare walls!"

"When did it happen?"

"Who knows? Oh, God, why wasn't I cremated like all
the other Jews?" She burst into hysterical weeping.

"Have you called the police?"

"What can the police do? They're thieves themselves!"

Masha hung up. It seemed to Herman he could still hear her crying.

4

WHERE was Tamara? Why hadn't she waited? He called her number again and again. Herman opened a book to quiet his anxiety. It was *The Sanctity of Levi.* "The fact is," he read, "that all the angels and sacred animals trembled before the Day of Judgment. And also in men, each limb fears the Day of Reckoning."

The door opened and Tamara entered the store. She was wearing a dress that seemed too long and too wide for her. She looked pale and haggard. She spoke loudly in a hoarse voice, barely restraining herself from shouting. "Where were you? I waited from ten to half past ten. We had a customer. He wanted to buy a set of the Mishnah, but I couldn't open the door. I telephoned you at Yadwiga's and no one answered. She may have killed herself."

"Tamara, I'm no longer in my own hands."

"Well, you're digging your own grave. That Masha is worse than you are. You don't take a man away from a woman who is in the last weeks of pregnancy. You have to be a bitch to do that."

"She has no more control over her actions than I have over mine."

"You always talked about 'free choice.' I read the book you wrote for the rabbi and it seemed to me that every second phrase was 'free choice.' "

"I gave him as much free choice as he ordered."

"Stop it! You make yourself sound worse than you are. A woman can drive a man insane. While we were fleeing from the Nazis, a man prominent in the Poalay Zion stole his best friend's wife. Later we were all forced to sleep in one room, about thirty people, and she had the chutzpa to lie with her lover two steps away from her husband. All three are dead now. Where are you planning to go? God has granted you a child after all this destruction—isn't that enough?"

"Tamara, this kind of talk is useless. I can't live without Masha, and I don't have the guts to kill myself."

"You don't have to kill yourself. We will bring up the baby. The rabbi will work out something, and I'm not exactly helpless. If I live, I'll be a second mother to it. You probably have no money?"

"I won't take another penny from you."

"Don't rush away. If she's waited this long, she'll wait another ten minutes. What are you going to do?"

"We haven't decided. The rabbi has offered her a job in Miami or California. I'll find work too. I'll send money for the baby."

"That's not the problem. I could move in with Yadwiga, but it's too far from the store. Perhaps I should bring her here to live with me. My uncle and aunt write such enthusiastic letters, I doubt that they'll be coming back. They've already visited all the holy graves. If Mother Rachel still has some pull with the Almighty, she'll surely intercede for them. Where does your Masha live?"

"I told you, in the East Bronx. She's just been robbed. They took everything."

"New York is full of thieves, but I don't have to worry about the store. A few days ago when I locked up, my neighbor, the one who has the yarn shop, asked me if I wasn't afraid of thieves and I said my only fear is that some Yiddish author might break in at night and put in some more books."

"Tamara, I must go. Let me kiss you. Tamara, it's the end for me."

Herman grabbed his valise and hurried out of the store. At this time of day, the subway was almost empty. He got off at his station and walked to the little side street where Masha lived. He still had the key to her apartment. He opened the door and saw her standing in the middle of the room. She seemed to have calmed down. All the closets were open, the dresser drawers pulled out. The apartment looked as if it were in the midst of being vacated, with the personal belongings packed and only the furniture still waiting to be moved. Herman noticed that the thieves had even unscrewed the electric lightbulbs.

Masha locked the door behind Herman so that the neighbors wouldn't come in. She went into Herman's room and sat down on the bed. Both the pillow and the spread had been stolen. She lighted a cigarette.

"What did you tell your mother?" Herman asked.

"The truth."

"What did she say?"

"The same old phrases: I'd be sorry. You would leave me, and all the rest of it. If you leave me, you'll leave me. Only the present counts for me. This robbery is no ordinary thing. It's a warning that we mustn't stay here any longer. In the Bible it says, 'Naked I came out of my mother's womb and naked will I return there.' Why 'there'? We don't return to our mothers' wombs."

"The earth is the mother."

"Yes. But until we return to her, let's try to live. We must decide right now where to go—California or Florida. We can go by train or bus. The bus is cheaper, but it takes a week to go to California and you get there more dead than alive. I think we should go to Miami. I'll be able to start working at the home right away. It's off-season and everything is half-price. It's hot, but as my mother says, 'In hell it will be hotter.' "

"When does the bus leave?"

"I'll call and find out. They didn't steal the telephone. They left an old valise too, and that's all we need. This is how we wandered across Europe. I didn't even have a valise, just a pack. Don't look so miserable! You'll find a job in Florida. If you don't want to write for the rabbi, you can teach. The old people need someone who will help them study the Pentateuch or some of the Commentaries. I'm sure you can earn at least forty dollars a week, and with the hundred I make we can live like kings."

"Well, then, it's decided."

"I wouldn't have taken all this junk along anyhow. Maybe it's a blessing in disguise that we were robbed!"

Masha's eyes became gay with laughter. The sun shone on her head, turning her hair a fiery color. The tree outside, which all winter long had stood blanketed with snow, was again adorned with glossy leaves. Herman looked at it in wonder. Each winter Herman had been convinced that the tree, which stood amid garbage and tin cans, had finally shriveled and died. The wind would snap off some of its branches. Stray dogs urinated on its trunk, which seemed to grow thinner and more gnarled with time. Neighborhood children carved their initials, hearts, and even obscenities into its bark. But when summer came, it was covered with foliage. Birds chirped in the thick growth. The tree had carried out its mission, never worrying that a saw, ax, or even one of the burning cigarette butts that Masha habitually threw out of the window might end its existence.

"Does the rabbi have a home in Mexico, by any chance?" Herman asked Masha.

"Why Mexico? Wait here, I'll be right back. Before I left, I gave some clothes to be dry-cleaned, and I took some of your things to the Chinese laundry. I still have a few dollars in the bank that I want to withdraw. It'll take about half an hour."

Masha left. Herman heard her lock the door. He began rummaging through his books and picked up a dictionary he would need if he were to continue working for the rabbi. He found all kinds of notebooks lying in a drawer, even an old fountain pen that the thieves had overlooked. Herman opened his valise and crammed the books into it, but then he couldn't shut it. He had an impulse to phone Yadwiga, but he knew it didn't make sense. He stretched out on the bare bed. He slept and dreamed. When he awakened, Masha still hadn't returned. The sun had disappeared and the room had darkened. Suddenly Herman heard noises outside the door, footsteps and shouts. It sounded as if something heavy was being dragged along. He got up and opened the outside door. A man and a woman held Shifrah Puah between them, half carrying, half leading her. Her face was sick and altered. The man called out, "She passed out in my taxi. Are you her son?"

"Where is Masha?" the woman asked. Herman recognized her as a neighbor.

"She's not at home."

"Call a doctor!"

Herman ran down the few steps separating him from Shifrah Puah. She stared at him with a stern expression when he tried to help her.

"Shall I call a doctor?" he asked.

Shifrah Puah shook her head. Herman backed into the apartment. The cab driver handed him Shifrah Puah's purse and overnight bag, which Herman hadn't noticed before. Herman paid the cab driver out of his own money. They led Shifrah Puah into the shadowy bedroom. Herman pushed the light switch, but the thieves had also removed these bulbs. The cab driver asked why no one turned on a light, and the woman went out to bring a lightbulb from her apartment. Shifrah Puah started to whimper, "Why is it so dark here? Where is Masha? Woe on my miserable life!"

Herman held Shifrah Puah by the arm and shoulder. Meanwhile, the woman returned and screwed in the lightbulb. Shifrah Puah looked at her bed. "Where is the bedding?" she asked in an almost healthy tone of voice.

"I'll get her a pillow and sheet," the neighbor said. "Lie down on it as it is for now."

Herman led Shifrah Puah to the bed. He could feel her body shaking. She clung to him as he lifted her and then lowered her onto the mattress. Shifrah Puah groaned and her face grew even more shriveled. The woman came in with a pillow and sheet. "We must call an ambulance immediately."

Again there was the sound of footsteps on the stairs and Masha entered. In one hand she carried clothes on hangers, and in the other a bundle of laundry. Before she could come into the room, Herman said through the open door, "Your mother is here!"

Masha stopped in her tracks. "She's come running back, has she?"

"She's sick."

Masha handed Herman the clothes and the bundle, which he laid on the kitchen table. He heard Masha shouting angrily at her mother. He knew he should call a doctor, but he didn't know one to call. The neighbor came out of the bedroom with her hands spread out in a questioning gesture. Herman went to his own room. He heard the woman complaining to someone on the phone.

"A policeman? Where will I get a policeman? The woman can die in the meantime!"

"A doctor! A doctor! She's dying!" Masha screamed. "She's killed herself, the bitch, just for spite!"

And Masha let out a wail similar to the one he had heard over the phone a few hours earlier, when she had told him about the robbery. It was a sound unlike her own voice—catlike and primitive. Her face became contorted, she tore her hair, stamped her feet, leaped at Herman as if to attack him. The neighbor held the phone to her breast, stunned.

Masha screamed, "This is what you wanted! Enemies! Bloody enemies!"

She gasped for breath and doubled over as if she were about to fall. The neighbor dropped the receiver and grabbed Masha by the shoulders. She shook her, as one would to relieve a child who was choking

"Murderers!"

· *CHAPTER TEN* ·

1

A DOCTOR arrived, the one who had attended Masha when she thought she was pregnant, and gave Shifrah Puah a shot. Then the ambulance came and Masha went with her to the hospital. A few minutes later a policeman knocked at the door. Herman told him that Shifrah Puah had already been taken to the hospital, but he said that his visit had to do with the robbery. The policeman asked Herman his name and address and what his connection was with the family. Herman stammered and turned pale. The policeman eyed him suspiciously and asked when he had come to America and whether he was a citizen. He wrote down something in a notebook and left. The woman next door had taken back her pillow and sheet. Herman was expecting Masha to phone from the hospital, but two hours passed and the phone was silent.

Evening came and, except for the bedroom, the apartment was without light. Herman unscrewed the lightbulb from the bedroom fixture to take it to his own room, but he bumped into a doorpost and heard the bulb filament rattle. He screwed the bulb into his bedside lamp, but it no longer worked. He went to the kitchen to look for

matches and candles, and couldn't find any. He stood at
the window, looking out into the night. The tree, whose
every leaf had reflected the play of sunlight a few hours
earlier, now stood black against the darkness. A single star
twinkled in the reddish, glowing sky. A cat walked across
the yard with cautious steps and crawled into a space between the scrap iron and the trash. Shouts, traffic noises,
and the muffled roar of the El echoed in the distance.
Herman experienced a melancholy more intense than he
had ever felt before. He couldn't remain in this vandal-
ized, unlighted house alone all night. If Shifrah Puah had
died, her spirit might come to haunt him.

He decided to go out and get some bulbs. Besides, he
hadn't eaten anything since breakfast. He left the apartment, realizing the moment the door closed behind him
that he had forgotten his key. He searched through his
pockets, knowing he wouldn't find it. He must have put it
down on the table. The phone began to ring inside the
apartment. Herman pushed at the door, but it was se-
curely locked. The ringing didn't stop. Herman pushed
with all his might, but the door would not budge and the
phone continued to ring.

"It's Masha! Masha!" He couldn't even remember to
which hospital they had taken Shifrah Puah.

The telephone stopped ringing, but Herman remained
standing at the door. He wondered if he should try to
break it down. He was sure that the phone would soon
ring again. He waited a full five minutes before he went
down the stairs. Just as he reached the street door, the
ringing started again and went on for many minutes. Herman imagined that he could hear Masha's fury in the insis-
tent ringing. He could see her face distorted in agony.

There was no sense in turning back. He walked in the

direction of Tremont Avenue and came to the cafeteria where Masha had worked as a cashier.

He decided to get a cup of coffee and then go back and wait on the stairs until Masha returned. He went up to the counter. He touched his vest pocket and felt a key, but it was the key to his apartment in Brooklyn.

Instead of ordering coffee, he thought he would phone Tamara, but all the booths were occupied. He tried to be patient. "Even eternity doesn't last forever," ran through his mind. "If the cosmos had no beginning, then one eternity has already passed." Herman smiled to himself. Back to Zeno's paradoxes! One of the three conversationalists at the telephones hung up. Herman quickly took his place in the booth. He dialed Tamara's number, but no one answered. He got his dime back and without thinking dialed the number of his Brooklyn apartment. He needed to hear a familiar voice, even a hostile one. Yadwiga wasn't at home either. He let the phone ring ten times.

Herman sat down at an empty table and decided to wait half an hour and then call Masha's apartment. He took a piece of paper out of his pocket and tried to calculate how long he and Masha could exist on the money they had. It was a futile effort since he did not know the price of the bus tickets. He figured, doodled, and every few minutes looked at his wristwatch. How much would he get for it if he were to sell it? Not more than a dollar.

He sat there, trying to sum things up. In the hayloft, he had had the illusion that some basic change would take place in the world, but nothing had changed. The same politics, the same phrases, the same false promises. Professors continued to write books about the ideology of murder, the sociology of torture, the philosophy of rape, the psychology of terror. Inventors created new deadly weapons. The talk about culture and justice was more revolting than the barbarism and injustice. "I am sunk in offal and I am myself offal. There is no way out," Herman muttered. "Teach? What is there to teach? And who am I to teach it? He felt nauseated in the same way that he had on the evening of the rabbi's party. After twenty minutes, Herman dialed Masha's number and she answered.

He knew from her voice that Shifrah Puah had died. It was toneless, the exact opposite of the overdramatic style in which she related the most ordinary things.

"How is your mother?" he nevertheless asked.

"I have no mother," Masha said.

Both were silent.

"Where are you?" Masha asked after a moment. "I thought you'd be waiting for me."

"God in heaven, when did it happen?"

"She died before she got to the hospital. Her last words were, 'Where is Herman?' Where *are* you? Come right back."

He rushed out of the cafeteria, forgetting to give the check back to the cashier, who shouted after him. He threw it to her.

2

HERMAN had expected to find the neighbors with Masha, but no one was there. The apartment was as dark as when he had left it. They stood close together in silence.

"I went down to buy lightbulbs, and locked myself out," he said. "Do you have a candle somewhere?"

"What for? No, we don't need one."

He led her to his room. It was a little lighter there. He sat down on a chair and Masha seated herself on the edge of the bed.

"Does anyone know yet?" Herman asked.

"No one knows and no one cares."

"Shall I call the rabbi?"

Masha didn't reply. He was beginning to think that in her grief she hadn't heard him, but suddenly she said, "Herman, I can't stand any more. These things involve formalities and require money too."

"Where is the rabbi? Still at the home?"

"I left him there, but he was supposed to fly some place. I don't remember where."

"I'll try to reach him at home. Do you have a match?"

"Where's my bag?"

"If you brought it home, I'll find it."

Herman got up and went to look for it. He had to feel his way like a blind man. He felt the surface of the table and chairs in the kitchen. He wanted to go into the bedroom, but was afraid. Could it be that Masha had left her bag at the hospital? He went back to Masha.

"I can't find it."

"I had it here. I took the doorkey out of it."

Masha got up and both of them fumbled around in the dark. A chair fell over and Masha picked it up. Herman felt his way into the bathroom and, out of habit, turned the light switch. The light went on, and he saw Masha's bag on the laundry hamper. The thieves had missed the bulb over the medicine cabinet.

Herman picked up the bag, surprised at its weight, and called to Masha that he had found it and that the bathroom light was working. He glanced at his wristwatch, but he had forgotten to wind it and it had stopped.

Masha came to the bathroom door, her face changed,

her hair disordered; she squinted. Herman handed her the bag. He could not look at her directly. He spoke to her, his face averted, like a pious Jew who may not look at a woman.

"I must put this bulb in the lamp near the phone."

"What for? Well—"

Herman unscrewed the bulb carefully and held it close to his body. He was grateful that Masha wasn't scolding him, crying, or making a scene. He screwed the bulb into the floor lamp and experienced a moment of satisfaction when it lighted. He phoned the rabbi, and a woman answered. "Rabbi Lampert has gone to California."

"Do you have any idea when he'll be back?"

"Not sooner than a week."

Herman knew what that implied. If he were here, the rabbi would take care of the formalities, probably assume the funeral expenses. Herman hesitated and then asked where the rabbi could be reached.

"I cannot tell you," the woman said officiously.

Herman turned off the light, not knowing why he did so. He went back to his room. Masha was sitting there with her bag on her knees.

"The rabbi left for California."

"Well—"

"Where do we begin?" Herman asked both Masha and himself. Masha had once mentioned that neither she nor her mother belonged to any organization or synagogue that handled its members' burials. Everything would have to be paid for: the funeral, the cemetery plot. Herman would have to see officials, request favors, credit, give guarantees. But who knew him? His thoughts turned to animals. They lived without complications and burdened no one when they died.

"Masha, I don't want to live," he said.

"You once promised me we would die together. Let's do it now. I have enough sleeping pills for both of us."

"Yes, let's take them," he said, not knowing whether he really meant it.

"I have them in my bag. All we need is a glass of water."

"That we have."

His throat constricted and he could hardly say the words. The way it had happened and the swiftness with which everything had come to a climax baffled him. He could hear the noisy clinking and scraping of keys, coins, lipstick, as Masha rummaged through her bag. "I always knew she was my Angel of Death," he thought.

"Before we die, I'd like to know the truth," he heard himself saying.

"About what?"

"Whether you've been faithful to me since we've been together."

"Have you been faithful to me? If you tell the truth, I will too."

"I'll tell the truth."

"Wait, I want to get a cigarette."

Masha took a cigarette out of a pack. She did everything slowly. He could hear her rolling the tip of the cigarette between her thumb and forefinger. She struck a match and in the glow of the flame her eyes looked at him questioningly. She inhaled, blew out the flame, and the match head glowed for an instant, illuminating her fingernail. "Well, let's hear," she said.

Herman had to make an effort to speak. "Only with Tamara. That's all."

"When?"

"She was at a hotel in the Catskills."

"You never went to the Catskills."

"I told you I was going to Atlantic City with Rabbi Lampert to attend a convention. Now it's your turn," Herman said.

Masha laughed a short laugh.

"What you did with your wife, I did with my husband."

"So that means he told the truth?"

"That time, yes. I went to ask him for the divorce and he insisted. He told me it was the only way I could get it."

"You swore a holy oath that he lied."

"I swore falsely."

They sat silently, each with his own thoughts.

"There isn't any point in dying now," Herman said.

"What do you want to do? Leave me?"

Herman didn't answer. He sat there, his mind blank. Then he said, "Masha, we must go tonight."

"Even the Nazis allowed the Jews to bury their dead."

"We're not Jews any more and I can't stay here any longer."

"What do you want me to do? I'll be damned for ten generations to come."

"We're damned already."

"At least let's wait till after the funeral." Masha barely managed to say the last word.

Herman stood up. "I'm leaving now."

"Wait, I'll go with you. Let me go into the bathroom a moment."

Masha rose. She dragged her feet as she walked. The heels of her shoes scraped along the floor. Outside, the tree stood motionless in the night. Herman bade it farewell. He tried one last time to fathom its mystery. He heard water splashing; Masha was apparently washing up. He stood quietly, listening intently, amazed at himself and at Masha's willingness to go with him.

Masha came out of the bathroom. "Herman, where are you?"

"Here I am."

"Herman, I can't leave my mother," Masha said quietly.

"You have to leave her anyhow."

"I want a grave next to hers. I don't want to lie among strangers."

"You'll lie near me."

"You're a stranger."

"Masha, I *must* go."

"Wait a second. As long as it is this way, go back to your peasant. Don't leave your child."

"I will leave everybody," Herman said.

$\cdot\ EPILOGUE\ \cdot$

THE night before Shevuot, Yadwiga gave birth to a daughter. The rabbi had suggested that if the child were a girl, she should be called Masha. He had taken care of everything: Shifrah Puah's and Masha's burials, Yadwiga's hospital costs. He had bought a baby carriage, blankets, a layette—even toys. Reb Abraham Nissen and Sheva Haddas had decided to remain in Israel, and Tamara had permanently taken over her uncle's apartment and bookstore.

Since Tamara did not want Yadwiga to live alone, she had arranged for Yadwiga and the baby to move in with her. Tamara worked in the store all day, and Yadwiga took care of the household.

Masha had left the usual note: no one was responsible for her death. She asked to be buried beside her mother. With the rabbi in California, they came close to being buried in the paupers' cemetery. Two days passed without anyone knowing what had happened. According to a story that was published in a Yiddish newspaper, Masha had appeared to Yasha Kotik, the actor, in a dream and had told him that she was dead. The following morning Yasha

Kotik telephoned Leon Tortshiner. Tortshiner, who still had a key to Masha's apartment, went there and found her body. It was Tortshiner who got in touch with the rabbi in California. This story was later refuted in a letter to the paper written by a neighbor of Masha's. The neighbor maintained that she had called the hospital, learned that Shifrah Puah had died and that no one had claimed the body. She had then called the janitor, who opened the apartment, and they had found Masha dead.

The rabbi became a frequent visitor to Tamara and to little Masha. He often parked his car in front of Tamara's store and came in to browse through the books. He sent her customers, and people who either gave her books free or charged little for them. The rabbi ordered a joint headstone for mother and daughter from a monument-maker on Canal Street, whose shop was located one block from Tamara's store.

Tamara had several times listed Herman's name in the missing-persons columns published in the Yiddish press, but without results. Tamara believed that Herman had either killed himself or was hiding somewhere in an American version of his Polish hayloft. One day the rabbi informed Tamara that, because of the holocaust, the rabbinate had eased restrictions so that deserted wives could be married a second time.

And Tamara had replied, "Perhaps, in the next world —to Herman."